"You did not favor me with a dance last night. I hope you'll save one for me at the party," Lord Kendrick said.

"I will certainly see if I can find time for a dance," Samantha promised. "But I expect to be very busy, my lord."

"I thought all young ladies wished to dance with eligible earls."

Did he consider himself eligible? She thought every lady within miles must be setting her cap at him. Given his history, she'd somehow considered him immune.

"I suppose they do," she acknowledged. "But I have no interest in attaching eligible gentlemen. Thank you for your company, my lord. I should return home."

He looked ready to protest, eyes narrowed, head high. But he nodded a farewell, and she turned the horse. She tried to look calm, but she couldn't keep herself from looking back. Once more he was watching her leave, but this time the determination on his face told her that he intended to learn her secrets, whether she wished it or not.

Books by Regina Scott

Love Inspired Historical

 The Irresistible Earl
 An Honorable Gentleman
The Rogue's Reform
The Captain's Courtship
The Rake's Redemption
The Heiress's Homecoming

*The Everard Legacy

REGINA SCOTT

started writing novels in the third grade. Thankfully for literature as we know it, she didn't actually sell her first novel until she had learned a bit more about writing. Since her first book was published in 1998, her stories have traveled the globe, with translations in many languages including Dutch, German, Italian and Portuguese.

She and her husband of more than twenty years reside in southeast Washington State with their overactive Irish terrier. Regina is a decent fencer, owns a historical costume collection that takes up over a third of her large closet and is an active member of the Church of the Nazarene. You can find her online blogging at www.nineteenteen.blogspot.com. Learn more about her at www.reginascott.com.

REGINA SCOTT

The Heiress's Homecoming

HHARLEQUIN® LOVE INSPIRED® HISTORICAL

Recycling programs
for this product may
not exist in your area.

™ LOVE INSPIRED BOOKS

ISBN-13: 978-0-373-82956-9

THE HEIRESS'S HOMECOMING

www.LoveInspiredBooks.com

Printed in U.S.A.

Trust in the Lord with all your heart
and lean not on your own understanding;
in all your ways acknowledge Him,
and He will make your paths straight.
—*Proverbs* 3:5,6

To my mother, who carries her burdens with love, grace and determination; and to my heavenly Father, who can carry all our burdens in His capable hands, if only we remember to ask.

Chapter One

Cumberland, England
June 1813

Oh, but he needed a diversion.

William Wentworth, Earl of Kendrick, gazed about the crowded hall of his ancestral estate. Every member of the gentry for miles around had come to celebrate his son's birthday with dinner and dancing. All but one member of the local aristocracy had also graced Kendrick Hall with their presence. Even though he had never met the missing Lady Everard, he was fairly certain she knew that any Everard was forever unwelcome in his home.

But his other guests did not seem distressed by her absence. They promenaded along the gilded walls, wandered out the three glass-paned doors to the terrace that ran along the back of the house and danced to the strains of a string quartet. The glow from the twin crystal chandeliers glinted off velvet, reflected off satin. Voices rose in conversation and good cheer. Yet Will kept remembering other balls, other dinners, some held far away, where jasmine scented the air. The memories made him long to pull off his dramatically tied cravat and dive into the pond behind the house to escape.

But tonight he must play host. After all, he had only a borrowed hostess. With a remarkable dearth of females in his family, he had had to prevail upon the kindness of his nearest respectable neighbor. He was merely glad that the elderly Mrs. Dallsten Walcott, who had known him since he was born, had been willing to help.

Still, he felt the breeze of fans plying as he gazed around the room, noted the speculative glances of a dozen ladies. They thought his long-awaited step into Society meant he was seeking to marry again. No chance of that. No reason. He had an heir, even if watching his seventeen-year-old son dance with Mrs. Dallsten Walcott made Will feel a great deal older than his thirty-five years.

Another reason he so badly needed a diversion.

Perhaps he should dance as well. Mrs. Dallsten Walcott was looking in his direction, lips pursed in determination. As the highest-ranking gentleman present, he supposed dancing was expected of him. But he had never done things simply because they were expected. Promenading held as little interest, and he knew engaging his neighbors in conversation was dangerous. After nearly a decade on the diplomatic circuit beyond the safe confines of Cumberland, Will had too many opinions that didn't align with theirs.

So he held up the wall, arms crossed over his green wool coat, and watched as his fifty-some guests thoroughly enjoyed themselves. The gold candle sconce beside him gave back a warped picture of his face—dark wavy hair, thick slash of brows, forest-green eyes. He thought the frown was the most accurate.

He shook it off, forced a smile. He ought to be proud

of this evening. Mrs. Dallsten Walcott had done a fine job. The music was elegant, the menu for the supper to come equally sophisticated. The parquet floor gave back a shine under the dancing slippers of his guests. Along each wall and the mantel of the marble fireplace, jade vases held gardenias from his conservatory, their perfume drifting through the hall.

But the fairest blossom was strolling down the opposite wall from him, her lithe figure reflected in the windows overlooking the terrace.

She had hair like the burnished gold of Egypt tumbling in curls behind her; skin like the palest ivory from Africa. In her cerulean satin gown, she reminded Will of sunlight on the Aegean Sea. She moved with the energy of sunlight, too, her steps sure and swift. The turn of her head told him she was looking for someone.

Will straightened off the wall. Who was she? He'd grown up knowing half the people in this room. The other half had either married into the Evendale valley or been born after Will had left at eighteen. Oh, how he hoped she wasn't married. She was exactly the kind of diversion he needed.

He took a step forward, then stopped himself. What was he thinking? A lady should not be used as a diversion. How many times had he watched his brother make that mistake? A lady was meant to befriend, to serenade, to court. He never planned on courting again. He should allow her to find the person she was seeking and stop wishing it was him.

"Well, that's done." His son hurried off the dance floor and braced his back against the wall as if intending to defend the space from desert chieftains. To Will, his son still seemed too young to be the heir to the earldom. His face looked soft under his thatch of black hair, his frame too thin. He was just beginning to understand what life might hold for him. Will envied him that.

"Do you find dancing with a lady so onerous?" he asked his son, returning to his spot along the wall.

James, as he had insisted he be called now that he had finished schooling at Eton, shook his head, further disheveling his hair. "Mrs. Dallsten Walcott isn't a lady, Father."

Will raised his brows, mouth curling up in a smile. "I'm sure her family will be sorry to hear that."

Jamie, as Will persisted in thinking of him, grimaced. "I didn't mean to disparage her. She simply isn't a lady of interest to me." He shifted against the wall as if finding his blue wool coat too tight or the gilded paneling too hard. "She is old enough to be my grandmother, and I have specific ideas for my bride."

Will felt as if the room was warming and adjusted his cravat. He truly wasn't ready for his son to choose a wife, even if Will had been Jamie's age when he'd first fancied himself in love. That had ended in tragedy. The only good to come of it was the young man standing beside him now.

"For tonight," Will said, "perhaps you should focus on being a good host."

Jamie's brown eyes, inherited from his mother, crinkled around the corners. "I will if you will. I don't think Mrs. Dallsten Walcott approves of you right now. You haven't danced once."

Will glanced across the room again and sighted his hostess. Though her hair was a silvery white, her carriage remained unbent, her steps firm. He didn't think her pride would allow it otherwise. Tonight in a poppy-colored gown with an inordinate number of flounces, she dominated the hall. She was glaring at him down her long nose, foot tapping, and the jerk of her head toward a bevy of belles clustered by the doors to the veranda told him her intentions.

"Perhaps I'm as fussy as my son in the lady I choose," Will said, clapping Jamie on the shoulder. He still had a couple inches on his son, and some of those broad shoulders on the lad were from the artful use of padding by their tailor.

Jamie, however, sobered. "I have been meaning to talk to you about that. I know it's poor timing, but would you be willing to break away for a few minutes and meet me in the library?"

This was not the diversion Will had had in mind, and he knew where his duty lay tonight, even if he found playing host difficult. But the look in his son's eyes was his undoing. He'd missed so many opportunities to be of use to the boy over the years, and he knew the days were swiftly approaching when Jamie would no longer bring his concerns to his father.

"Of course," he said. "I'll leave now to throw Mrs. Dallsten Walcott off the scent, and you follow when it's safe."

Jamie's smile was relieved.

Will wandered through the room, pausing to chat with this gentleman, compliment that lady, all the while keeping a wary eye on his hostess. He was disappointed to find that the beauty who had caught his attention earlier had vanished, and he could only hope she'd found what she'd been seeking. He made his way out of the hall, across the center corridor of the house and into the west wing, where his library sat.

The faint music from the dance cut off as he shut the door behind him, and he felt the crowded shelves closing in. A shame he could not take more pleasure in the library at Kendrick Hall. The books were excellent, he knew, with everything from thick tomes on history to more recent novels of adventure. Unfortunately most of his time in this room was spent on estate business. He consoled himself with the thought that his ancestors must have felt a similar need to flee, for the rear wall was entirely made up of a bow window overlooking the grounds, with a center door that led out onto the terrace.

The shutters were closed over the view tonight, the estate ledgers put away in one of the glass-fronted bookcases. Either Jamie had alerted their butler or his staff had anticipated Will's needs because a merry fire was burning in the grate of the white marble fireplace, and the lamp on his desk cast a golden glow over the room.

But in the absence of the noise from the party another sound caught his attention—a soft whimper and sniff. Will took a step deeper into the room. "Who's in here?"

He heard the gasp, and then that golden head popped into sight over the back of the satin-striped sofa that faced the fire. Tears wet her fair cheeks, and her rosy lips were parted in surprise.

The look propelled him forward. Will strode around the sofa, went down on one knee before her. "Tell me who made you cry, and I promise he will regret it even more than I do."

She smiled through her tears, such a brave upturn of those lovely lips. "You are too kind, sir, but I fear there's nothing that can be done."

He knew the feeling. There was nothing that could be done when his wife had died moments after bringing their son into the world. There was nothing that could be done when his older brother had been murdered, and Will had had to return home to comfort his father and take up his new role as heir. There was nothing that could be done when a bout of influenza had carried off his father two years ago.

I'm so sick of hearing that nothing can be done, Lord!

He took her gloved hands and held them in his own. Her fingers were long and slender, but he felt a supple strength in them. "Perhaps," he murmured, "if you were to tell me the problem, we could find an amicable solution."

She searched his gaze as if looking for hope. Those dark brown eyes reminded him of Saharan wells, giving restful relief from heat and travel. She had every right to pull back from his grip, order him to mind his own affairs. He only hoped she could tell that his intentions were honorable.

And yet his lips seemed to have other ideas. Before he even knew it, he was leaning closer. Like filings to a magnet, she drew closer as well, until he caught the scent of roses and their faces were mere inches apart.

The library door opened with a crack as loud as thunder, and Will jerked back. The lady stared at him, two roses blooming in her cheeks, and for an odd moment, Will had the insane notion that they were the source of the captivating scent.

Jamie strode into the room, gaze lighting on the sofa. "Oh, good. You're here."

Will stood, even as the lady rushed to her feet.

"Of course I'm here," she said, turning to face his son as she smoothed the wrinkles from the blue of her gown. "Isn't this where you said you'd meet me?"

Will felt as if he'd stepped under one of the icy waterfalls that plunged from the fells. So that was why she was at the party. She'd been searching the hall, for Jamie. She was waiting in the library, for Jamie.

Was she crying over his son as well?

"I suggest," he said to Jamie, pulse pounding in his temple, "that you explain yourself. Immediately."

Something of what he was feeling must have shown on his face, for his son hurried around the sofa to take up his place at the lady's side. With Jamie standing so close, it was apparent the woman was older than he was, somewhere between twenty and thirty, Will would have guessed. What would a woman who had to have seen much more of Society want with his untried son? His unease ratcheted up another notch.

"It's all right, Father," Jamie said, raising his chin as if to defend himself and the lady next to him. "I asked her to join us."

"Father?" The word came out in a squeak, and all color fled from the woman's face. She turned on Jamie. "You never said anything about your father."

What was all this? Was this woman less than a lady? Why was she here? What hold did she have on his son?

And what hold had she already gained on Will that he wished so desperately for her to be innocent?

Samantha, Lady Everard, wanted to dash across the colorful Oriental carpet at her feet and escape. Never in the eight years since she'd first made her come out in Society had she ever been so embarrassed. Given the antics of her three guardians and cousins, that was saying a very great deal. She glared at her longtime friend Jamie, who immediately quailed.

"Samantha, Lady Everard," he mumbled, "may I present my father, William Wentworth, Earl of Kendrick?"

Samantha dipped a curtsey, lowering her gaze to the shine of the earl's evening pumps. "An honor, my lord."

When she straightened and looked up, she found he had taken a step back, and his face had stiffened. She wasn't sure what had upset him, her presence in his home or her friendship with Jamie. But she could feel his disapproval radiating out of him with as much heat as she'd felt when he'd leaned toward her.

For a moment there she'd thought he might actually kiss her, this stranger who had stumbled upon her. That wasn't altogether surprising. She never had the least trouble turning a gentleman up sweet. She simply hadn't found one she was willing to marry.

And knowing who he was assured her that he'd never offer her marriage. If the stories were true, he'd already won and lost his true love. The local ladies must be in mourning at the thought of a handsome earl on the shelf. She'd certainly noticed him when she'd first entered the hall and had begun searching for Jamie. A head taller than most of the men in the room, he was difficult to miss.

But there was something else about him—that sable hair waving around his head as if it refused to be tamed, that lift of one corner of his mouth, the light in his green eyes that said he was game for adventure.

Not, unfortunately, at the moment. Unless she missed her guess, he was now thoroughly annoyed.

"I believe we agreed Lady Everard would not attend," he said to Jamie.

What was this? Would he ban her from his home? Did he hold her in even greater contempt than she'd expected? Samantha glanced at her friend in time to see him frown.

"I thought she couldn't attend," Jamie protested. "I didn't know she had returned to Evendale until I stopped by the manor to give Mrs. Dallsten Walcott my opinion on the silver we intended to borrow."

Ah, that was it. She probably made them uneven at table. "So I arrived unexpectedly and late as well," Samantha summarized, returning her gaze to her host and offering him her most charming smile. "Forgive me, my lord. If it's any conciliation, I didn't intend to stay long, just until I spoke to Jamie, I mean Lord Wentworth."

Her honest speech should have earned her a pardon at least, but Lord Kendrick's green gaze only darkened.

Beside her, Jamie grimaced. "James. You promised."

She had promised, but she found it hard to call him that. Though his height had surpassed hers by a good six inches, he was still eight years her junior, and just as likely to remind her of the boy she'd left behind when she'd moved to London.

"James," she said with a smile to appease him, but she felt his father stiffen. Whoever would have thought the famous world traveller William Wentworth would be so censorious, or so devastatingly handsome? Jamie— James—must take after his mother.

"James," Lord Kendrick said, very likely through clenched teeth, "I believe you wished a moment of my time."

Samantha touched her fingers to her lips. "Oh, dear, I must have misunderstood. I thought you said you wished to talk to me about a matter of great urgency, James."

"I did," Jamie promised her with a nod to his father as well. "I wished to speak to you both, in private. You see, I know why you've returned, Samantha, and I thought Father and I could help."

He knew? The breath stopped in her chest. How could he know? Had she told him once, years ago, about her father's will? Did anyone except her solicitor, her guardians and their wives know what this month meant to her, that she stood to lose everything she held dear?

Her gloved hand seemed to be moving toward her throat; she consciously lowered her arm. She would not let them see her pain. She'd slipped already, giving in to the dismals on the sofa, but she would not repeat her mistake, not with Lord Kendrick glowering at her as if she'd somehow stolen something from his precious home.

Lord, please help me to be strong!

"I'm here for the annual summer party at Dallsten Manor," she told Jamie. "All my cousins and their families are coming. I have sufficient help, I assure you."

He shook his head, then turned to his father. "That's not why she's here. She turns five and twenty the day after the party. That's the problem."

No! She would not discuss her life with them. Her family hounded her on a daily basis it seemed, concerned for her future, for her state of mind. It was no one's business but hers how she chose to lead her life. When she turned five and twenty, her cousins' guardianships would finally end, but her choices now were still her own.

Samantha pushed past him, and the rustle of her skirts fueled her agitation. "You should know better than to reveal a lady's age, sir. This discussion is at an end. And I repeat—I need no help."

"Then why," Lord Kendrick said, the tone guaranteed to stop her at the door, "were you crying?"

Samantha felt the tears threatening again, pricking at the backs of her eyes. She straightened her spine and put her hand to the door latch.

"You were crying?" Jamie strode to her side to stare

at her face so intently Samantha felt compelled to turn her head. But that only meant her gaze collided with Lord Kendrick's and held. His look had softened, as if he knew the pain inside her. But he couldn't help her. She knew what she must do.

"I'm fine, Jamie," she said. "Leave off, and let me go."

"How can I?" Jamie demanded. "I knew this business troubled you. You don't have to lose the manor, you know. We can find someone to…"

"Stop!" Samantha ordered, heat washing over her. "Now."

"But," Jamie began.

Samantha held up her hand. "I have nothing further to say in the matter, to either of you." She picked up her skirts and swept out the door. The life she'd known might be ending in a fortnight, but she was not going to beg for assistance, particularly from Lord Kendrick, who could never love her, no matter what she did.

Chapter Two

Will reacted first, the consequence, he feared, of too many years fending for himself. "Lady Everard, wait!"

What was he doing? What did he hope to gain? He should rejoice that she was leaving his home and his son untouched. Already in the corridor, she paused to glance back at him. Something called to him from those dark eyes, as if the ache inside her sought understanding. Perhaps he'd been holed up in Kendrick Hall for too long, but some part of him longed to help.

Why? He knew she was trouble. He'd heard the stories over the years about the wild and wily Everards. And he suspected they were connected with his brother's death. He should let her walk away. Isn't that what he wanted?

"Yes, Samantha, please wait," Jamie said, reaching out a hand. "I didn't mean to upset you. I just wanted to help."

Her gaze met his, and the anger melted. "There's nothing to be done, Jamie. I've made up my mind. Please let the matter go."

Will had seldom seen his son's face so mulish. His brows were gathered, his lips tight and his head was every bit as high and proud as hers as he dropped his hand to the side of his coat. "How can I let it go when your choice will take you away from me…away from Evendale?"

If she noticed his lapse, she was wise enough not to comment on it. "I will come visit. I promise."

"It won't be the same."

Will winced at the adolescent whine. With every movement, every word, his son proved how young he was. And Will didn't want him any more attached to this woman.

"James," he said, "the lady asked you to drop the subject. I suggest you comply."

He regretted his suggestion immediately, for his son blanched. Jamie snapped Lady Everard a bow. "Never intended to hurt you. Sorry."

Now she paled, and Will could not understand the reason. "There's no need to apologize," she replied. "I know you have my best interests at heart. Please tell Mrs. Dallsten Walcott I'm sorry I missed the party. I should go." Her curtsey was a mere bob of her head before she fled.

"You didn't need to berate me in front of her," Jamie said in the silence that followed, his gaze on the floor. "She already considers me a child."

Jamie's actions spoke louder than Will's chastisement, but Will didn't think the boy would appreciate the fact. He kept his voice gentle. "Sometimes those who watch us grow up are the last to see us change."

"I suppose so." His deep sigh could have felled a forest.

Under other circumstances Will would have been hard-pressed not to smile at the dramatic performance, but now he could only wonder how far things had progressed between his son and their lovely neighbor. "I realize you've known her for years," he ventured. "Your grandfather wrote me letters and told me about your antics as children."

Jamie nodded, clearly avoiding Will's gaze. "She was always there, as long as I can remember."

When he hadn't been. Will had run off with the diplomatic corps shortly after Jamie had been born, and only his brother's death had brought Will home. He tried to ignore the guilt that tugged at him. "I suppose it's natural that you'd come in contact with her. The Everards are our closest neighbors."

Jamie shook his head, one corner of his mouth lifting. "She was more than a neighbor. She was my best friend. And she was always up for a lark. We used to ride together and play catch-me-who-can in the woods. Grandfather even had me take lessons from her governess when we were between tutors." He sighed again, and another forest tumbled.

"But she's been in London the past few years, hasn't she?" Will asked, almost afraid to hear the answer. From what he knew of the Everard family, it would not have surprised him to learn that his son and the lady had been meeting in private.

"Eight years," Jamie agreed so heavily he made the time sound like decades. He glanced up at his father, defiance shining in his eyes. "I wrote to her."

Will leaned his hip against the sofa, trying not to overreact. Neither his son nor Will's consequence would thank him for it. "And did she return your sentiments?"

Jamie gazed out the door. "She wrote back, but she never claimed anything more than friendship."

Relief was palpable. He could only hope the lady

would remain nothing more than a friend. "And may I ask your intentions now?"

Jamie shrugged. "It doesn't matter. I should have known better than to try, but I thought perhaps she might see me differently with her back against the wall."

She felt trapped? Was that why she'd been crying? Despite his intentions, Will straightened and came around the sofa to join his son by the door. "What do you mean? What's troubling her?"

Jamie flushed. "Apparently she doesn't wish me to speak of it. I cannot abuse her trust, Father. I hope you understand."

Will was afraid he understood all too well. Jamie was in love with Samantha Everard. He was tempted to put it down to calf-love—that tempestuous emotion that sometimes plagued the youth. But he had not forgotten the feelings he'd had for Jamie's mother, and at an equally young age. He would never have claimed that was anything short of love.

"You need say no more," Will promised him. Indeed, at the moment, he was less interested in hearing from his son and more interested in hearing from the lady herself. But he needed no audience save hers.

"Perhaps you should return to the party," he suggested to Jamie. "You are the guest of honor, after all."

Jamie nodded, but Will was certain his son would take little joy from the remainder of the evening.

He escorted Jamie back to the hall; introduced him to the wife of a local baronet, a lady who would in no way affect his emotions as they danced; ignored yet another imperious look from his hostess; and darted for the entryway. If Lady Everard was waiting for her carriage, he wanted to catch her before she departed.

He had never met any of the Everards personally,

but what he suspected would be enough to give most men pause. He'd been in the process of marrying and mourning when Arthur, Lord Everard, had moved his wife and young daughter into Dallsten Manor, the estate to the south of the Kendrick seat.

While he was away trying to forget his lost love, Samantha Everard had grown into a beautiful woman, one who had gathered an offer of marriage from more than one gentleman, he'd heard. Yet despite her wealth, charm and beauty, she had accepted no man as husband. He wasn't sure why and feared the reason would only hurt his son. He could understand Jamie's infatuation, but he could not allow it to go any further.

As he had hoped, she was waiting in the entryway. One of his footmen must have retrieved her evening cloak, for the black velvet that draped her made her seem all too slender, almost ethereal, as if one of the fairies rumored to live in the forests nearby had come to visit.

She certainly had more energy than a mythical creature. Instead of standing regally as a lady normally would, she was striding back and forth in front of the white marble columns that separated the entry from the wood-paneled main corridor of the house. She moved so quickly, in fact, he wondered that her kid leather slippers didn't wear out against the black-and-white marble tiles.

But at least her reflection in the gilt-framed mirror on the opposite wall proved she was the only guest waiting. With the late supper soon to be served, none of his other visitors were ready to depart. The only other people in the space were the footmen who stood at attention in their coats and breeches on either side of the wide-paneled door that fronted the drive, and Will knew he could count on their discretion.

"Lady Everard," he said, approaching her, and she pulled herself up in obvious surprise, skirts swirling about her ankles like a gentle tide. The smile that brightened her face stopped his movement, his thoughts and very nearly his breath.

"Lord Kendrick," she said. "You didn't have to abandon your other guests for me. Your staff is wondrously efficient. I expect my carriage any moment."

He thought the footmen stood a little taller at her praise. He wanted to stand a little taller as she gazed up at him. This was ridiculous! He wasn't an eighteen-year-old lad on his first year in Society. And he feared something far darker lay beneath that pleasing smile.

"I wished a word with you before you left," he said, lowering his voice. "I must ask your intentions concerning my son."

Her golden brows shot up. "*My* intentions? Isn't it generally the lady's father who asks that question, of a suitor?"

She was right of course, and she could not know he'd just asked Jamie the same question.

"Generally," he acknowledged. "But these are unusual circumstances. The gentleman is usually the elder and therefore more experienced."

Now her brows came down, and he felt as if a thundercloud was gathering. "Are you implying I am too experienced for your son, my lord?"

In some matters, he very much feared that for the truth. Oh, he had no doubt she was still a lady; her three guardians would have horsewhipped any man who had tried to change that. But she had seen things Jamie had yet to discover, things Will hoped he never would.

And thank You, Lord, for that!

"I merely meant," he said, "that you have had more time in Society than Lord Wentworth, and you must know he isn't ready for a serious courtship."

She cocked her head, curls falling against her creamy neck, and he had to pull his gaze away. "So you'd prefer he merely dally with me," she mused, though her voice held an edge, "perhaps increase his reputation with the ladies while sullying mine. Heaven forbid that he actually marry me."

This was getting worse by the minute! Will tugged down his waistcoat and raised his chin, trying to look every inch the Earl of Kendrick even while using his best diplomat's voice. "Suggesting my son dally with you would be most ungentlemanly," he assured her. "But if it's a husband you're seeking, I should point out that as a baroness in your own right you could do far better than Lord Wentworth."

He thought that would appease her. It was the truth, after all. Jamie might be the heir to an earldom, but only Will and his steward knew how tight the purse strings had become. Unless Will was very careful, his son would inherit nothing but an empty title.

But Lady Everard did not appear appeased. "Your son," she said, each word precise with tension, "is a paragon—clever, loyal and kind. I assure you, I could do far worse."

Was she intent on capturing Jamie, then? He ought to feel protective of his son, annoyed by her presumption, aghast that she would parade her intentions before him like a challenge. But the emotion striding to the front of his mind was nothing short of jealousy.

He drew himself up, shoved his feelings down deep.

"I must ask you to leave my son alone. I will not countenance a marriage between you."

She blinked, then a laugh bubbled up, soft and lilting. Another time, he was certain he would have been enchanted.

"How funny," she said, steepling her fingers in front of her lips. "I would have thought a gentleman who had seen so much of the world would have acquired more sense along the way."

Will was prepared to take offense, but she leaned closer, and the scent of roses seemed far too soft for the hard feelings he was trying to muster.

"Ask yourself this," she murmured, gaze on his. "If I truly wished to marry into your family, why would I pursue the cub instead of the lion?"

Will recoiled. Her gaze danced with laughter; her smile could only be called smug. She knew she'd shocked him. Even with his years of experience as a diplomat, he had no idea how to respond.

The clatter of horses' hooves outside announced her carriage. She straightened. "Thank you for a most diverting evening, my lord," she said, and she turned and followed one of his footmen toward the door as the other servant threw it wide for her.

Will could only stare after her. He should speak to Jamie, confess his concerns, forbid the boy to see anything more of the beautiful Lady Everard. But as he moved to return to his other guests, he passed the gilt-framed mirror, and he wasn't entirely surprised by the smile lining his face.

Samantha cast a quick look over her shoulder before the door of Kendrick Hall shut behind her. Lord Kendrick was smiling, and she felt an answering warmth inside. She could imagine laughing over a game of chess, pacing him across the countryside on horseback, dancing with her hands on his, the admiration of his gaze filling her to overflowing.

Oh, no! This would never do. She simply could not entertain such thoughts about the Earl of Kendrick.

William Wentworth would never be in charity with her. At times she was amazed Jamie was still willing to speak to her. After all, she was the reason the previous Lord Wentworth, William's brother, had been killed.

Surely he knew. Surely that was why he was so concerned that Jamie seemed to care for her. Lord Kendrick didn't understand it was merely an abiding friendship she and his son shared. She'd watched young James grow up with only his grandfather to guide him, while his father was busy defending British interests in far off places like Constantinople and Alexandria. How Jamie had pined for a moment with his father, much as she had pined for more time with hers. Come to think of it, she had every right to be annoyed with Lord Kendrick!

How could he have abandoned his son on his wife's death? Jamie had been an infant! William Wentworth had only returned after his brother's death, she was sure, because tradition required him to take up his place as the new heir. Did he care nothing for family? Was he only concerned she was pursuing Jamie because of her own past?

She shook her head as she settled herself against the velvet-covered seat and the carriage headed down the drive for the road to Dallsten Manor. Her thoughts moved faster than the lacquered wheels. Jamie's father, this new Lord Kendrick, was not what she had expected. He looked nothing like his son; he acted nothing like his father, who had always treated her with the utmost kindness, even after her connection to his older son's death.

And as for any resemblance to his dead brother, she had refused to think about the former Lord Wentworth for a very long time. She'd only lost her composure tonight when Jamie had cut short his sentences, an annoying habit that had, alas, been his late uncle's.

She needed no reminders of the mistakes she'd made, of the tragedies she'd inherited along with the Everard legacy. Those mistakes were the main reason she'd refused her suitors over the years. Each had had something to commend him: a pleasant disposition, a commanding presence, a devotion to duty. Her latest unintended conquest, Prentice Haygood, had followed her about so loyally she'd resorted to hiding in the ladies' retiring room at balls to avoid hurting his feelings!

Some of her suitors had been handsome, and some had been wealthy and some had been both. Far too many, however, had been fortune hunters, and she'd come to the point where she could smell the breed at twenty paces. Those she had no trouble refusing.

But one other sort of follower had plagued her last days in London. Her home had been broken into, her rooms pawed through. Nothing had been taken, but she could not shake the feeling that someone was watching her. She'd made inquiries, even set a trap in her home to catch the villain, going so far as to leave a window open and waiting with her strongest footman in the dark, but to no avail. Only her impending birthday had forced her north to the one place she'd ever felt truly at home: Dallsten Manor.

Unfortunately she had found an entirely different problem awaiting her in Lord Kendrick. She wasn't surprised to be attracted to him. Both Jamie and his grandfather had delighted to tell her about his adventures. The stories had circled the valley when she was a girl—his insistent courtship of Peggy Demesne, who was only the miller's daughter; their eloping to Gretna Green to marry despite his father's wishes; her death a year later birthing Jamie; and his journeys throughout the world to forget his heartbreak. William Wentworth was the stuff of legend in the Evendale valley.

Or had been, until her family's scandals eclipsed his.

She hugged her velvet cloak closer as the carriage trundled through the night. Emotions fired too easily in her family, for good and ill. Emotions, she was convinced, lay at the heart of her family's past problems. She would not trust her feelings with her future. Though it cost her everything, she would not marry on a whim, not even to save her fortune.

Chapter Three

Will would have preferred to have put the lovely Lady Everard from his mind. Unfortunately, Jamie's attitude at breakfast the next morning prevented that. The lad's cheeks and mouth sagged, his shoulders slumped over his coddled eggs and salmon. His responses to Will's attempts at conversation consisted of grunts and questionable movements of his head.

"Oxford," Will announced, keeping his gaze on the freshly baked bread he was slathering with butter. "Fine school. I think it will do very well for you."

"Oxford?" The silver-rimmed china clattered as Jamie set down his cup.

Will glanced up to see that he had his son's attention at last. "Oxford. Divinity school. With all these martyred sighs I thought perhaps you were planning on being a man of the cloth."

Jamie's mouth turned up as he shook his head. "I don't think I'm cut out for Holy Orders, thank you, Father. And you said I didn't have to return to school if I didn't wish it. You never attended Oxford."

He hadn't, and now that the title had come to him, he wondered if his earlier choices had been wise. But at eighteen, he could not have imagined the road he would travel. "So you still plan to stay here with me, learn more about managing our estate, our holdings."

Jamie nodded, hands braced on the damask tablecloth. "I'd like to understand my duty better, yes. But I intend to take a little holiday before jumping in."

Will raised his brows. "Planning to go on a Grand Tour of Europe, are you?"

Jamie grinned, pulling back his hands. "Nothing so elaborate. I'd just like to fish, ride, visit neighbors. That sort of thing."

Will set down his butter knife. "Neighbors like the Everards."

Jamie colored as if he'd been caught with his fingers in the sugar bowl. "Lady Everard is our neighbor, so yes, I planned to visit her as well as the Gileses, Mr. Ramsey our old vicar and others who knew me before I went away to Eton."

"Very…neighborly of you," Will managed.

Jamie raised his chin. "I thought so."

Will watched as the boy attacked his eggs. Jamie might protest all he liked, but Will was certain more than a friendly nature motivated him to pursue Lady Everard. He had to find a way to break through to his son.

"Perhaps I'll come with you," Will ventured. "I feel in an uncommonly neighborly mood as well."

For some reason his son did not seem amused by the prospect. But he finished breakfast and excused himself, promising to rejoin his father after Will's morning ride.

Will hoped that ride would at least clear his mind of his concerns. Nothing like pounding across the turf to remind him of the reason he was born. He was a Wentworth, and this estate had belonged to his family for ten generations. He glanced back at the hall as he wended his way through the boxed hedges for the stables behind the house.

A sturdy brick edifice four stories tall, with squat wings clinging to the center, Kendrick Hall had been built for his great-grandfather. The numerous high-arched windows capped in white, and white stone columns marking the center block, managed to give the place a look of elegance in keeping with the current age. But though the house was newer than its neighbors, Wentworth blood had defended the grounds from Scottish tribes over four hundred years ago.

And now it was Will's turn to defend it from the rising debts. He nodded to his head groom as he mounted Arrow, his favorite horse. He knew others whose heritage had been stolen by a father who gambled, a brother who invested unwisely. That was not the case with the Kendrick estate. His father had been a good if unenlightened manager. But times were changing, and the Evendale valley, so close to the fells of Cumberland, was struggling to keep pace.

Will set Arrow to a canter and guided him out around the house for the front. There he could see snatches of the oak woods to the north and the lone line of oaks flanking the long drive to the road. He had only to move beyond them, and he could see all the way to Dallsten Manor.

So he could not fail to notice the other rider pelting across the green pastures between the two houses. Even if he had doubted the identity, the flash of sunlight on golden hair would have given her away.

The gelding beneath him tossed his head as if wishing to follow. Will felt a similar desire to give chase.

He knew Arrow was swift enough to catch her. But he wasn't sure he wanted the conversation that would follow. Neighbors or not, the less time he spent in Lady Everard's company, the safer he'd feel.

But would Jamie be any safer if Will let her be? Jamie had no understanding of the female mind; Will had met enough ladies on his travels to have some familiarity. Lady Everard had implied last night that she would be more interested in him than in his son, a fact that had refused to leave his thoughts for much of the night.

Should I keep an eye on her, Father? Try to understand why she's here, what she hopes to gain?

Something inside him jumped at the idea. Still, Will hesitated, watching her. She certainly had no concerns about her own safety. Though she had crossed onto his lands, she had forsaken a groom or lady to attend her. Her horse galloped across the field, sheep scattering before them, and approached a low hedge that separated the patches of grass so the flocks could be rotated among the pastures.

Surely she'd slow; surely she'd stop. He found himself rising in the stirrup irons as if he could hold her up by sheer force of character.

The horse sailed up and over the hedge, and Lady Everard flew up and out of the saddle to land on the ground.

Will felt as if his breath had been knocked from him as well. Arrow was moving before he realized he'd directed the dappled gelding. Down they went, through the trees, over a stream. Every length Will sent up a prayer that he would find her unharmed. He galloped to the hedge and leaped from the saddle.

She had managed to raise herself into a sitting position and was gazing about her as if dazed. Will crouched beside her. Her tall-crowned hat had fallen, her curls hung free about her shoulders, and her cheeks were bright. She blinked at him as if surprised to find him there.

"Lady Everard," he murmured, tightening his fist on the reins to keep from touching her. "Are you all right?"

She wrinkled her nose and puffed out a sigh. "I am remarkably disappointed. I've taken that hedge any number of times. Why was today any different?"

He wasn't sure whether to hug her to him in relief or shout at her for risking her life. He settled for rising and going to fetch her horse, which was waiting for her a few yards away. When he returned with the black-coated mare, Lady Everard had retrieved her hat and was struggling to take another step, the skirts of her blue riding habit heavy with the mud of the field.

"Easy!" He dropped both reins and reached for her, but she held out her free hand to prevent his touch.

"I'm fine," she said, straightening to her full height, which still put her under his chin. She took a hesitant couple of steps and nodded. "Yes, quite fine." She dimpled up at him. "But thank you for your concern."

Will shook his head at her cavalier attitude. Didn't she know she could have broken her neck? "You're certain?"

"Reasonably. Though I could use your help to mount."

That was it? He couldn't think of a lady of his acquaintance who would take such a fall so calmly. His Peg had refused to ride, saying the great beasts frightened her, and he'd felt distinctly manly at the time that he was so comfortable in the saddle. In his travels he'd met any number of women who rode or drove wagons pulled by horses, donkeys or oxen, but those women had never been among the aristocracy.

"Your servant, Lady Everard," he said, bemused. Knowing his horse was well trained enough not to wander off, he handed her her horse's reins and bent to cup his fingers.

Hat back on her head, Samantha Everard put her foot in his hands. For all her bravado, it was a surprisingly small foot. Even encased in a sturdy brown leather half-boot, it fit easily in his grip, and she seemed to weigh next to nothing as he lifted her into the saddle.

She spread her sodden skirts as she settled into place. "Thank you, my lord. I appreciate your kindness."

But not necessarily his presence. Already she was gathering the reins, preparing to ride off. He should let her go, hurry back to Kendrick Hall and all those tedious estate duties. But those duties would not help him understand her, or protect his son.

"Then perhaps you would grant me a favor," he said.

She arched a brow. "A favor?"

He lay his hand on her stirrup, gazed up at her with his best smile and was surprised to hear his heart pounding louder than when he'd seen her fall. "Allow me to ride with you. I'd like to apologize for my behavior last night and become better acquainted."

It should have been easy to urge Blackie to a run and dash away, but Lord Kendrick's face, turned up to her, was bright with hope. Those green eyes positively twinkled in the summer sun, as if being with her was the most delightful thing he could imagine. Besides, her hip was beginning to protest its collision with the ground, and she didn't relish galloping at the moment.

"Very well, my lord," she said.

Returning to his horse, he swung himself up into the saddle as if from long practice and eased alongside her. His dapple gray was a fine animal, with dark intelligent eyes and a ready step. She was certain he'd give Blackie a good run, if she'd have dared to race today. But perhaps she should try to remember she was a lady for a change.

Together they set off across the pastures toward Kendrick Hall. The air was still cool so close to the mountains, scented with damp earth and growing things. London never smelled this good. No country estate she'd visited matched the crisp scent either. She found herself drawing it in. It smelled like home.

"You're certain you're fine," he asked again, as if noticing her deep breaths.

Samantha felt herself coloring. "I've taken a fall or two in my time, sir. There's no need to fuss over me."

Immediately she regretted the tartness of her words, but he merely smiled. "Habit. It seems I've grown a bit too much into the fatherly role."

Just as Jamie was outgrowing it, she realized. She remembered how she'd had to accustom herself to her three guardians when her cousins had first arrived at Dallsten Manor on her father's death. Lord Everard had kept his nephews in the dark about his wife and daughter. Certainly Samantha had never dreamed she had a family until her father had died and his will demanded that she work with her cousins to save her inheritance and theirs.

The will had required her to be presented to the queen, to be welcomed in all the homes who had refused admittance to her scandalous father and to garner an offer of marriage from three eligible gentlemen. One had been from her old friend Toby Giles, one from her cousin Vaughn and one from the brother of the man who rode beside her. Only one requirement remained, and she knew she would never fulfill it now.

"Still, there's no need to apologize," she told him as they crossed the stream, the horses' hooves splashing in the sparkling mountain waters. "You were only trying to protect Jamie. I used to do the same thing when we were younger."

He held the reins lightly, but his gaze flickered over her. "Did you?"

Could he not see her in that role? "Certainly. He was so cute when he was little, so earnest." She smiled, remembering. "He would do anything I suggested. I had to be very careful, I promise you."

He seemed to sit taller in the saddle. "And now you've returned," he said, and something simmered in his warm voice. "But not to stay, it seems."

The light of day made this conversation no easier than it had been last night. She said the lines she'd rehearsed. "I thought it was time I took a more active role in the summer party. It's a family tradition, and it's been years since I even attended."

"So I understand. Eight, isn't it?"

Did he think to upbraid her? She offered him a smile and said sweetly, "Less than the nine or more years you were away."

He grimaced, a quirk of his gentle mouth that reminded her of Jamie. "Your point. I should be the last one to question why someone would want to leave Evendale."

Or return. She knew why he'd come back, and though she was glad Jamie had been reunited with his father, the knowledge of the part she'd played was a weight on her heart.

"And how go plans for the big event?" he asked as if realizing she was too quiet. Her—quiet! How her cousins would laugh if they knew. She certainly had no trouble talking to anyone else, and she very much feared it wasn't her guilt that was keeping her tongue-tied.

She could see Kendrick Hall rising ahead of them and directed Blackie to stop.

"Well enough," she answered him as he pulled his horse up beside hers. "There will be a puppet show, a whirligig and more pies than anyone should safely eat."

"And dancing in the evening?"

She blushed at his tone and wasn't sure why. "Certainly, my lord. That is tradition, too."

"And woe betide us for changing tradition," he said with a chuckle. "As you did not favor me with a dance last night, I hope you'll save one for me at the party."

A dance? With him? Ever since her father had instituted the annual summer party, she'd dreamed of dancing. When she'd left for London, she had been too young, in her governess's eyes, to participate. The party had been held the past eight years without her as she'd attended one house party after another, from Cornwall in the south to Carlisle in the north, all to fulfill the last requirement of her father's will. She'd had to delegate the party to her housekeeper and Mrs. Dallsten Walcott.

Now at last and possibly for the last, Samantha was the hostess.

"I will certainly see if I can find time for a dance," she promised. "But I expect to be very busy, my lord."

He barked a laugh. "Well, that's a leveler. I thought all young ladies wished to dance with eligible earls."

Did he consider himself eligible, then? She thought every lady within miles must be setting her cap at him.

Funny. Given his history she'd somehow considered him immune.

"I suppose they do," she acknowledged. "But I no longer need to attach eligible gentlemen."

"Then you have an understanding," he said, and once again she was all too aware of his green gaze as he studied her. She had an understanding all right, but not of the sort he meant. She had come to the realization that marriage was not for her.

"Suffice it to say that I will not be marrying anytime soon," she replied. "Thank you for your company, my lord. I should return home."

He looked ready to protest, eyes narrowed, head high. Still he nodded a farewell, and she turned the horse. She tried to look as calm, but she couldn't keep herself from looking back. Once more he was watching her leave, yet this time the determination on his face told her that he intended to learn her secrets, whether she wished it or not.

Chapter Four

Unfortunately the Earl of Kendrick wasn't the only person intent on discovering more about Samantha's personal affairs. She had barely reached Dallsten Manor and was heading for her room to change out of her mud-encrusted riding habit when Mrs. Dallsten Walcott met her at the foot of the main stair.

The house was much improved since she'd left, thanks to the vision of her cousin Jerome and judicious use of funds from her inheritance. Jerome had a reason to want to preserve the manor. He had fallen in love here with Mrs. Dallsten Walcott's daughter, Samantha's former governess, Adele. And Adele had been raised in the house, which had belonged to her family before hard times had forced them to sell to Samantha's father. So it was no wonder Jerome and Adele shared Samantha's fondness for the place.

In the past eight years the Everards had rebuilt the crumbling pele tower that stood at the north corner and added fine wood paneling to the lower half of many of the walls. They'd also augmented the formerly spartan staff with footmen, gardeners and maids of every variety.

Now their work was evident, for every wood surface gleamed, from the parquet floor to the banister on the elegant stair. Even the ancient wall tapestry of knights attacking a stag had been cleaned, the colors once more proud.

But never as proud as the lady standing sternly on the stair.

"Why am I not informed of your goings out?" Mrs. Dallsten Walcott demanded, face nearly as pink as her fashionable wool gown.

Samantha stifled a desire to stick out her tongue at the elderly woman who had known her most of her life. For one thing, the gesture was unkind—she knew how Mrs. Dallsten Walcott tended to cling to people and things as a way to stave off her fears of loneliness and poverty. For another, Samantha had entirely outgrown such childish displays, most days.

"It was only a ride," she said, pausing below her chaperone and feeling a bit more like a schoolgirl every moment. "I didn't think you'd wish to join me."

Mrs. Dallsten Walcott put her formidable nose in the air and sniffed. "Certainly not. I never felt the need to pelt across the grounds willy-nilly like some hoyden."

Like me, Samantha thought, but the appellation of hoyden merely made her smile. Truth be told, she liked the fact she felt free to race across the grounds. Lord Kendrick hadn't minded either. He'd seemed genuinely concerned about her fall, of course, but he'd never scolded her for jumping hedges, even if the act was a challenging feat from a sidesaddle.

"If you have need of me, I'd be delighted to help," she told Mrs. Dallsten Walcott, "as soon as I've changed." She spread her skirts to emphasize the state of her disarray and a chunk of dried mud obligingly fell to the floor with a plop.

Mrs. Dallsten Walcott took a step back as if she feared the dirt would attack her. "I merely wish to congratulate you on your strategy and offer my guidance in achieving it." She eyed Samantha's riding habit. "You appear to need some assistance."

Samantha dropped her skirts. "Strategy?"

"To marry young Lord Wentworth." She wagged a finger at Samantha. "You may have the others fooled into thinking you'll give away the manor, but I know better."

Why would none of them leave her alone on the matter? It wasn't their portions of the Everard legacy at risk if she failed to meet the last stipulation of her father's will and marry before her upcoming birthday.

Her oldest cousin, Jerome, would keep the estate her father had left him, which had only grown more prosperous under his management. Her cousin Richard would keep his ship and the two he'd purchased with his inheritance. Cousin Vaughn had no doubt already spent the money her father had left him on the estate he'd been given when he'd been elevated to marquess. She was the only one who stood to lose—her childhood home and the bulk of the fortune. But better that than to risk her future or her very life.

Samantha pushed past her chaperone and started up the stairs.

"I am not marrying Jamie," she flung over her shoulder. "And I don't need anyone's help."

She said it loudly and with great conviction, but she might have been whistling down the wind for all the good it did. Mrs. Dallsten Walcott swept up beside her, keeping pace as Samantha stomped down the long corridor for her bedchamber, shedding more mud with each step.

"Certainly you need help," the elderly lady scolded. "He's a mere youth, true, but even young men can be clever about evading matrimony. And you only have a fortnight."

Samantha paused beside the painting of Mrs. Dallsten Walcott's father, who had a similarly unforgiving look in his eyes. "Madam, I refuse to have this conversation with you."

Mrs. Dallsten Walcott folded in on herself, and her lower lip began to tremble. "Very well. I know you have no use for me even though I was your mother's dearest friend and only confidante when your father abandoned her here for his other life in London. You needn't heed my advice, although I'm certain I've only ever had your best interests at heart." She slipped a lace-edged handkerchief from the sleeve of her gown and dabbed at her eyes.

Other women would have begged her pardon, rushed to assure her of her place in their affections. Samantha had known her too long. She put her hands on her hips.

"Crocodile tears will not move me, madam. I know where your loyalty lies—with this house and the name of Dallsten."

Mrs. Dallsten Walcott raised her head, and as Samantha had suspected, no tears glistened on her soft cheeks. "And if that were true, would you blame me?" She flapped her handkerchief across the air. "How can you even consider giving all this away!"

The guilt threatened to overwhelm her. She was an Everard, and this was her home just as much as it was Mrs. Dallsten Walcott's. She'd learned to read and ride here, lost a father and found a family. How could she let this house be sold to another?

For where your treasure is, there will your heart be also.

The guilt abated. She had to remember that Dallsten Manor was only a house. Its presence or loss only affected her and a few others. They would mourn, and it would be over. Marrying in desperation or out of any other emotion had the potential to hurt so many more people, and more than one generation. She knew that now.

She laid her hand on Mrs. Dallsten Walcott's shoulder and was surprised how frail it had become. "I'm sorry. I know how much you love this house and how you've enjoyed living in it the past eight years while I've been gone. But I'm not marrying before my twenty-fifth birthday. Very likely, I'm not marrying at all."

This time Samantha was fairly sure the water welling in her chaperone's blue eyes was real. "But we'll lose the house, all the furnishings, the paintings, the sculpture," Mrs. Dallsten Walcott said, sucking in a breath as if the idea was too much to bear.

"All but the dower house," Samantha agreed, the words like acid on her tongue. "You have the use of that in your lifetime, along with any family mementos you care to claim." She leaned closer. "We both know how many of those the dower house can hold."

A slow smile lit her chaperone's face as she blinked back her tears. Samantha knew she was also thinking about the time, eight years ago, when Mrs. Dallsten Walcott had managed to cart most of the house's valuables down to the dower house for "safekeeping." Only Jerome's diplomacy and Samantha's offer to let the lady live in the main house again had made the woman feel comfortable in returning the items to their former places.

"Clever girl," she told Samantha now. "I've always said so. I'll need your help."

Samantha straightened. "You'll have it. Whatever you like, we'll move it down to the dower house immediately, just as was agreed in the original deed from my father. I imagine you know exactly where to find all the important pieces."

Mrs. Dallsten Walcott nodded as she tucked her handkerchief away. "I have the list in my head. I shall put it to paper, and we can start checking things off this very day. But you will need to forego our efforts tomorrow for tea."

Hand on the latch to the door of her room, Samantha eyed her. "Tea? I don't recall an appointment over tea."

Mrs. Dallsten Walcott waved a hand. "The invitation came while you were out. Lord Wentworth has invited you to tea tomorrow at Kendrick Hall." She beamed as if this was a tremendous honor.

Samantha raised her brows. "Reading my mail now, are you?"

Her chaperone drew herself up. "And how else am I to keep watch over you, young lady? There's a reason Adele allowed you to come north alone ahead of the others."

There was indeed, and it had little to do with the fact that Mrs. Dallsten Walcott was available to play chaperone for propriety's sake. Adele was hoping the time alone at Dallsten Manor would make Samantha change her mind about marrying.

"I didn't come ahead to play at tea," she said. "We have work to do if we're to have everything ready for the summer party in a fortnight."

Mrs. Dallsten Walcott waved her hand again as if the effort amounted to nothing. "That is well in hand, thanks to all your work in the intervening months. You have done quite well in that regard, so you have no reason to avoid tea tomorrow. I have already accepted for you."

Heat licked up her. It seemed no matter how old she was, her life was not her own. Well, perhaps it was time to make it her own.

"Since you accepted, you can explain why I don't show up," Samantha informed her chaperone, pushing open the door and marching into her room.

She thought the lady would wait to continue the argument until after Samantha had changed, but Mrs. Dallsten Walcott followed her into the bedchamber, ignoring the maid who came hurrying from the dressing room.

"But he's the heir to an earldom," her chaperone protested. "Surely you can see the benefits of such a match!"

The benefits were evident—the combination of their lands to provide a larger estate for both houses, the fulfillment of her father's will. She could live among her beloved fells, surrounded by friends and family.

But she would have cheated Jamie out of finding a bride who could truly love him. Surely her way was better! *Help me be strong, heavenly Father!*

She pasted on a smile as she raised her arms to allow her maid to help her out of her soiled habit. "I'm sure Lord Wentworth will make a wonderful husband, for the right young lady. I am not that lady."

Mrs. Dallsten Walcott went so far as to stamp her foot, and the maid cringed.

"Oh, how can you be so stubborn?" her chaperone cried. "Adele let this chance slip through her fingers.

She was engaged to the former heir to Kendrick Hall, and she let him get away. Do not make the same mistake!"

Samantha had nearly been engaged to the former heir as well, something she could never forget. Lord Gregory Wentworth had been years older and a sophisticated gentleman who'd had years to master London Society. She'd been fascinated from the moment he had been introduced to her. He'd seemed so attentive, so sure of himself and her.

But she'd later learned that his pursuit of her had been dictated by his mentor, a villain intent on treason who had already hurt her family. The former Lord Wentworth's role in his powerful mentor's evil plan had been to keep her cousin Vaughn so busy worrying about Lord Wentworth's courtship of Samantha that Vaughn forgot his quest to find the villain who had murdered her father, his beloved uncle.

The plan might have worked but for two things. Vaughn hadn't been jealous; he'd already fallen in love with the villain's daughter, of all people! And Lord Wentworth had fallen in love as well, with Samantha. The knowledge that he would put her before his mentor's plans had driven the villain to kill him. Samantha could not help feeling that she should have done something, anything, to save Lord Wentworth. Perhaps, if she'd been more observant, if she hadn't been ruled by her emotions, if she hadn't been so fixated on gathering her third proposal, she might have discovered his connection to the treason plot and acted before he'd been killed.

Now she turned her back on Mrs. Dallsten Walcott as the maid pulled off her habit.

"The gravest mistake, madam, would be for me to

marry," she said, gaze on the far pink wall. "And nothing you or anyone else says will change that."

Though she heard Mrs. Dallsten Walcott stalk from the room, Samantha was fairly sure the argument wasn't over. But she knew she'd already won. And lost.

Will reacted with nearly as much determination when he was informed later that day about Jamie's invitation to have Lady Everard join them for tea. He had returned from his ride sure that he could find a way to uncover the secrets he saw lurking in the lady's deep brown eyes, if only to protect his family. That effort would require him to meet her again, gain her trust. But he had not expected his son to steal a march on him.

"And what exactly is the purpose of this event?" he asked Jamie as they sat in the library discussing estate business.

Jamie shrugged, lounging with great satisfaction in the leather-upholstered chair. "I told you—I want to reacquaint myself with our neighbors. Tea seemed a good way to start."

"Will you pour or shall I?" Will quipped.

Jamie colored. "Mrs. Dallsten Walcott will be joining us. She can pour. And I would be delighted for you to attend, Father. Unless you have better things to do."

Nothing more important than protecting his son from possibly predatory females. And attending would give him a chance to study Lady Everard more closely.

"Of course I'll attend," he told Jamie. "This is my home. I'd insult the ladies by not making an appearance." He slapped his son on the knee. "Count on it. I'll be there to support you."

Jamie nodded, but somehow he did not look comforted.

He looked even less happy when he and Will gathered in the withdrawing room the next day to await their guests. Will's mother had designed the formal room, from the elaborate pattern of the inlaid wood floor to the gilded chevrons on the white paneling of the lower walls and white marble fireplace. The creamy floral wreaths on the red silk wall hangings were mirrored in the sculpted wreaths edging the high ceiling.

Will hadn't paid the decor all that much attention growing up. Peg had hated the room, particularly the snowy carpet in the center with its red silk fringe. She'd been afraid to walk on it lest she soil it. He had to agree it was rather impractical. He should have removed it years ago, but it reminded him of Peg.

Today Jamie refused to sit on any of the elegant white, curved-back chairs or sofa. He paced from the windows overlooking the fells to the doorway into the corridor, peering out each and pausing only long enough to tug at various articles of clothing. Already his cravat was wilting, his blue patterned waistcoat was rumpled, and his tasseled boots had lost their shine. Will felt for him.

"You'll be fine," he offered, stretching out his own tooled leather boots where he sat near the hearth. He hadn't dressed the part of the earl today, choosing instead a tweed coat and chamois trousers. But the boots had been with him too many years to forego. Far more elaborate than the ones his contemporaries generally favored, they were as soft as butter and as comfortable as old slippers. He'd had them made his first week in Constantinople, and they'd been with him ever since.

When Jamie didn't respond, Will glanced up. His son was frozen on the carpet, and their guests were at the door.

"Lady Everard and Mrs. Dallsten Walcott," said their butler, a relict as formal as the room.

Will could understand why his son was gaping. He was hard-pressed not to gape himself. Samantha, Lady Everard, had been a vision in her cerulean ball gown. Now it seemed as if joy had entered the room. Her pale muslin gown was covered in a fitted blue jacket that brought out the gold of her hair. The collar was a frivolous affair with multiple points edged in lace; it was as whimsical as her smile.

He found himself smiling back and forced a more serious look. He'd met women from every part of the Ottoman Empire and places in between, from dusky-skinned princesses to platinum-haired grand duchesses. Why did this woman make them all fade in comparison?

"Samantha." Jamie rushed forward to take her arm and lead her into the room. "Thank you for coming."

"Well, it seems I promised," she said with a sidelong glance at her companion.

Mrs. Dallsten Walcott, resplendent in royal purple as if she planned to take tea with the Regent, swept up to Will and curtseyed. "Lord Kendrick, how kind of you to invite us to your lovely home."

Will bowed. "It is only lovely because you grace us with your presence, dear lady."

She batted her lashes at him as she rose and tapped his arm with one finger. "I spoke with the Widow Trent yesterday. She was utterly charmed by your attentions at the party the other night."

He could not think who she meant. The only woman he remembered meeting was gazing at him from across the room in obvious amusement. "She is kind to think of me," he replied.

Mrs. Dallsten Walcott tittered. "It isn't kindness that

makes a lady remember a handsome gentleman, my lord."

"Oh, I don't know," Samantha put in. "Any lady would remember a kindness after a sudden mishap. Such an act is unlooked for and most welcome, like a breeze on a hot day."

It was not the day but his face that felt hot at that reference to their ride the previous day. No, he couldn't be blushing! He waved to the chair closest to the tea cart, and Mrs. Dallsten Walcott took it while he made sure to sit the farthest from Lady Everard. He told himself it was his duty to keep an eye on things, but some part of him warned it was self-preservation.

Still, the tableau would have been amusing under other circumstances. Their staff had set up a cart with the dainty silver tea urn his mother had preferred and her favorite rose-covered china cups and saucers. A plate of delicate tea cakes, frosted in a creamy yellow, lay ready for the passing. Normally his son would have been the first to reach for them.

But Jamie was watching Samantha as if she was the tea cake and he was starving. Mrs. Dallsten Walcott was studying the pair of them with narrowed eyes that seemed to hold more speculation than censorship. And Samantha was eying Will, mouth turned up at one corner, twinkle in her dark eyes as if she was in complete agreement with him that the situation was ridiculous.

Even as he fought the urge to adjust his cravat or waistcoat, she turned her smile on Jamie.

"Everything looks marvelous. Would you like me to pour?"

"Of course," Jamie said as if waking from a dream.

She set about pouring the steaming brew into the cups, her movements sure and easy. She'd probably poured tea a hundred times since she'd made her debut in Society, yet the smiles she bestowed on Mrs. Dallsten Walcott and Jamie said they were the most important people she had ever served. Will was on his feet and moving toward her before she even held out his cup.

His fingers brushed hers as he reached for the china, and he heard the sharp intake of her breath. Her gaze met his. He could not seem to look away. As if from a long distance he heard the soft thud of a cup and saucer hitting the carpet.

"Oh, gracious!" Mrs. Dallsten Walcott cried. "Samantha, how could you!"

Samantha turned red and dropped her gaze, now empty hands falling into the lap of her pale gown. "I'm so sorry, my lord."

"My fault entirely," Will said, squatting to pick up the unbroken china. The stain of the spilled tea was spreading across the pristine carpet. He couldn't help grimacing, but the act had more to do with his own behavior than hers.

What was he thinking, mooning about, gazing into her eyes like a lovesick schoolboy? He had thought he'd learned something in the nearly twenty years since he'd fallen in love the first time. At the moment he felt no wiser than his son.

He had to be wiser. He had to protect Jamie. And now it appeared he had to protect himself as well. For if he wasn't careful, Samantha, Lady Everard, might wedge her way into his heart, and that would be a mistake.

Chapter Five

Samantha sat quietly, trying not to bite her lip, as Mrs. Dallsten Walcott poured another cup of tea for Lord Kendrick and chatted about commonplaces. Why had she dropped that cup? She'd served tea dozens of times, once to His Highness the Duke of York! Her hands had never so much as trembled. But one look in those deep green eyes and she'd lost all sense of place, aware only of the pounding of her heart.

Lord, please, not like this. You know the danger of trusting feelings that come so quickly. Help me!

"It's nothing," Jamie whispered beside her. "Please don't concern yourself. My father says my mother hated that carpet. I don't know why he kept it."

She nodded, but she focused her gaze on the ugly brown stain. Likely William Wentworth, Lord Kendrick, kept the carpet for the same reason she kept the iron canopy over her mother's bed—so he would never forget. She could not allow these fleeting feelings to overpower her resolve.

"Cake?" Lord Kendrick asked, holding out the silver-rimmed plate to her. "They used to be Lord Wentworth's favorite."

Lord Wentworth? The image of his brother, cleft chin, blue eyes, superior air, came to mind despite her best efforts. She hadn't known the schemes that were about to endanger her family then. Certainly she hadn't suspected Lord Wentworth had been anything but sincere in his courtship. Did Lord Kendrick understand she'd once hoped his brother might offer for her? That he had in fact offered the day before his murder?

She searched Lord Kendrick's face for judgment, for blame. But he was merely smiling at her, all encouragement, as if trying to allay her concerns after the tea contretemps.

"They're still my favorites," Jamie proclaimed, reaching past her to take the tray from his father. He held it before her. "Try one, Samantha. They're delicious."

Oh, of course. She had to remember Jamie was Lord Wentworth now. The former Lord Wentworth was dead, and if she were wise she would not mention the reasons to his brother. She managed a smile for Jamie's sake and selected one of the little iced cakes. The taste was a perfect blend of tart and sweet, much like her life of late.

"Delicious," she assured Jamie, who was watching her. By his smile, she would have thought she'd offered him the moon.

As he returned the plate to the tea cart, she picked up her spoon to stir her tea and was surprised to find that the implement was made of rosewood. Something glimmered at the tip. Looking closer, she saw amber inlaid into the end.

"Something to remember my travels," Lord Kendrick said, as if he'd been watching her.

"A gift from the sultan of the Ottoman Empire,"

Jamie said with some pride. "You recall how Father served in Constantinople."

"And Egypt," Samantha replied, fingering the satiny wood of the spoon. She shot Jamie a grin. "You always hoped he'd bring back a mummy."

"No mummies, alas," Lord Kendrick said with a smile.

Jamie laughed, eyes bright. "But he has a whole room full of wonders. Would you like to see them?"

"I'm sure Lady Everard has better things to do than look at a moldery bunch of keepsakes," his father said.

She doubted they could be moldery. "I'd love to see them," she told Jamie, hopping to her feet. Jamie rose just as eagerly, with Lord Kendrick only a few seconds behind.

Mrs. Dallsten Walcott heaved a martyred sigh as she set aside her tea and rose to follow them from the withdrawing room.

Samantha had visited Kendrick Hall many times growing up. It was much grander than Dallsten Manor, with easily twice as many rooms. Each room she'd seen was paneled in silk or fine woods, the hearths all varying types of marble, with liberal use of gilding on every conceivable surface. In short, it was elegant, imposing and far too formal for her tastes.

She could not say the same for the room Jamie showed her now, located just down the corridor from the withdrawing room. The moment she stepped past the paneled door, she felt as if she'd been transported to another land.

Crimson and azure tapestries woven with gold hung from the walls; carpets patterned in fanciful flowers and bright-plumed birds graced the parquet floor. Tall bronze vases with fluted mouths held feathers from peacocks and ostriches. Tables inlaid with ivory and ebony supported delicate statuary and finely wrought boxes of gold and silver. The very air was scented with sandalwood and incense. Mrs. Dallsten Walcott turned up her aristocratic nose.

But Samantha wandered deeper into the room, gaze darting from one piece to another. Here was the William Wentworth the valley legends proclaimed—the world traveler, the mysterious adventurer. This room she thought, unlike any other in Kendrick Hall, truly reflected its master. That he was well aware of it was evident by the smile tugging at the corners of his mouth as he too gazed about fondly. These were not just mementos; this was his life on display.

"Look here," Jamie urged, taking her hand and pulling her to where several curved sheaths of beaten gold hung from mahogany arms on the wall. He lifted one down and drew on the jeweled hilt until the sword flashed in the light from the far window. "Father won this from a Janissary by defeating him in combat."

"How interesting," Mrs. Dallsten Walcott said, but she gravitated to a set of jeweled pins shaped like butterflies.

Samantha was far more interested in the swords. It wasn't hard to picture Lord Kendrick, blade raised like a knight of old, ready to protect England. "A Janissary?" she asked, rubbing a finger along the metal sheath.

Lord Kendrick's hands passed over hers and took the sword from Jamie. "A soldier hired to protect the Ottoman Empire and those who serve her," he explained. "Janissaries are assigned to the foreign embassies and envoys as guards. They can be your best source of help in trouble. And I didn't defeat one. The swords were a gift, like much of what you see here." He returned the sword to its place on the wall.

"A gift for valor," Jamie assured Samantha even as she wondered why Lord Kendrick didn't seem to like his son touching his things. "Father fought to keep the French out of Egypt. Here, I'll show you." He hurried off to the leather-bound trunk along the opposite wall.

"You are too humble, I think," Samantha teased Lord Kendrick, her hand falling to rest on a carved chest.

His mouth turned up at one corner. He had a nice mouth—firm lips above a firmer chin. She could imagine him ordering a battalion to action as easily as he called for tea.

"It isn't humility to know one's place in history," he countered. "That's one thing I learned in the diplomatic corps. No matter how important the ruler, there's always someone else who fancies himself more important. And sometimes he's right."

"And just as often he's wrong," Samantha replied, thinking back to her family's struggles against the powerful nobleman who had thought to help Napoleon conquer England. That man had intended to rule England himself one day, even if he had to kill a few Englishmen like Lord Kendrick's brother along the way. Of course she couldn't tell Lord Kendrick or Jamie about that. Everyone involved had been sworn to secrecy.

"You needn't worry, Lady Everard," Lord Kendrick murmured, hand covering hers on the chest. "We will beat Napoleon. It's only a matter of time."

He thought she'd meant the current war. She should find a way to explain or agree, but everything in her seemed to be focused on his gentle touch. The warmth seeped into her skin, relaxed muscles she hadn't realized she'd held tight. Would his embrace be just as warm?

"Here you are," Jamie declared, and Samantha sprang away from Lord Kendrick, her face heating. There she went again! She had to master these emotions. She'd thought she'd become more skilled at it, but after spending her whole life acting on her feelings, shutting them off now wasn't easy, even understanding their danger.

She was merely thankful that Jamie didn't seem to notice her lapse. Neither did her chaperone. Mrs. Dallsten Walcott, returning to join them, was obviously more interested in the scroll Jamie was unrolling. Samantha could only hope her host was as oblivious. She chanced a glance at him, but his gaze was on the scroll.

And what a sight it was, nearly two feet high and bound on golden rods. Gold and crimson figures ran along each margin and the top. Across the page danced fanciful writing in bold brown ink. She had never seen its like.

"What does it say?" she asked, peering closer.

"To Lord William," Lord Kendrick read, long finger gliding along the words as he translated. "You have my everlasting gratitude for your help in settling the Egyptian question and my deepest affections for your friendship."

"It's from the ruler of the Ottoman Empire," Jamie explained as Lord Kendrick's hand fell to his side.

"The sultan, until he lost his place and life to a rebellion," Lord Kendrick murmured, straightening. Samantha could hear the sorrow in his voice.

"Father was gone from there by then," Jamie said as if the entire culture had ceased to be of interest once his father had departed. He carefully rolled up the scroll. "All the English left when the Turks started supporting the French. We even sent in the Navy."

Lord Kendrick stepped back, jaw tightening. "The sultan was the most progressive ruler in that part of the world in the past hundred years. He would have seen reason without shoving a frigate down his throat. As it was, the Navy had to retreat in defeat from the Ottoman shore batteries after losing more than forty men. And the ambassador and his staff were forced to flee the country."

He must have been one of those staff. Small wonder he hesitated to relive those days. His usual diplomacy had all but deserted him, and it was clear he was not a man willing to concede defeat.

It was a trait she unfortunately shared with him. She could only hope the two of them would never have cause to oppose each other, for the results could be devastating.

Will was glad to shut the door on his memories and chivvy his son and guests back to the more traditional surroundings of the withdrawing room. The way Samantha Everard's eyes had brightened as she'd gazed around his room had made him want to stand straighter, point out his triumphs as proudly as Jamie.

And he knew he had reason to be pleased with his accomplishments. His work had built friendships between high-ranking members of the Ottoman Empire and Britain, safeguarded British citizens and protected antiquities from French conquest. His encouragement of the sultan's reforms, however, had also resulted in rebellion and the deaths of friends and colleagues. He could never fully celebrate the good without being drawn into regret over the bad.

So he returned to the safety of his withdrawing room, which held far more benign memories. His efficient staff had refreshed the tea and replaced the stained carpet with one from a guest bedchamber. While the gold-and-brown pattern did not match the rest of the decor, it warmed the room, and he found he liked it better.

Mrs. Dallsten Walcott seemed to think she should rise to the position of his hostess again, for she poured everyone another cup of tea the moment they had settled into seats and promptly began quizzing Jamie as if he were the visitor in her home and not the other way around.

"And what are your plans now, Lord Wentworth?" she asked, fingers curled around the handle of the flowered cup. "Do you plan to enter the diplomatic corps like your father?"

Jamie smiled, but his gaze was on Lady Everard. "Oh no, ma'am. I'm here at Kendrick Hall to stay. This is my home."

Samantha kept her gaze on her tea, and her look was not nearly as bright as it had been in the other room. By now, Will was certain she was not one to shrink away from conflict. Was she trying to discourage his son, or draw him out with her silence?

"I imagine you will make a very fine earl one day," Mrs. Dallsten Walcott said with a nod to confirm her opinion. "Once you have set up your nursery, of course." She tittered like a young girl.

Samantha shot her a narrow-eyed glance. "I'm sure James has other plans at the moment."

Mrs. Dallsten Walcott took a sip of her tea and said nothing. She didn't have to. Her arched brows spoke for her.

"Lord Wentworth is planning to help me manage our holdings," Will felt compelled to put in. "He also intends to reacquaint himself with his neighbors. Isn't that right, James?"

"Exactly right, Father," Jamie agreed. "I have a lot of catching up to do, with friends, with family. And I think I've nearly forgotten how to fish. Remember how Grandfather used to take us up to the Evendale, Samantha?"

That brought her head up. "Oh, yes," she said with a grin to Jamie. "And I remember how many times you fell in."

Will nearly winced as his son colored. "I still caught my fish, didn't I?" Jamie challenged.

"Always," she assured him. "And they were delicious cooked for dinner. I remember that, too!"

He set down his cup and saucer on the little ornamental table beside him. "Count on it, then. I'll catch you a dozen of the biggest fish in the Evendale so you can have them every night for a week."

Samantha's spine straightened so quickly the points of her collar stuck out. Jamie had clearly overstepped himself, and Will thought he knew why.

"Perhaps Lady Everard would prefer to catch her own fish," he offered and hoped his son would take the hint.

Samantha beamed at him, obviously pleased he'd understood. He refused to preen.

Mrs. Dallsten Walcott was less willing to agree. "Of course she doesn't!" she all but scolded and threw in a shudder for good measure. "You catch those horrid smelly creatures, Lord Wentworth, as a gentleman should. Lady Everard and I will stay safely in the manor."

Jamie, unfortunately, did not have the sense to hide his pride at her words. He visibly brightened, chin coming up.

Samantha scowled at him. "Do not look so pleased, sir. You should know I'm not one to let others have all the fun or make all the effort."

His son must have realized his error, for he lowered his head. "Of course. Forgive me. I'd be delighted to take you fishing. And if you don't care to fish, perhaps there's something else we might do together."

The yearning in the lad's voice cut into Will. He thought he understood what had bonded his son and Lady Everard when they were younger, despite the differences in their ages and genders. Jamie had been an only child being raised by his grandfather; she had been an only child being raised by her governess, with only occasional visits from her father. With Kendrick Hall so close to Dallsten Manor, it was natural the two should band together.

But now their lives were different. Jamie had been away at school, and Will knew that Eton was a far cry from the rest of the world. Samantha Everard had seen more of that world, if only in England. The way Will had found her crying in the library said she'd seen heartache. Could Jamie appreciate the woman she'd become?

If she had a similar thought, she didn't show it. Nor did she take the opportunity Jamie had offered to monopolize his attentions. "There's always the summer party," she offered with a gentle smile. "Everyone comes to that."

Again, Will felt his son's pain. "Yes, I suppose so," Jamie said, looking away.

But in doing so, he missed the struggle Will could see in Samantha. Her golden brows lowered, and her hand twitched in her lap as if she longed to reach out to Jamie. What was going on inside her? Was she interested in capturing Jamie's heart, or not?

As if making a decision, she put a hand on Jamie's arm. "Tell you what—you always wanted to learn to fence. Why don't I teach you?"

Will brought his cup to his mouth and took a sip to hide his groan. Lady Everard might have more experience in Society, but both of them needed lessons in diplomacy!

Jamie washed white and pulled away from her touch. "I learned to fence at Eton, thank you very much. What kind of man do you think me that I need a girl to teach me?"

"A girl?" There went her back up once more.

Mrs. Dallsten Walcott tittered again. "How silly. I'm certain it was just a jest. Tell Lord Wentworth it was just a jest, Samantha."

Samantha's lips were so tight Will didn't think a word could have escaped. Indeed, all her emotions were leaping in her dark eyes. This needed to end.

He set down his cup. "I'm sure you'd agree, madam," he said to Mrs. Dallsten Walcott, "that there's no need to apologize for an acquired skill. Nor would Lady Everard be the first woman to acquire it."

Mrs. Dallsten Walcott gasped as if he'd suggested all men start wearing petticoats.

Samantha, however, relaxed in her seat. "It's excellent exercise," she said, but more as if she were stating a fact than justifying her pastime. "So is boxing."

He thought Mrs. Dallsten Walcott might have apoplexy. Even Jamie was regarding his friend with something akin to shock.

"It certainly is," Will temporized. "James is rather good at that as well." He gave his son a nod of encouragement. "But he excels at the blade. I imagine he'd be delighted to show you, Lady Everard."

Once more she beamed at him, and he felt as if he were the most clever fellow on the planet. When she turned that smile to Jamie, the room seemed to dim.

"What do you say, Jamie?" she asked. "Shall we fence?"

"Now, now," Mrs. Dallsten Walcott interrupted. "This has gone far enough. A match between a man and a woman is unseemly."

Though Will knew many who would agree, hearing the sentiment expressed so vehemently made him question it. Why shouldn't a lady fence with a gentleman, if both were willing and skilled? He'd never been one to confine a person, by age, class or gender. Why start now?

Samantha frowned at her chaperone. "I've fenced with men before. Cousin Vaughn taught me the basic moves years ago, and I've had bouts with my cousins Jerome and Richard as well."

"And I'm certain you taught them a thing or two," Will said before Mrs. Dallsten Walcott could protest further. "It sounds as if you quite enjoy the sport."

"More than I should," she admitted with a bubbly laugh, her composure restored. "You must fence as well, my lord."

Will shrugged, but Jamie spoke up. "He's an expert. You should join us Monday afternoon for our weekly bout."

Will tensed and wasn't sure why. He had no doubt he could hold his own with the blade. He was starting to fear he would have far less luck with his heart. He held his breath as she gazed at Jamie.

She had to see how much her answer meant to the lad. Emotion simmered in Jamie's eyes, tension tightened the skin across his nose. He wanted her to fence with him, more than anything.

"Very well, then, James," she said. "If it pleases you."

Will let out his breath and thought Jamie was doing the same. But he was no longer sure which of them was anticipating the match more.

Chapter Six

The tea party over, Jamie insisted on accompanying their guests to the front door, so Will tagged along and watched while Jamie bent over Lady Everard's hand and stammered his goodbyes. Will didn't think it was his imagination that she uttered a sigh of relief as the door closed behind her and her chaperone.

Perhaps she found it difficult to be the focus of Jamie's attempts at courting. It was becoming increasingly clear to Will that any hope for a love match between her and Jamie lay entirely with his son. Lady Everard saw the lad for what he was—an untried colt with the potential to win races, but not today, and certainly not in the fortnight she planned to be in Evendale.

He didn't relish watching Jamie figure out as much.

He supposed he could tell his son. He'd have to call on every ounce of the diplomatic skill he'd acquired in his nearly ten years of service. Convincing the Pasha of Egypt to free British sailors kidnapped by the very pirates he funded was child's play next to telling Jamie he had to let Samantha Everard go.

"An amazing woman," Will said to Jamie's back as his son rushed to the window to watch the ladies climb into their waiting coach. "Who would have thought she fenced?"

Jamie glanced back at him and made a face. "And why would she think I still didn't? I don't need her to tutor me."

Will rubbed his hands together. "You'll show her as much on Monday, I know."

Jamie nodded, but he stood at the window long after Will heard the Everard carriage depart.

The matter of Samantha Everard remained on Will's mind the rest of the day, but he could find no easy way to speak to his son about her. He could only hope Sunday might be a day of rest for him and Jamie. Sundays were generally reserved for worship and family in the Evendale valley.

Will had participated in cathedral services, where voices echoed off stone arches that seemed as massive as one of the fells. He'd prayed in a tiny cave while a desert sandstorm howled at the entrance and grit closed his throat. Until he had returned to Kendrick Hall, he had almost forgotten the peace to be had in the little stone chapel at the edge of their estate.

His great-great-great-great-grandfather had ordered the hewing of the reddish stones that made up the walls. His great-great-great-uncle had replaced the previous dark pews with ones of polished oak. His great-great-grandmother had endowed the stained-glass windows that cast jeweled reflections on the worshiping congregation. His contribution for the moment consisted of a stone monument in the churchyard, where Peg had been laid to rest seventeen years ago this week.

No, that was unfair of him. He'd been involved in the parish since the day he'd returned. One of his first duties on becoming earl had been to install a new vicar when the previous man had left for a well-earned retirement. Mr. Pratt was a small man with a bare pate and trembling hands. Unfortunately even after several years in leadership, he consulted Will before making any decision.

Today Will and Jamie had already taken their seats in the Kendrick pew near the front of the church when a murmur ran through the waiting congregation. Samantha, Lady Everard, was making her way up the center aisle, a green velvet spencer over her gray lustring gown, peacock feathers waving from her velvet cap. She smiled at everyone and took her place beside Mrs. Dallsten Walcott in the Dallsten pew directly in front of Will. The scent of roses drifted over him.

It seemed a little peace was too much to ask.

As services began, Will wasn't surprised to find Jamie fidgeting. They had all heard the words many times before, though Will usually found something new to intrigue him.

But it didn't appear to be familiarity that bored his son. Jamie kept leaning forward, tilting his head, and Will was sure it wasn't to better hear the sermon that followed the readings. No, Jamie was trying to catch a glimpse of Samantha Everard's face, perhaps meet her gaze. To his sorrow Will had done the same thing when he'd been Jamie's age—using any excuse to turn and look at Peggy several rows back.

To Lady Everard's credit, however, she did not look at Jamie. Her gaze was on the vicar or the *Book of Common Prayer* whenever Will glanced her way, and Jamie's heavy sigh told Will that she hadn't favored the lad with a look even when Will had been focused on the vicar. From what he could tell by her bowed head and sweet voice, she seemed to take her worship seriously.

Normally so did Will. His father had raised him with a healthy respect for the church, and what he'd seen on his travels had only underscored the need to honor his Savior. But lately he felt his prayers laden with more questions than answers.

Why couldn't Peg have lived to see their son become a man?

Why were they in danger of losing Kendrick Hall when he had worked hard to manage well?

Why had his brother been killed eight years ago?

Why couldn't he get his mind off Samantha Everard?

Forgive me, Lord. You've seen me through robbery and rebellion. I know You have a plan for me now. I just can't see it at the moment.

As if on cue the final hymn started, the congregation rose and voices swelled. Sunlight glittered through the stained-glass windows, casting a rainbow over the front pew, and Samantha Everard.

Was she part of the Lord's plan for Will's future?

He dropped his gaze to the flagstones at his feet. Even if he could convince himself to open his heart again, his place was here in Evendale. She had made it plain she wasn't staying beyond a fortnight. And he could not hurt his son by evincing interest in the woman Jamie loved. Will needed to let go of these feelings she was raising in him.

Unfortunately letting go was the hardest thing for him to do.

Samantha sighed contently as the service ended. She'd worshipped at St. George's, Hanover Square, with most of the denizens of London's wealthy West End. She'd even spent a few occasions at the grand Westminster Cathedral. But there was nothing quite so satisfying as this church where she'd been raised. The light from the stained-glass windows always made her feel as if God was sending a blessing just for her.

Around her, the congregation was filing out, the murmur of their voices lapping at her like warm waves. The people of the valley would gather for a moment in the churchyard, she knew, to exchange greetings, pass messages about friends and family. She clung to the peace of the sanctuary a moment, closing her eyes.

Lord, I've made so many mistakes the past few years. I've been impetuous, headstrong and obstinate. Each time, I've come to You, and You've forgiven me. Help me now to do what's right, for all of us.

She opened her eyes to find Mrs. Dallsten Walcott regarding her quizzically. "Is something wrong, dear girl?"

Samantha smiled. "No. Just appreciating this place, our people." She wrapped her arms around the lady and gave her a hug. She knew it was impetuous, but she was fairly sure God looked kindly on such acts of love.

Mrs. Dallsten Walcott did so as well, it seemed, for she was smiling when Samantha released her.

"Come along now," she said as if to hide the lapse in her normally composed demeanor. "I want to introduce you to the new vicar. He hasn't Mr. Ramsey's presence, but he's very good about knowing his place."

By that Samantha guessed the new vicar knew how to toady up to the lady. Though the Dallstens had once been one of the most prestigious families in the area, Samantha's father, the former Lord Everard, had changed that when he'd purchased their impoverished estate and installed his wife and young daughter in the manor. Mrs. Dallsten Walcott had gone to live in the dower cottage at the foot of the drive, her provenance supplied by her daughter's work as Samantha's governess.

In other places the change in her status might have been enough to cost Mrs. Dallsten Walcott the respect of the community. But the local families still held the Dallstens in high esteem, which was evident by the number of people waiting to greet Samantha's chaperone when she and Mrs. Dallsten Walcott exited the church.

But Jamie and his father were not among them. She'd known they'd been right behind her in church; Jamie and his grandfather had always sat in that pew when she'd been growing up. Then as now, his presence had brought comfort.

Jamie's father was another matter. At times she'd found it difficult to concentrate on her worship, knowing Lord Kendrick might be looking at her back. Was her cap on straight? Was she standing reverently enough? Oh, but she shouldn't worship to please anyone but her heavenly Father!

Yet the moment she spotted him and Jamie standing in the shade of an elm along the edge of the churchyard, she felt a similar wish to please Lord Kendrick. She wanted him to approve of the way she smiled and exclaimed over new babies, recent marriages and good fortune. She hoped he would join her in commiserating over deaths, illness and hard times. But though she felt his gaze on her as she followed Mrs. Dallsten Walcott from group to group, he remained on the edge of the yard.

What was he waiting for? Why didn't he approach her? She could not have given him a disgust of her by admitting she fenced, or he was not the man she thought him. What kept him away?

She wasn't sure whether to be relieved or dismayed

when Mrs. Dallsten Walcott finally drew her up beside Jamie and Lord Kendrick. Jamie looked dapper in a navy coat and trousers, his cravat tied in some complicated knot she thought must have given his valet fits.

But Lord Kendrick outdid his son. He wore a dove-gray cutaway coat over black trousers, his cravat simply but elegantly tied, the buttons on his silver-shot waistcoat gleaming in the sunlight. And those boots! The scarlet leather was tooled with fanciful birds and sweeping palms. She was certain there wasn't another pair like them in England.

Lord Kendrick and Jamie had been talking with another fellow dressed more humbly in brown coat and trousers, and it wasn't until he pulled off his top hat to reveal carrot-colored hair that she recognized him, and every other thought flew from her mind.

"Toby!" Samantha enfolded her friend and former suitor in a hug, then stepped back to eye him. "Oh, it's been ages. How are you?"

His grin was as bold as ever. "Quite fine, thank you."

Lord Kendrick's smile was amused. "I take it you know the gentleman."

Samantha blushed, realizing she'd been her usual enthusiastic self, a fact that had caused more than one of her acquaintances to cringe. Of course London was a far more formal place than the Evendale valley, and she had known Toby most of her life.

"She knows me to her sorrow, I'm sure," Toby replied for her. "I once laid my heart at her feet."

Lord Kendrick raised a brow.

Samantha couldn't help laughing at Toby's exaggerated sigh. "You remember it decidedly differently, Mr. Giles. As I recall, my cousin Vaughn made a cake of himself over some imagined slight, and you felt obliged to offer for me to appease him."

Now Toby laughed as well. "I'm sure it would have taken a lot less than the threat of your cousin to get me to propose in those days. But life moves on. I've a missus about somewhere." He glanced around the churchyard and beckoned to someone. "We can't all wait for Lady Everard, eh, Lord Wentworth?"

Jamie turned a darker red than Toby's hair.

Samantha nudged him with her elbow. "Lord Wentworth isn't waiting for me either. I'm sure he has his sights on the perfect young lady."

Jamie gazed at her. "I recently made such a decision, actually."

"And here are Mrs. Giles and her delightful children," Lord Kendrick put in smoothly, stepping back to make room for the brood. Samantha counted at least six, but she could easily have been mistaken, for the group cavorted around her like a pack of hounds, and it was difficult to estimate the number.

"There's Molly and Polly, Dick and Nick, Ed and Ned and Hepsibah Elizabeth," Toby said proudly. He leaned closer to Samantha. "The last is named for her grandmother."

Nick and Ned—or was it Dick and Ed?—started a tussle, and Toby waded in to stop it. Samantha backed up and bumped into Lord Kendrick, and his hands came down on her shoulders to steady her.

"There's a happy bunch," his warm voice murmured beside her ear. "I always wanted a large family."

"So did I," she murmured back. "Jamie and I would have done anything for siblings."

Too late she realized he might take that as judgment. His hands and his presence withdrew. Stricken, she turned to face him. His smile had faded, and his look was deeper, sorrowful, as if a cloud covered the forest green of his gaze.

"I'm so sorry, my lord," she said. "I meant no disrespect."

He shrugged, but she thought it cost him. "You spoke the truth," he replied. "I left Jamie alone far too long. If duty hadn't recalled me home, I might never have seen my son grow up."

Now she felt the sting. She knew the duty that had called him home—the death of his older brother. She should apologize for that as well, yet how did one apologize for playing a part in murder?

"There we are," Toby proclaimed, a son tucked under each arm, their feet dangling. "Come meet the missus."

Samantha pasted on a smile and turned to greet Toby's wife, a pale, thin woman with luminous eyes. But she couldn't help remembering someone else entirely—Lord Kendrick's lost brother and her other suitor, Gregory Wentworth.

Will joined in the conversation with Samantha and the Giles family, but it was clear something had troubled her. The light of her usual energy had dimmed. Why?

Was it her memory of how he had abandoned his son? He was ready to own his part in the matter. His behavior had come home to him when he'd returned to Kendrick Hall after news of Gregory's death had finally reached him, only to find Peg's eyes gazing back at him from his son's too-solemn face. It had taken him the better part of a year to gain Jamie's trust. It had taken far longer for him to forgive himself.

Perhaps that was why he was so determined that

Jamie not repeat his mistakes. Jamie was too young to consider marriage. Will had to help him see that.

Before he could think of his next step, Samantha Everard stiffened. She had been contemplating her shoes, a dainty pair of green kid leather with rosettes on the toes, when her head jerked up as if she'd scented something on the breeze. Will glanced around, but could see nothing different in his neighbors. The only change was the sun pulling out from behind some clouds, bringing a glow to the stone church, the churchyard and the woods beyond.

She picked up her skirts as if she intended to run a race.

"It's time!" she cried. "Come on, Jamie!" As if assuming his son would follow, she darted past Will, weaving through the headstones of the cemetery beside the church.

Will glanced between her rapidly disappearing form and his son. Jamie had been teasing one of the older Gileses' boys and had completely failed to notice the departure of his lady love. Mrs. Dallsten Walcott was lecturing Mrs. Giles on the proper way to discipline children, even though Will was fairly certain she'd never applied those techniques herself. He could point out that the woman she was chaperoning now had just disappeared, alone, or he could hasten after Lady Everard himself.

He didn't think further. He hastened.

He caught a fleeting glimpse of her ahead of him as she ran into the wood. Where was she going? She'd forsaken the path that wound toward Kendrick Hall, instead plunging through the trees toward the fells. The undergrowth was sparse here, so he couldn't fear she'd take a fall or lose her way. In fact she seemed to know exactly where she was going.

He caught up to her in a clearing that ran against a draw in the hillside. Tree limbs dangled over a pool of water, surrounded by stone. Shadows danced across the green expanse, and the air was moist and loud with the sound of falling water.

He wasn't sure she could hear him approach, so he cleared his throat. She kept her gaze on the cliff side, where a freshet tumbled down over black stones.

"I wasn't quick enough," she said, voice as heavy as the spray-dampened branches hanging over the water. "We missed the rainbow."

So that's what she was after. Will shook his head. What other woman would climb through a forest, dressed as she was for church, on the chance of finding a rainbow in the spray of a waterfall? She sounded so disappointed to have missed it that he wanted to find that rainbow for her, if only to see the matching glow on her face.

"Perhaps if you give it a moment," he said, glancing up at the sun and noting its angle to the water.

"Oh!" She whirled to face him, cheeks darkening. "I thought you were Jamie."

"My son has been detained," Will said with a bow. As he straightened, he nodded toward the falls. "Take a few steps to the left and see what happens."

She nodded happily, as if Will had granted a fervent wish. "Good idea."

To his surprise, she seized his hand and pulled him to the left with her. She positively vibrated with anticipation. He found himself waiting with equal eagerness.

"Watch now," she whispered as if afraid of scaring the rainbow away.

Across the stream, color began to sparkle in the air. Deep red, vibrant orange, bright yellow, vivid green, blue and purple. A rainbow more pure and clean than the one he'd seen in the chapel arched across the spray, framing the falls in splendor.

"Isn't it magnificent?" she murmured, giving his hand a squeeze. "I've never seen anything more beautiful."

"I have," Will said, watching her. He was glad she didn't question him, or he'd have had to find a diplomatic way of evading an answer. For how could he admit that in all his travels, from the palaces along the Bosporus Sea near Constantinople to the pyramids of Egypt, the most beautiful sight he'd ever beheld was her?

Chapter Seven

She'd found the rainbow. Samantha sighed with pleasure. Sunshine at precisely half past eleven was rare in
the Evendale valley, where misty mornings were more
often the norm even in the summer. Sighting the rainbow was just as rare.

"How did you know this was here?" Lord Kendrick
asked, and she could hear a similar awe in his voice.

The memory was a mix of pain and joy. "I found it,"
Samantha admitted. "I escaped from services one day
at exactly the right time."

"I'm surprised your mother let you out of her sight,"
he said, but his voice held more humor than censor.

"She seldom attended services with Adele and Mrs.
Dallsten Walcott and me," Samantha replied, remembering. "I didn't understand then, but now I think she
didn't like the whispers."

"Whispers?"

His voice remained kind, interested, so she answered
though she kept her gaze on the cool water.

"There were rumors, unfounded as it turned out, that
my mother and father were not legally wed, that I was

illegitimate. Even knowing the truth, my mother didn't like hearing them."

"I imagine you didn't either."

Now he sounded more censorious, but she hoped his frustration was aimed at the gossips.

"I am very thankful my governess Adele Walcott sheltered me from much of it," Samantha told him. "But after Mother died, nothing could console me. I ran away from the manor several times. I wanted my father so desperately."

"Fathers can be important to a child."

The pain in his voice drew her gaze to his face. His muscles were still, chiseled. His gaze was fixed on the waterfall, as if he'd ceased to see its beauty and instead saw a boy who had been just as lonesome for his father.

"Yes, they can," she agreed. "That's why I'm glad you returned to Jamie. I wish I'd had more time with my father. I still miss him."

The waterfall's mist seemed to be thickening. She could feel dampness on her cheeks. Moving to wipe it away, she realized she still held Lord Kendrick's hand. Letting go was more difficult than she'd expected.

As if he felt the loss of her touch as keenly, he turned from the water to eye her. "So you ran away from church and found this. Did it please you as much then?"

A smile tugged at her lips. "Yes. I thought it was meant just for me, a gift from God. I never told anyone, until Jamie."

He cocked his head, eyes narrowing. "Why James?"

Did he still wonder at their friendship? "I guess I thought he needed it, too," she said with a shrug, then turned her gaze back to the falling water. "Perhaps we all need to remember there is beauty in the world."

"Do you doubt it?" He spread his hands. "Look

around you—the fells, the springs, the lakes. There is no more beautiful spot in England."

Her smile broke free, and she drew in a breath of the moist air. "I feel the same way. I've been to house parties near the Cliffs of Dover, hunting parties in the Scottish moors. There is no place like home."

"And yet you seem to be leaving again," he pointed out, hands falling to his sides.

She felt her smile slipping. She'd almost said too much. The waterfall, her memories, his uncondemning presence had conspired to make her forget herself.

"Only after the summer party," she said and knew she sounded entirely too delighted with the prospect. "Goodness, but we seem to have stayed here overlong. Forgive me for detaining you. We should return to the churchyard."

He leaned forward, met her gaze, his own probing. "Is there no one you confide in?" he challenged. "Your cousins, their wives?"

He was so intent, as if he wanted to exorcise her secrets. She backed away from him, felt a sapling sway from her touch. "There is no need, I assure you. Now, come along. I'm sure the others will wonder about our absence, my lord."

He stood a second longer, watching her, and she felt the stories welling up inside her. How freeing it would be to lay them at someone else's feet, to pour out her concerns and listen to his calm voice reason them away.

But reason was not the issue in this case, and no amount of sharing would change what must be.

Lord, please help him let it go!

As if Lord Kendrick had seen the struggle in her, he offered her his arm. "Of course, my dear. Forgive me for adding to your burdens. This way."

As they started away from the falls, the sun went behind a cloud, and her rainbow vanished.

Jamie and Mrs. Dallsten Walcott were among the last in the churchyard when Samantha and Lord Kendrick returned. Of the two, Samantha thought Jamie looked the most concerned. He rushed forward, took both her hands in his.

"Are you all right?" he demanded. "Where have you been?"

"Lady Everard showed me a fine waterfall," Lord Kendrick said as if to defend her. "I hadn't even realized it existed."

Jamie dropped her hands as if her touch had scalded him. "You took him to see our rainbow?"

He sounded as shocked as if she'd plotted the overthrow of the crown. "I invited you," she informed him. "Either you failed to hear me, or you have better ways to spend your time these days."

Immediately she felt as if she'd kicked a puppy, his look turned so forlorn. Even Lord Kendrick seemed concerned, for he took a step closer to his son.

"Please forgive me," Jamie begged, gaze on Samantha's. "I would have been delighted to join you."

"Perhaps next Sunday," Lord Kendrick said.

Always the diplomat. She appreciated that. She found it too easy to speak first and regret it afterward, as her reaction to Jamie had just proved.

She dropped a curtsey, including them both in the gesture. "Next Sunday to be sure. It was a pleasure seeing you both. If you'll excuse me, I have kept my dear chaperone standing quite long enough." She rose and turned purposefully toward Mrs. Dallsten Walcott. The lady's thin lips were twitching as if she fought to keep words from tumbling out as well.

"But you'll still come over tomorrow?" Jamie called, voice laced with a desperation that nearly made Samantha wince.

"Tomorrow," she promised, taking her chaperone's arm and all but dragging her to the carriage.

"Clever girl," Mrs. Dallsten Walcott said as she settled into her seat across from Samantha.

Samantha had been peering out the window. Lord Kendrick had escorted his son to their carriage as well. Though Jamie kept turning his head to look her way, his father never did. She puffed out a sigh.

"And now what have I done?" she asked her chaperone, facing forward as the carriage started away from the church.

Mrs. Dallsten Walcott nodded sagely. "You made him jealous. It brings a fellow around every time."

What nonsense! "I sincerely doubt Lord Kendrick has any reason to be jealous of his son," she scolded.

Mrs. Dallsten Walcott tittered behind her gloved hand. "Of course not! I meant you were using the father to bring the son to the point of proposing. A promising approach."

Samantha felt her shoulders bunching, her fists tightening as if some part of her longed to physically fight the accusation. "I am doing no such thing! I have no designs on anyone with the name of Wentworth."

Mrs. Dallsten Walcott dropped her hand to reveal a pout. "The more fool you, then. They are both excellent catches."

Samantha refused to dignify the comment with a response.

She let Mrs. Dallsten Walcott chatter the rest of the

way home, but the happy sounds didn't improve Samantha's mood. The sunny summer day seemed darker somehow, and she knew it wasn't from her chaperone's intimation that Samantha was attempting to trap one of the Wentworth men into marriage.

So many things had happened in this valley, good and bad. She'd thought she'd faced them all over the years. But each memory seemed more painful here, where they'd been made. She supposed she should have been expecting these feelings of loss and sorrow. She'd come to make her peace, after all. But she didn't want to wallow in her past!

So she attempted to focus on her other reason for coming ahead of the others—to ensure everything was ready for the summer party. She'd been planning for months, arranging for music, fireworks, flowers and food. Now she immersed herself in the work for the rest of the day, checking the rooms where her family was to stay to confirm all was in readiness, reviewing plans for laying out the various booths and events, even counting the sacks of flour and sugar that had been purchased to make pastries for the children.

By dinner she caught Mrs. Dallsten Walcott and their housekeeper Mrs. Linton casting her bemused glances. They had been holding the party for years without her. They surely didn't need her help. But she wanted to help. This time, of all the years, she wanted everything to be perfect. Very likely this would be the last summer party at Dallsten Manor, for who knew if the next owner would continue the tradition?

On Monday, however, she was quite ready for a new challenge. She donned the outfit she used to practice her swordplay—white gown with stiffer skirts that wouldn't get in her way while she moved, and a padded leather vest that protected her chest. She carried her foil, wire mask, leather gloves and flexible-soled shoes with her in the carriage.

At Kendrick Hall a helpful footman saw her up to the top floor and a room at the front of the house. All furnishings had been removed save a long padded bench against one wall. A rack of fencing foils rested near the door, and nearby hung several pairs of padded gloves used for pugilistic displays. She had a pair of those at home, too, specially made for her smaller hands.

Someone was in the room ahead of her. He was standing in the center of the space, feet positioned properly on the wood floor. He wore a muslin shirt, padded vest like hers and buckskin breeches, and his wire mask was already in place. From across the room, and with no furniture for perspective, she had a hard time telling his height.

"Jamie?" she asked, venturing into the room.

In answer, he saluted her with his foil.

Samantha smiled. "Give me a moment, and I'll join you."

She went to the bench and sat to remove her half-boots. He flexed his shoulders and tossed the blade from hand to hand. Bending to slip on her fencing shoes, she felt her smile growing. *Show off! Well, he'd find she gave as good as she got.*

A moment later she joined him on the floor. She held out her foil for his inspection as she approached. "It's baited. Is yours?"

He extended his arm, and she spotted the button of leather on the tip.

"Very good, then." She lowered her blade and glanced at the door. "What about your father? I thought he was going to join us."

Though she knew it was polite to wait for her host, she almost wished Jamie would agree to simply start fencing. From the moment Vaughn had handed her the blade, she had never had any trouble facing an opponent. But somehow fencing with Lord Kendrick watching made her tremble just the slightest.

"No need to wait," said a warm voice.

She stiffened as she turned back to the man facing her. Now that she was focused on him instead of the blade she could see the twinkle of those green eyes inside the mask, as much humor as challenge. Lord Kendrick slipped off his mask and smiled at her.

"Forgive me," he said. "I couldn't resist."

She could not be angry with him, not when he was so obviously contrite. "And what have you done with Jamie?" she asked.

"He'll be along shortly," he promised. "Until then, perhaps you'd like a sparring partner to help you warm up."

Him? Excitement skittered along her skin, and gooseflesh pimpled her arms even under her heavy clothes. She should refuse. Fencing with Jamie was the same as fencing with her cousins. Fencing with Lord Kendrick felt different, like riding a racehorse instead of a dependable hunter, exhilarating and forbidden at the same time.

What was she thinking? It wasn't forbidden! He'd made the offer; she hadn't coerced him into it. There should be no difference between facing him and facing Jamie across the floor.

Or so she told herself as she took up her spot opposite him, set her mask in place and raised her foil.

Will slipped his mask back on, extended his foil and laid it against Samantha's. She stood calm and composed, sure of herself and her skills. But the bout would tell just how formidable those skills were. He pushed against her blade; she pushed back. He smiled.

He disengaged and thrust toward her left shoulder. She parried but didn't back away. The laugh that escaped her told him she knew what he was doing.

The next few minutes proved that she knew what she was doing as well. They moved about the room, foils clinking as they hit, breaths coming thickly through the masks. She darted and spun about him, quick and light as a dancer. But with each blow, Will saw that she was always on the defensive. Did she fear to offend him by attempting a strike, or had her cousins perhaps only taught her to defend herself? He thrust again, and she turned to avoid the blow.

And then he found her blade at his throat.

"You are beaten, my lord," she said, triumph in her voice.

The minx! She'd been testing him, seeking a weak spot, and when she'd found it she hadn't hesitated to use it to her advantage.

"I believe the rules call for a strike between the shoulders and hips," he countered.

She pulled up her sword as if in surprise. "You play by the rules?"

"Spoken like an Everard," Jamie said, striding into the room. His son had on a similar white shirt, padded vest, buckskin breeches and a mask tucked under his arm.

Samantha pulled off her mask and turned to face Jamie. "Oh, good. A fresh opponent. I've already beaten your father."

"I was blinded by your beauty," Will said with a bow that extended his blade to the side.

"I'll have to remember that excuse," Jamie said, taking up his favorite foil. "If I ever need it."

Will gave him a bow as well as he surrendered the floor to his son.

He watched carefully as Jamie and Samantha took their places opposite each other. It had been a hard lesson for him to learn in the diplomatic corps—sometimes arriving at a solution to a difficult problem required not decisive action but careful observation. An incursion taken as an act of war might instead be only a desperate attempt to save a stricken outpost.

He thought Samantha's bout with Jamie would be telling. He was fairly certain now she had no designs on his son, but if he'd mistaken her motivation, surely he'd see evidence. A woman bent on capturing a man's heart might defer to him, make it appear he was the stronger. On the other hand, a self-absorbed beauty might blame her loss on fatigue from the previous bout.

Samantha did neither. She fought, with grace, precision and enthusiasm. The clang of their blows echoed around the room. Will found himself edging to the right or left, grimacing when Jamie's blade came perilously close to her shoulder, smothering a shout of triumph when she pushed the boy back with the flick of her wrist alone. She was fire, she was lightning. She was bold, undaunted. He'd fought men with less skill, less daring. Even the Janissaries would have quailed before her.

How could the spirit of a warrior have made its home in the body of a beautiful woman?

With a lunge Jamie penetrated her defenses and struck her square in the heart. She put up her blade with a laugh and pulled off her mask. The action must have caught her hair pins just right, for her tresses began to tumble in a shower of gold.

"Oh, well done, Jamie!" she cried, hair flowing down her back. "Please accept my apologies for thinking there was anything I could teach you."

As Jamie removed his own mask, Will could see he was grinning from ear to ear. He swept her a bow. "Apology accepted."

It was a courtly gesture, but Will couldn't help thinking his son had it all wrong. Samantha, Lady Everard, could teach them both a great deal, if they were willing to learn.

But Jamie wasn't finished. Flushed with his victory, he went down on one knee, blade tip on the floor, hands braced on the hilt like a knight before the queen.

"I hope I've proven to you my devotion and my ability to take care of you," he said, gaze on hers.

No! Will felt as if Jamie's blade had thrust through his own heart. This couldn't be the prelude to what Will feared. He started forward, to do what, he wasn't sure.

"Jamie," Samantha said. The tenderness in her tone hit Will with the force of a blow, stopping him where he stood.

"Samantha, Lady Everard," Jamie said, chin up and eyes imploring, "will you do me the honor of marrying me?"

She bent and pressed a kiss to Jamie's forehead, and Will felt physically sick. What was wrong with him? He'd decided she was a fine woman. He knew Jamie sincerely cared for her. Their lands and estates would benefit from the union. Everything said this would be an excellent match.

Everything but his heart.

She pulled back. "James Wentworth, I have never met a finer man. You have been my friend through thick and thin, and we both know there were a lot of thin times. I will always treasure your friendship, but I cannot marry you or anyone else, I fear. Please try to understand."

With a nod of respect to Will, she snatched up her half boots and hurried from the room.

Will stood there, stunned. Why refuse Jamie? Why disdain marriage? She'd asked his son to understand, but Will found it impossible.

Nearly as impossible as the joy singing through him that she had refused.

Jamie climbed to his feet. "What was that?" he asked Will.

Will made himself shrug. "I have no idea," he answered truthfully. "You cut a dashing figure, made a fine speech. The lady's feelings and your own were evident."

"Much good it did me." Jamie tossed his blade aside. "Why did I even try?"

His son's pain reached inside Will. For all a part of him wished he was the one girding up his courage to propose to this amazing woman, Will knew what was expected of him as father and follower of Christ. He strode to his son's side and put his hand on Jamie's shoulder.

"You love her. Go after her. Discover what concerns her and make it right."

Jamie nodded. "Excellent advice." He took a deep breath. "Thank you, Father."

Will watched him stride from the room and told himself not to wish it was him instead.

Chapter Eight

Samantha hurried through Kendrick Hall, intent only on escaping. The pain on Jamie's face at her refusal cut sharper than any blade. Someday she'd explain her reasons to him. He might well be the only one who'd understand why she would likely never marry. But she couldn't explain today, and never in front of Lord Kendrick.

The view down the paneled corridor was blurring, the lovely paintings and sculptures melting. She paused to dash the tears from her eyes. She was so tired of being the one to wound, to disappoint! But she couldn't agree to walk the path others had laid out for her.

Trust in the Lord with all thine heart; and lean not unto thine own understanding. In all thy ways acknowledge Him, and He shall direct thy paths.

The verse came readily to mind. Had it been the vicar who had quoted it yesterday or had it been in one of the readings? Either way she was no longer sure of the Lord's path. All she knew was that she had to avoid the emotions that had caused so much pain over the years, particularly to her mother.

"Samantha."

She closed her eyes at the sound of Jamie's voice behind her, said a prayer for strength. Then she opened her eyes and turned to meet his gaze. A lock of dark hair had fallen over a pinched face, and his fists were tight at his sides as if he didn't trust himself to reach for her.

"I'm sorry," he blurted out. "I never wanted to hurt you."

Samantha offered him a smile. "It's all right, Jamie. You honored me with your proposal."

"Yet you refused," he said.

She nodded. "I must. I think of you as the brother I never had."

"A little brother," he said bitterly.

She put out her free hand. "A younger brother," she corrected. "A charming, clever, wonderful younger brother of whom I'm terribly proud. But that is a far cry from what you should expect in a wife."

He took a step closer, seized her hand and held it tight. "I don't care. You're the one I want. Can't you see? I think about you all the time."

Oh, but she knew that feeling. Once she'd thought the sun rose and set on her cousin Vaughn. But it had been calf-love, an all-consuming fire that burnt more than it warmed. When she'd seen the blazing light of his love for his wife, Imogene, and hers for him, she'd known what she felt couldn't hold a candle to it.

She shook his hand to emphasize her words. "And I am truly honored you care for me so much. I could never have done enough to deserve such a friend. But that is what we are—friends. I ask you to respect that."

"You ask too much." He pulled away.

"Do I?" She cocked her head, eying him. "Then perhaps we define love differently. I believe the Bible calls it charity, and it is patient and kind, rejoicing in the right."

"Enduring all things," Jamie agreed with a prodigious sigh.

Samantha grinned at him. "Hoping in all things. If that is the love we have for each other, it will never fail."

He raised his gaze to hers, dark eyes intent. "Are you giving me reason to hope you'll change your mind?"

Samantha shook her head. "No, Jamie. I'm trying to get you to see that my feelings for you will never change. You will be my dear friend, always."

He nodded slowly. "Then I suppose I must accept that."

She hadn't realized her shoulders were so tight until she felt the tension easing at his words. "Oh, yes, please! I'd like us to put this all behind us. We do have a summer party approaching, you know, and I believe you offered to help me."

"An offer you also refused," he pointed out, but she thought he stood a little taller, too, as if a weight had been lifted.

"How silly of me," Samantha replied with a smile. "I can always use the assistance of my friends. My family will arrive any day. Will you come over and help me greet them?"

He shrugged. "I'm glad to help, but I have no idea what I can do to make them feel more comfortable here."

She couldn't keep the laughter from her voice. "Well, Jerome and Adele are bringing their children, and Vaughn and Imogene will have the twins. I'm sure we'll need help in the schoolroom."

Jamie rolled his eyes. "Delightful. I barely graduate from school, and you want to put me right back into it."

"Look at it this way," Samantha said, a giggle slipping out. "You have the most recent experience of all of us. You're practically an expert!"

He laughed at that, and she could only hope his heart was on the road to mending.

A shame she could not say the same for hers. She managed to fend off Jamie's offer to see her to the door and made her way down the main stairs to the entry hall alone. She could not regret refusing him. Jamie deserved a wife who loved him as a man.

She'd once hoped she and his uncle might share that kind of love. Of course now she knew that his courtship had been initially motivated by the need to keep her cousin Vaughn off balance and off the trail of the traitor. The truth about his courtship had caused her to begin questioning whether a true love would ever be hers. The fortune hunters who had followed her had only magnified her concerns. All her life she'd lived by her emotions—loving quickly, feeling deeply. But it seemed where marriage was concerned, her emotions were not to be trusted. Her mother's death had proven as much.

As a child she hadn't understood what had happened to Rosamunde, Lady Everard. Samantha had been six when her governess, now wife to her cousin Jerome, had told her her mother had died. A tragic accident, Adele and the servants had said. Oh, how Samantha had cried. It had taken days for the word to reach London and her father to come to comfort her.

She thought he might scold her for crying. Mrs. Dallsten Walcott had already told her a lady didn't carry on so. The vicar had murmured words about being strong. But her father had taken her in his arms and rested his platinum-haired head on hers.

"You cry, daughter," he'd said. "If that makes you feel better, you cry all you want. Just know I'm crying with you."

A tear slipped down now as she stopped at the foot of the stair. *And who will cry with me now, Papa? Especially now that I know it wasn't an accident at all.*

For her mother hadn't fallen down the stairs as Adele had intimated. Her mother had committed suicide.

Just the thought of it still shook her. Sucking in a breath, she glanced around and sighted a padded bench in the corridor beside the stair. She went to sit on it, so heavily her skirts spread about her, and forced herself to change out of her fencing shoes. The laces of her half boots felt stiff under her fingers, her hands clumsy. She just wanted to go home. But somehow she'd lost where home was.

"Allow me."

She straightened to find Lord Kendrick between her and the footman waiting to open the door. Like Jamie he still wore his fencing costume, the vest straining across his chest. But instead of the tormented look his son had given her, his green eyes were solemn, his hands hanging loosely as if he were ready to do anything she needed. He knelt in front of her and laced her half boots, quickly, efficiently. Somehow that only made her throat tighter.

"Are you all right?" he murmured as he rose.

"I'll be fine," she said. "And so will Jamie. Thank you for your concern."

"You don't look fine," he said. "Pardon my intrusion, but you look done in."

All at once, she felt done in. The burdens she carried seemed to press upon her, threatened to shove her to her knees. "No, I…" she started, but the tears were coming again, and she couldn't seem to stop them.

He sat beside her, slipped one arm around her as if protecting her from all her sorrows. The touch, the kindness, the unquestioning silence, was her undoing, and she found herself sobbing. She buried her face in his vest, trembling. His hand rubbed up and down her arm, offering commiseration, solace. She felt as if the darkness was fleeing from her, vanquished by his strength and allowing her own strength to rebound.

At last she pulled away from him, took a deep breath and tried to gather the shreds of her dignity.

"Forgive me," she managed. "I've soaked you, and I don't even have a handkerchief."

"Not much room in a fencing vest for one," he agreed, patting his chest as if to emphasize the point. "Shortsighted, really. I imagine more than one fellow has been tempted to cry after losing a match."

The idea was so silly she choked a laugh. "Perhaps you should suggest it to your tailor. It will be a great innovation."

One corner of his mouth turned up as he removed his arm from around her. "Ah, yes. I shall leave my mark on history as the earl who invented pockets in fencing waistcoats. We can call them Kendricoats."

She found her breath coming easier and shook her head at him wryly. "You truly are a clever fellow, my lord."

"Perhaps," he said, gaze studiously on his hands resting on his buckskin breeches, "you could call me Will. You already call Lord Wentworth Jamie."

She felt herself blushing. "A very kind offer, to be sure. But then, you are continually kind to me. But if you are to be Will, I must be Samantha."

He inclined his head, then raised his gaze to hers. "It would be my honor. Just remember, Samantha, that you are an amazing woman. Please forgive anything my son or I might have done that would make you think otherwise."

Will regretted the words the moment they left his mouth. He wasn't sure why he'd left the exercise salon by the back stairs after counseling his son to make things right with Samantha. Some part of him had wanted to stand beside Jamie if he needed that support. Another part feared to find his son and Samantha in each other's arms. He wasn't sure how he'd react to that, but he'd promised himself to behave like the gentleman he believed himself to be.

Instead he'd found Samantha alone and looking so bereft he'd felt compelled to offer comfort. She'd stopped crying at last, the tears glistening on her fair cheeks like sea spray on pearls. She'd even given him a smile, her eyes shining with that light that called to him. Now she dropped her gaze, and one arm wrapped around her waist as if something inside hurt.

"You are neither of you to blame," she murmured. "I have reasons for my choices. Please don't press me on them."

Did she know he longed to do just that? He wanted to know what kept a woman of her beauty, position and, by all accounts, income from marrying and marrying well. Of course some might have wondered the same thing about him. But he knew why he had no interest in marrying again. The marriage of a man in his position was meant to ensure the line, to unite families for security and prestige. He had an heir in Jamie. He needed no more prestige than being the Earl of Kendrick. And he was proud enough that he would not marry for income to secure the estate.

Now he eyed her, sitting in such a tight ball beside him, as if trying to huddle away from the things she did not want him to know. "It must be difficult being the keeper of so many secrets," he said.

Her head jerked up, her eyes wide and panicked. "How did you know?"

Something inside him tightened. So, she did hide secrets. Why did that so disappoint him? Just because he tended to live his scandals in the open didn't mean others were as oblivious to Society's demands. He should simply be grateful she'd refused Jamie and so was no danger to his family. Her affairs were no concern to him now.

But he could not let the matter go.

"I spent nearly ten years on the diplomatic circuit, remember?" he answered her. "There, many things are not what they seem. A smile to the wrong person can mean a dagger in your back."

She shuddered, and he wasn't sure if it was from his words or the loss of warmth from his touch. Certainly he was already missing her closeness. He felt as if a cool breeze had blown down the corridor, past the paintings of his ancestors, the marble bust of his mother on a pedestal along the wall.

"My secrets won't put you in danger," Samantha promised, and rather primly too, her hands folded in the lap of her fencing gown. "They are my burden to carry."

Why? She had cousins, family. Why was she alone responsible for the Everard miscellany? She might have inherited the title, but if her cousins were any kind of gentlemen, they would be helping her with the duties, just as his brother and Will had helped their father, just as Jamie was helping Will now.

"They have a saying in Constantinople," he offered, leaning back. "What burdens one camel is lighter for two."

She cast him a glance from the corners of her eyes. "By that you mean I should share my concerns with you. Thank you, but no."

The dismissal was curt, but he should accept it nonetheless. Still something protested that she should not have to take this road alone, that he was meant to walk it with her. Wasn't that his duty as a gentleman? Why have this experience, this knowledge of the world, if not to share it, to make life easier for another?

"I suppose you have no reason to trust me," he ventured, keeping his gaze carefully away from hers and fixed on the far paneled wall. "We don't know each other well."

"Both true," she allowed.

"Yet you've known my son his whole life," he continued, crossing his legs at the ankles, "and I believe you were a great favorite with my father. He wrote of you frequently."

"He did?" She sounded surprised.

Will found himself smiling, remembering. "My father was a dedicated correspondent. Being so far away, I found letters from home a great treat. It was the same for all embassy staff. We used to read the letters to each other, just to get the feel of being in England. His were particularly popular."

"Why?" she asked, turning toward him.

He chanced a glance her way. She was obviously intrigued by his story, one leg bent at the knee so she could lean toward him.

"He had a way of making you feel as if you knew everyone he wrote about," he explained. "Your friend Mr. Giles's adventures put the other members of the embassy in stitches. And I think more than one of them hoped to come back and meet you."

She blinked, golden lashes fluttering. "Me? Why-ever me?"

Will shot her a grin. "A sweet young heiress, pretty, vivacious. What fellow wouldn't fall in line?"

He thought she might dimple at the prospect, but the color that had been returning to her cheeks fled once more, and she pushed herself to her feet. "Far too many, I fear. Your father was a darling man, and I was very fond of him. But you mustn't think his letters told all the truth, my lord."

"Will," he said gently, rising as well as propriety demanded.

"Will," she conceded. "That girl your father wrote about went to London eight years ago. She is not the woman who returned."

He wasn't so certain. Oh, surely she had learned something from her time in London. Families often sent their daughters for a year or two to acquire town bronze, as they called it. She seemed to have gathered sufficient amounts. She carried herself with confidence most of the time; she had no trouble conversing with strangers or people she hadn't seen in years. But had the heart his father had praised, the sweetness, the kindness, the joy of life, truly been lost along the way?

"We all grow older," he said. "We can only hope our characters grow as well."

She nodded as if she appreciated his understanding. "That's it exactly. Sometimes it seems that everyone around me wants to hold on to that wide-eyed girl. I want to be more than that. I want to take responsibility for my life."

Will spread his hands. "Then do so."

She shook her head. "It isn't that easy. There are expectations, hopes. My father's will." She rolled her eyes.

"He left some stipulation?" Will asked with a frown.

"One too many," she replied darkly. "But nothing that need concern you." She bent to retrieve her fencing shoes. "Thank you for your kindness, Will. I should go."

He caught her arm as she straightened. "Something is troubling you. You've alluded to it twice, and I see the sadness that comes over you from time to time."

She eyed his hand, and he released her. "My sorrow could merely be melancholy for the past."

Yet she didn't claim it was. She clearly didn't want to lie, but at the same time she had no desire to tell him the truth. He longed to convince her to share her burdens, but now was not the time. He knew by the height of her chin, the stiffness in her frame that she had closed off any opening he might have taken.

Will bowed to her. "I can see that I've offended you, Samantha. Forgive me. I know that Jamie cares for you deeply. For his sake I would not see you troubled. If there is anything either of us can do to help you, you have only to ask."

She smiled then, a gentle upturn of her lips that made his heart lighten. "That is very kind of you, but as I've said, I'm fine. I know exactly what I'm doing. I don't need any help." She curtsied. "Good day, my lord."

He watched her walk to the door, saw the footman open it for her and escort her down to her waiting carriage. Her back was straight, her shoulders unbowed.

But he saw the weight she carried, the effort she

made to hide it. It was as if something dark was squatting on Samantha's shoulders, digging its claws into her.

She was bright, she was strong, she was determined. She obviously knew what was plaguing her. She seemed to think she had a strategy for defeating it. He should let her go her way and encourage Jamie to go his.

But as the carriage started away from the house, something else moved among the oaks lining the drive. Will pushed past his footman, who stiffened in obvious surprise, to get a better look.

A man on a powerful roan horse was following the Everard coach. Even though the day was bright and growing warmer, the fellow wore a hooded cloak that obscured his head and body. Only the fact that he rode astride assured Will it was a man.

What was this? Did the lady so fear for her safety she needed an outrider for protection? Who threatened her? And if she had not hired her shadow, what was the fellow about? What brash confidence or evil purpose made him comfortable following her onto Wentworth land?

It seemed the mystery associated with Samantha Everard was only deepening. By the quickening of his pulse, Will knew he intended to solve it.

Chapter Nine

"See that my horse is saddled," Will ordered his footman. "I want Arrow out front in two minutes."

The footman gaped, then dashed off with a cry of "Right away, my lord."

Will kept an eye on the departing carriage. He'd lost sight of the man following it, but he thought the fellow had to be close. All Will had to do was catch that coach.

His groom came running from the back of the house, leading a prancing Arrow. Will was in the saddle and heading across the lawn moments later. He didn't want to startle his quarry by galloping down the drive, but he knew another way to approach the carriage. He urged Arrow into the pastures.

A carriage had to travel in a U to return to Dallsten Manor—down the drive from Kendrick Hall, along the country lane between the two houses and back up the Dallsten Manor drive. Will on Arrow was unfettered. They pounded across the turf, angling to cut off the coach before it reached the other drive. The cool mountain air streamed past, but Will felt no chill. He was acting for once, not sitting in his office looking at problems that had few solutions.

Was that why he intended to solve this problem? He had no reason to discover Samantha Everard's secrets, after all. With her having refused Jamie's suit, she was no threat to his family. And her stated intention of leaving the area after the summer party made her opinions no threat to the future of the valley either. Yet surely as a gentleman he should see a lady protected, even if it was only from the sorrow that seemed to dog her steps. Either way, Will couldn't rest until he knew the truth.

As he neared the road, he slowed Arrow. He could see the carriage approaching, the empty road before and behind it. Where was the outrider? Had Will mistaken the fellow's purpose? Had he been after something at Kendrick Hall instead? All the more reason to find him and demand an accounting!

Will chucked to Arrow, felt the horse gather speed beneath him. They flew toward the road and the hedge that separated it from the pasture. Will never hesitated. As the carriage thundered past, Arrow gathered himself and launched into the air, and then they were up and over and onto the road.

Will turned the dappled gray to face the way back, but the road remained empty, save for the dust of the carriage's passing lingering in the air. And though he rode up and down the lane twice more, he caught no further glimpse of the mysterious horseman. Perhaps it had been Kendrick Hall the man had been watching. Just to be safe, Will rode home and alerted his staff to keep an eye out for the fellow.

But his failure to discover the identity of the man on the roan horse didn't mean he was willing to let the matter of Samantha Everard go. He had a feeling the person most likely to know her secrets and share them was Jamie. Unfortunately he doubted his son would be amenable to being questioned about the woman who'd just refused his offer of marriage. Indeed, Will was a little concerned about how Jamie would take the crushing blow.

So he kept an eye on his son the rest of the day. Jamie was surprisingly composed, going riding, finding his old fishing rod and trimming it for his purposes. Will even caught him humming to himself at one point. If Jamie was so unmoved, Will felt comfortable approaching the boy over dinner.

The dining room was another of his mother's projects. She had felt that food and companionship should be the centerpiece of any meal, so the rest of the room was remarkably free of the furbelows she favored elsewhere. The walls were plastered in white, the ceiling gray with white laurels at each corner. The mahogany table was generally draped in white and could easily seat thirty.

He and Jamie sat at one end, Will at the head and Jamie at his right. And by the way his son tucked into the first course, Will thought his stomach was also unaffected by the loss of his dream.

"Do you still plan on visiting all the neighbors?" he asked his son over a spoonful of mulligatawny soup.

Jamie nodded as he swallowed some of the curried mixture of chicken and vegetables. "I do. But first I promised Samantha I would help her with her family's visit."

So it was still about Samantha, and his son had not lost his desire to do the lady a service. Did he think to change her mind?

"I was under the impression Lady Everard needed no help," Will said, testing the waters.

"She asked me specifically," Jamie assured him,

chest puffed out with the honor of it. "I intend to ride over in the morning early to see what she needs."

"Then I'll join you," Will said, digging into the braised lamb his cook had sent up with the soup.

Jamie laid down his spoon and glared at Will. "Now, see here, Father. You've followed me about all day. Don't think I didn't notice. I'm not a wounded dove."

Will kept the smile from his face and voice. "I should hope not."

Jamie nodded as if satisfied he'd made his point, then picked up his spoon and set about emptying his bowl. "So there's no need for you to trail after me all over Cumberland," he insisted between mouthfuls. "I'm sure you have other matters to keep you busy."

Will raised a brow as he set down his own fork. "Shunting me off in my old age, is that it?"

Jamie blushed. "I didn't mean to disparage you. But I don't need a tutor anymore. I can take care of myself."

"Of that I have no doubt," Will assured him. "But Lady Everard looked rather sorrowful when she left today, and I'd like to be certain there's no enmity between our families."

Jamie's color fled, and his spoon stilled. "I didn't mean to hurt her."

"Of course you didn't," Will replied. "You honored her with an offer of marriage. Unfortunately that seemed to upset her more than anything else."

Jamie sighed as he went after his lamb. "I don't think it was my offer that upset her. She's made up her mind not to marry, and she's not likely to change it. I've seen that look in her eyes before."

Will took the opening his son had offered. "Oh?" he asked, casually poking at his mashed potatoes.

"She can be very stubborn," Jamie obligingly replied,

pushing back in his chair. "If she thought something was right, there was no dissuading her it was wrong." He glanced at the ceiling as if picturing her at a younger age. Will could imagine she had been a handful for her governess—all that energy and determination.

"I remember there was an old story about a troll living in our woods," Jamie said, "and she set out to find it. I think I was about six then, so she would have been fourteen."

"Old enough not to believe in trolls anymore," Will mused.

Jamie shook his head. "Not her. She always loved believing in the impossible. She had me convinced she'd found the lair, that stone gamekeeper's cottage about a mile from here. I never saw old Mr. Michaelson the same way again." He shuddered for good measure.

Will chuckled. "He was my least favorite among your grandfather's servants when I was your age. I was glad he'd retired and moved elsewhere by the time I returned." He sobered and set aside his plate. "But I doubt it's a troll in the woods that troubles Lady Everard now."

"No," Jamie agreed darkly, "and what's troubling her isn't likely to be resolved the way she's going." He pushed away a plate that had been thoroughly cleaned of food.

"Nothing you can do to help?" Will asked, reaching for his crystal glass, as if the topic held no more interest than their usual conversation.

Jamie snorted. "I tried. You heard her. She refused to marry me. How many more offers do you think she'll get by the twenty-fifth?"

"The twenty-fifth?" Will seized on the date. "Why must she receive an offer of marriage by June twenty-fifth?"

Jamie clamped his mouth shut long enough to shake his head. "Sorry, Father. I've said too much. Please don't press me or her for the matter. She won't thank either of us for it."

Will knew the matter was closed for the moment, but he could not be disheartened. He'd gained a bit of leverage to use when he spoke to Samantha Everard the next day. From his experience, the right leverage, applied correctly, could open the floodgates of information.

So he let the matter go then and insisted on joining Jamie in the morning. Together they rode to Dallsten Manor after breakfast. Though it was early to be paying calls by London standards, Will knew, Evendale ran on its own clock. Therefore he wasn't surprised when they were ushered into the Dallsten Manor withdrawing room to find Mrs. Dallsten Walcott there ahead of them.

It was a decidedly feminine room, with walls that hinted of pink, and classical cameos peering down from the ceiling. The settee and chairs were edged with gilt, the hearth wrapped in white marble. He thought he caught the scent of roses in the air, even though their hostess was yet absent.

"Lord Kendrick," Mrs. Dallsten Walcott chirped, hands behind the back of her gray-striped day dress. "Lord Wentworth. What a delightful surprise."

Jamie and Will both bowed, but she made no move to sit, shifting from foot to foot as if anxious to escape their presence. "Lady Everard will be down shortly," she promised, edging around them. "Please make yourselves comfortable." Even as Will watched, she backed out the door. What was she doing? As chaperone it was her duty to stay and see to Lady Everard.

"She's pocketing the goods again," Jamie murmured as she disappeared from sight.

Will frowned at his son. "What are you talking about?"

He nodded to a rosewood table under the window, where an embroidered cloth showed the mark of something heavy. "There used to be a statue there, of David. I liked to look at it when I was a child. I'm guessing that's what she had behind her back."

Will stiffened. "She's stealing from the house? Is she so lacking in funds?"

Jamie shrugged as if he'd never considered why one might take a priceless object. At that moment Samantha entered the room. Today she wore a plain blue dress with a delicate lace collar; the subdued garment only made her beauty more obvious. Her smile was as bright as usual, but as she ventured closer Will could see that shadows hung under her eyes. Whatever was troubling her had not been resolved, as Jamie had predicted.

"Good morning to you both," she greeted them. "To what do I owe this honor?"

"You'd asked for help with the summer party," Jamie reminded her. "We're here to offer our support."

Her gaze swung between the two of them and rested on Will. "Both of you?"

Will inclined his head and spread one arm. "Always willing to do a service for a lady."

Her smile quirked. "How kind. And Jamie? You're ready to be put to work in the schoolroom?"

He made a face. "If that's what you need."

Samantha laughed, a sound as welcome as spring rain. "It is, indeed. You know where it is. Would you go up and see if there's anything missing we'd need to keep the young ones safe and entertained while they're here?"

He nodded his agreement and glanced at Will.

"Go ahead," Will encouraged him. "I'd like to speak to Lady Everard a moment."

Jamie's gaze narrowed in obvious warning, but he left the room.

Will turned to Samantha to find her regarding him nearly as warily. "Is there some problem, my lord?"

Will grimaced. "I thought we had agreed on Will."

Her smile was sweet, but he felt the sting of her tart response. "Very well, Will. What do you need of me?"

"First," he said, clasping his hands behind him, "Jamie seems to think there may be some items missing."

She started. "Has he been in touch with Jerome? Were things taken from the London house after all?"

"You've had thefts in London as well?" Despite himself, Will dropped his hands and took a step forward. "When was this?"

She waved a hand. "Before I came north. But it sounds as if we're talking at cross purposes. What thefts are you talking about?"

He nodded toward the empty table. "Here in Dallsten Manor."

She looked at the table, then returned her gaze to him, cheeks brighter than her smile. "Oh, that. There is no need for concern. I am well aware of where those pieces have gone."

Interesting. Was she trying to find a way to help the elderly lady without hurting her pride? Or was there some other reason for Mrs. Dallsten Walcott to take the pieces?

"And the things in London?" Will asked.

"Those are a different matter, which was most likely settled by me coming north. Was there anything else?"

She seemed in a decided hurry to get rid of him. He

ought to take offense, but he couldn't help thinking she was only trying to protect herself.

"I am not your enemy, you know," he said softly. "Why are you so intent on refusing my help?"

She smiled sadly, as if she knew he would not like her answer. "Because I have no need for your help. Thank you again for your kindness. I'll make sure Jamie gets home when he's finished here."

She was dismissing him. He hadn't been dismissed since the bey of Bendigo had refused to free captives taken as slaves from a British caravan in the Sahara. Then Will had gathered a party of armed men and gone by cover of night to free the captives himself. Perhaps he ought to forgo diplomacy in this case as well. It wasn't getting him very far.

"So you have everything in hand for the twenty-fifth," he said, watching her.

She took a step back, and her head came up, skin tightening around her lovely lips. "Jamie told you. The rat! Oh, I could drop him off the pele tower!"

Given that his son had likely reached the top of the opposite tower, where the schoolroom lay, Will thought his heir was safe for the moment. From the fire in her eyes, he wasn't as sure about his own safety.

"James is remarkably closemouthed when it comes to your secrets," he assured her. "But he did let slip that the date was significant to you. Why?"

"It's my birthday," she said. "Silly of me to make so much of it, but what lady likes the thought of giving away her age?"

She wasn't telling him the whole of it, he was certain. He was equally certain she would be a woman who would never have to worry about her age; she would only grow more lovely as the years went by.

He inclined his head. "Of course. Please forgive me. I assure you that James and I only wish to be of help. How can I convince you of that?"

She eyed him as if weighing the worth of his character, and he stood a little straighter.

"Why?" she challenged. "Why are you so insistent on helping?"

Will spread his hands. "It is my duty as a gentleman, Jamie's father and your neighbor."

"It won't wash," she countered. "I've met any number of so-called gentlemen who thought only of themselves. I refused your son yesterday, so you owe me no family obligation, and I doubt we'll be neighbors for long. You will have to do better than that for excuses to meddle in my affairs."

He didn't know whether to press the fact that she intended to leave the area or to take umbrage over her assumption he meant to meddle. At the moment umbrage seemed to have the upper hand.

"Very well," he said. "The truth is that I wish to help you, madam, because you are the most beautiful, infuriating, intriguing woman it has been my pleasure to meet across three continents, and I begin to wonder what I would have to do to prove it to you."

Samantha stared at him, heart hammering. He thought she was beautiful! She intrigued him! Of course, she apparently infuriated him as well, but she chose not the dwell on that. He was quite enough to dwell on.

She'd caught her breath when she'd seen him jump that hedge yesterday. He'd embodied everything she'd ever read about his brave adventures, every story his father had delighted to tell about him. She'd known then that she had growing feelings for Will, and now it seemed he reciprocated. She wanted to dance around the withdrawing room, shout it out the door, carry it up the fells.

Run as far and as fast as she could.

So she did the one thing she knew was guaranteed to cool any feelings he might have for her. She smiled sweetly and said, "Your brother had similar thoughts about me, my lord. A shame he didn't live to fulfill them."

He recoiled as if she'd struck him. She supposed she had. But if he couldn't remember the reason he should avoid her family, it was her duty to remind him.

"You will excuse me now, I'm sure," she said. It took every ounce of strength to move around him and walk toward the door, but she knew it was for the best. Getting caught up in these emotions was no good for either of them. Better to cut the strings now, before they grew any stronger.

"Lady Everard." The detached voice felt like a blow, but she turned to glance at him. His face was calm; all warmth and interest had fled. It was as if a stranger stood there. Once more she wished she could run away, hide, anything to avoid the pain building inside her.

Help me, Lord. You know what I'm doing is right.

Then why did it feel so wrong?

"I had assumed you were unaware of the circumstances surrounding his death," he said. "If you know more, tell me."

Samantha swallowed. All those who had been involved in the case had been sworn to secrecy, on penalty of being tried for treason if they confessed their parts to anyone but an appointed agent of the Crown. By his statement, Will must not have been made privy to the secret. It was grossly unfair! His brother's death was involved! But she could not break her oath, even for his sake. The scandal would hurt more than he could know.

"I'm sorry," she said. "I'm not at liberty to discuss the matter."

"No, only to throw it in my face, it seems."

She would not cringe. She had made this mess; she must live with it. Oh, why had she brought up his brother? Couldn't she have found a kinder way to fend off his attentions? Why couldn't she have been gifted with her cousin Jerome's gilded tongue or her cousin Richard's patience? No, she was too much like her cousin Vaughn and her father, acting first and thinking it over later.

Perhaps that was why she returned to Will's side. He stood stiffly, warily, his beautiful boots planted deep in the carpet, as if he expected her to attack.

Instead she kept her voice calm. "I never set out to hurt your family—your brother, Jamie or you. I wish you would believe that at least."

"I'd like nothing better," he said, and she thought she could hear the truth of it in his voice. "But there are too many secrets between your family and mine, secrets you refuse to share."

"Because they are not mine to share! Because sharing them would only hurt others who do not deserve more pain!"

"Because you do not trust me," he said.

Heat pulsed in the air, and she trembled with it. "You don't understand."

"Don't I? I'm not a vengeful man, Samantha. I have no wish to harm you or your family either. I have stated my desire to be your friend, begun to prove it, I hope, by my actions. But a friendship without trust is false."

"Trust is like a fencing foil," she countered. "It isn't effective unless you extend it."

He inclined his head. "Excellent point. Perhaps we both have something to learn in that area. But I have no secrets—my life, alas, is an open book."

And hers was a book locked tightly shut. She could not afford to give him the key.

"I will consider your offer of friendship, Will," she said. "But more I cannot promise."

He bowed, and she curtsied. For once, she had the opportunity to watch him retreat. Yet somehow, she still felt as if she was the one running away.

Chapter Ten

Wﬣat was she hiding? What did she know about his brother's death? Was that knowledge why she kept crying, why she refused to further an acquaintance with Jamie or him?

Will wanted answers, but he knew withdrawal was the surest way to earning her trust.

Lord, guide me in this!

He took two steps down the corridor from the withdrawing room and found Jamie standing here, face set.

"You were hard on her."

Will raised his chin. "You heard the conversation?"

"Some of it," Jamie admitted, closing the distance between them. "It didn't take me long to determine the schoolroom is lacking a few things a young gentleman might need, such as toy soldiers and a decent ball. I intend to send over some things from home."

"Then perhaps we should go," Will said, starting past him.

Jamie caught his arm. "A moment. You and Samantha seemed at cross purposes. Why?"

Will knew he had to go carefully. He didn't want

Jamie to think he had feelings for Samantha, especially when her refusal to marry must be fresh in the lad's mind.

"It's a long story," Will said. "If you're finished here for the moment, say your goodbyes to the lady and we can talk on the ride home."

Jamie nodded, and a short time later he and Will were riding back across the fields for Kendrick Hall.

"She seemed unaccountably delighted to be rid of us," Jamie said. "I thought I knew what was troubling her, but you seem to have hit on something more. What is it?"

"She mentioned your uncle," Will replied. Just remembering hurt. He'd all but blurted out that he had feelings for her, and she'd said the one thing calculated to douse the warmth. He did not think it was a coincidence. Something about him frightened her. But again, he could not discuss that with Jamie without hurting his son.

"About Uncle?" Jamie asked. "He'd left for London before she was more than a child. Did she even know him?"

Will felt as if he was picking his way through the darkest night, he had to chose his words so carefully. "Yes. They met in London. Tell me, what do you know about your uncle's death?"

"Only that he was killed." Jamie guided his horse over the little stream in the center of the field. "I wondered why. Was it a theft gone wrong or had he made an enemy? I just don't understand why you think Samantha would know the answer."

So, his father, Jamie's grandfather, hadn't told the boy everything. Will should have expected that. Jamie had been all of eight when his uncle, the former Lord

Wentworth, had been killed. Was he any more ready to hear the truth at seventeen?

As if Jamie knew his thoughts, he drew his horse closer to Arrow. "You don't have to shield me, Father. I'm not a child."

No one would have believed the statement by the way he thrust out his chin, as if he'd been denied a treat. But if Jamie was to spend the rest of his life next door to the Everards, perhaps he should know the whole story.

"Very well," Will said. "Here's what I was able to piece together from your grandfather and discreet inquiries in London. My brother, Gregory, was in town for the Season. He and your grandfather had talked about him taking a wife, so no one was surprised that he began courting—no one, that is, except the Everards."

"Samantha's family?" Jamie pulled his horse farther away. "Why would they care if Uncle began courting?"

"Because he began courting Samantha."

Jamie reined in with a jerk that set his mare to champing at the bit. Will slowed Arrow and allowed his son to catch up.

"Uncle was courting Samantha?" he demanded. "She was sixteen! He had to be ages older."

"Thirteen years older to be precise," Will said. "Not unheard of. You know your mother and I were the same age at seventeen, but that was a rarity."

"On too many counts," Jamie muttered.

Will frowned. "I hope you'll have the good sense not to disparage your mother."

Jamie colored and hung his head. "Of course I wouldn't disparage her, Father. I only meant that, growing up, there were a lot of stories told about you both. Some I didn't like."

Will kept Arrow at a steady trot. "We'll have to discuss those as well, then. Just know that your mother and I did nothing shameful. We were in love, we eloped to Scotland to marry against our parents' wishes, they agreed to accept the marriage when we returned and you were born a year later."

"A full year?" Jamie pressed.

So that was his concern. Will remembered the gossip. Some had insisted he had a reason to rush Peg over the border to Gretna Green, that she had tricked him into marriage by becoming pregnant. He knew that he and Peg had exchanged nothing more than fervent glances and heated kisses before the day they'd wed.

"A full year," he assured his son. "I have your mother's marriage certificate. I'll show you when we return."

Jamie settled into his saddle. "So Uncle Wentworth tried to court Samantha. Of course she refused."

"She never had the opportunity to accept," Will corrected him. "I don't know whether he actually offered for her, but there was an altercation at White's over a lady, and Vaughn Everard challenged him to a duel."

Jamie's horse pranced, and Will knew his son's hands must have tightened on the reins. "Uncle cannot have been cruel to her. No man could!"

Will had seen a few too many men who were cruel to women, so he wasn't sure of his brother's innocence. Gregory had tended to see women as a means to an end, never as a person deserving of his love and loyalty. What was more, Vaughn Everard may have earned the reputation of being a hothead in his youth, but something had goaded him into challenging Gregory to a duel.

"We do not know Samantha was the lady they argued over," Will cautioned. "All we know is that your uncle and Mr. Everard met on Primrose Hill outside London the next morning, and he wounded my brother."

"What!" At Jamie's cry, his horse galloped ahead, and it was a moment before he could get the beast under control and return to Will's side. When he did, Jamie's face was bloodless. "Vaughn Everard killed Uncle?"

Will held up one hand. "The authorities say otherwise. The wound was serious, but not fatal. My brother was very much alive when he reached our London house. He tried to hide his injury from the staff, telling only his valet. The valet had gone down to the linen closet for sheets to use as bandages. When he returned to the room, he found my brother dead, bleeding from multiple wounds. He and the attending physician swear those wounds were not the result of the duel."

"Everard must have followed him," Jamie declared, voice tinged with the fire of vengeance. "Followed him and murdered him."

"Perhaps," Will said, using all his skill to keep his own voice level. "The witnesses to the duel say he disappeared immediately afterward but returned a short time later. That would not have given him time to do the deed."

"He could have gone after Uncle," Jamie protested. "Found a way into the house."

"He could have. But the magistrates sent for him for questioning and found him on Bond Street."

Jamie made a face. "Well, that makes no sense. I can't see Everard killing someone in a fit of passion and going shopping afterward."

Will had reached the same conclusion. "And the magistrates deemed him innocent."

"Then who killed Uncle?" Jamie demanded. "And why?"

"That," Will said, "is just one of the things I hope to convince our friend Samantha to tell us."

Samantha knew she should be glad the two Wentworth men had left her alone. Jamie had promised to return when her family arrived to lend a hand with entertaining them. And she should be relieved to be spared further quizzing from his father.

Then, too, there were still a number of items Mrs. Dallsten Walcott needed ferried down to the dower cottage. Samantha could have ordered a servant to carry that painting, this vase, but she thought the fewer people who knew where the pieces had gone the less likely her family would be to protest. It was the lady's right under the agreement with Samantha's father, but she knew Mrs. Dallsten Walcott had taken advantage of that agreement before, and so did her family. It would be easier to move the pieces now, before the rest of her family arrived and questioned the changes, as Will had done.

But whatever she did, Will seemed to follow her. As she carried a miniature of Adele's grandmother down the drive for the dower house, she caught herself wondering whether anyone had ever captured those forest green eyes on canvas. When she approved Mrs. Linton's menu for the welcoming dinner, she wondered whether Will was as fond of roast duck as she was. He even intruded on her prayers that night, for when she asked the Lord's blessing on those she loved, his face was the first to come to mind.

This would never do! She couldn't fall in love with the Earl of Kendrick in less than a week! She didn't want him to fall in love with her and end up hurting him as she'd hurt Jamie. But in their world love meant marriage, and marriage was the one thing she could not afford. That fact had been brought home to her by a number of memories, stored up from when she'd been a child.

She climbed from her bed and went to the chest at its foot. Inside lay a small wooden box. She ran her fingers over the satiny surface, traced the intricate heart carved around the keyhole. She had never locked the box; Adele had not given her the key when she'd brought Samantha the box. She opened it now and drew out the miniature of her mother. Rosamunde Defaneuil's hair might have been a darker shade of blond, but it curled around a face very like Samantha's, and her smile promised excitement, adventure.

"The most beautiful, vivacious, sought-after girl in the Evendale Valley," Mrs. Dallsten Walcott had assured Samantha more than once. "Before Adele was born, of course."

But unlike Adele who had been forced to work as a governess in her own home, Samantha's mother had made a spectacular match. Arthur, Lord Everard, had been in the area hunting and had gone on a whim to the Blackcliff assembly. One look, the story said, and he and her mother had fallen in love.

Samantha set her mother's picture back in the box and shut the lid. The love her parents had shared had been the heart of a maelstrom. Neither had come out unscathed. Nor had she.

She shuddered as she put away the box and padded back to her bed. Even when she snuggled deep under the goose-down comforter, the memories intruded. Each time her father returned to London and left them both behind, her mother had been devastated. Her despondent sobs had echoed down the corridors.

"I want to see my mother," Samantha would say to Adele. "I want to give her a hug."

Adele's face was always so sad when she'd return from taking the message to Lady Everard. "Your mama says she is not quite up to visitors right now. But I promised her you love her very much. Perhaps we could draw her a picture to cheer her."

Samantha had drawn pictures. She had learned songs on the pianoforte to play for her mother when she felt better. She had learned how to say "I'm sorry" and "I love you" in French. None of it had mattered. Her mother was lost to her, and would soon be lost to the world.

When she was older, she thought she knew one of the reasons her mother was so sad. She'd been all of nine when she'd first heard the rumors. She'd been in the village shopping with Adele and had tarried in front of the bakery while Adele spoke to a neighbor. Looking into the window at the sweet treats displayed there, Samantha had been surprised to find two girls nearly her age looking back from inside. She'd smiled at them, always hungry to make a friend.

The taller of the two drew the other closer, and Samantha could hear her words come faintly through the glass. "Don't encourage her. Father says her father is ashamed of her. That's why he stays so long in London. She must have done something awful."

She'd wanted to march inside and scold those girls. Her father wasn't ashamed of her! He was a baron; he had to spend time in London in Parliament and at his other estates. She'd said as much to Adele as they'd ridden home in the carriage.

Adele had hugged her close. "Your father loves you," she'd said. "There are always stories about people who live their lives for all to see. You know the truth. Hold it in your heart and hold up your head."

The trouble was, now she did know the truth about how her mother had died, and she found it hard to take anything but sorrow from it. How could her mother's suicide bring anything other than pain?

Her cousins often told her how much she reminded them of her father—his desire for adventure, his joy for life. She thought she carried some of her mother's traits as well—the need to be loved, bouts with the dismals. But what she feared most was that she had enough of both her mother and father to make marriage, a good solid marriage, impossible.

With such thoughts on her mind sleep was hard that night. Unfortunately that meant her spirits were at their lowest the next morning. No matter what she did, she felt them weighing her down. Even her maid remarked on her attitude when she brought Samantha her usual chocolate and buttered toast for breakfast.

"I'll be fine," Samantha assured her, straightening her spine and raising her chin. She would be fine. She had promised herself she would never get as low as her mother had.

Her mother had focused on loss to the point she had forgotten what she'd gained. Samantha tried to remember things for which she was thankful—her cousins, the friends she'd made in London, even the fortune her father had left her. Though she stood to lose the bulk of it if she wasn't married in eight days, she would retain several of his many estates. Their income would be enough to keep her clothed and fed in style throughout her life. Jerome's oldest son would eventually inherit and become Baron Everard. And her family would finally know peace.

Help me remember that, Lord. Help me stay the course You've laid out for me.

For My yoke is easy, and My burden is light.

She knew the verse. She just wasn't sure she believed it at the moment.

Determined to shake off the dismals, she took her usual morning ride, being careful to stay on the forest trail and turning Blackie before reaching Wentworth land. Her mare protested, as if she too longed to ride up to Kendrick Hall and spend a few minutes in teasing conversation with its master. But Samantha was not about to give in.

Instead she rounded up the last few items Mrs. Dallsten Walcott wanted to be sure were saved from sale, delivered them personally to the dower cottage and cringed when she saw how crowded the place had become in the past few days. She had just reached the top of the drive and the manor when she heard the crunch of carriage wheels behind her.

Turning, she saw a sturdy brown travel coach with yellow wheels passing her. It was large enough to hold six passengers, and already another coach trundled up the drive strapped with luggage and undoubtedly carrying additional servants.

She smiled as she took up her place before the door to welcome her first guests. She was certain she knew which cousin was about to poke his head out the door. It wouldn't be Vaughn. He always traveled in something more sporty, and half the time he was at the reins. And not Richard and Claire either. They might need as large a coach for Claire's wardrobe, for she was never in less than the first state of fashion, but they tended to arrive with more fanfare.

Her suspicions proved true as the door opened and

the footman lowered the steps. The first passenger to disembark didn't even use them, leaping from the coach to throw himself into her arms.

"Auntie Lady Sam!" Justin Everard, her cousin Jerome's oldest son, hugged her tightly, and she patted the back of the seven-year-old's navy coat.

"Good catch," his father said to Samantha, climbing down after him before turning to offer his hand to his wife. Samantha had always thought Jerome was the most distinguished looking of her cousins with his raven hair and sharp blue eyes. The silver sprinkling his temples had only made him more so. Dressed in a navy coat and fawn trousers like his son, he cut a fine figure.

Samantha felt her smile growing as his wife descended to the drive in a whisper of emerald wool. Adele always looked the same to her, every dark hair in place, movements elegant and refined. She had been Samantha's beautiful governess growing up and was her dear friend now that Samantha was grown. She returned Samantha's smile and glanced up at the house, heart in her dark brown eyes.

Guilt shadowed Samantha's joy. Dallsten Manor was Adele's home. Samantha's refusal to marry would force them to sell it. The proceeds would go to charity, but that would be small consolation for losing a house that had meant so much to them both.

Before Samantha could do more than call a welcome, Adele was turning to take the baby from their nurse while Jerome helped their other two children to alight. With one hand holding onto their five-year-old son and the other their three-year-old daughter, he led his family toward the house, Justin keeping up a constant spate of questions about the visit, the stables and the upcoming party.

A longing tugged at Samantha's heart even as Justin's hand tugged on hers. If she never married, she'd never know the delight of holding little hands, guiding her children as they grew.

"Auntie Lady Sam?" Justin asked, peering up at her when she paused in the entryway. "Is something wrong?"

Adele and Jerome were regarding her as well. Samantha forced her lips to turn upward and ruffled his dark hair with her free hand. "How could anything be wrong when my family is here? We're going to have so much fun!"

The boy brightened at that, but by the looks they exchanged, Adele and Jerome were not fooled.

Samantha had far too much on her hands the next few hours to worry about what they might do with their concerns. Coach after coach arrived, bearing family and their servants and luggage. Samantha greeted each of her guests with a laugh and words of welcome, helped direct them to the rooms assigned to them for their stay and promised to talk more over dinner. She answered Mrs. Linton's questions about seniority in the servant's hall, mediated a squabble between two of the oldest children as to which bedchamber was "best" and sent up reminders to her cousins' wives that dinner that night was to be informal.

She was in the entry hall, sorting through a last-minute problem concerning dinner with Mrs. Linton when the footman let Jamie in.

"I saw the coaches," he explained. "I thought you might need some help. But if I'm in the way, just say so."

Samantha could have hugged him. She'd planned a number of parties over the years, but never one of this duration or number of people. She'd seriously underestimated the amount of work. The event hadn't even officially started, and already she felt stretched!

"You are most welcome," Samantha assured him with a nod of thanks to Mrs. Linton, who hurried off. "Two of my cousins' wives are settling their children and the third is helping to settle the extra staff. I expect my cousins to come thundering down the stairs shortly, complaining of nothing to do. Can you set up a game of billiards or some such?"

"On my way," Jamie promised.

"Thank you!" Samantha called as he hurried toward the south stair.

"And have you a task for me as well?"

A shiver of pleasure ran through her at the warm voice. Oh, how she'd missed Will, and it had been less than a day since she'd told him she wasn't sure they could even be friends. Obviously he bore her no ill will or he wouldn't be here offering his help now. How could she possibly refuse him again?

She turned with a smile for the door, ready to accept his offer of help this time. But another man stood just behind Will on the parquet floor of the entry hall, and her smile froze on her face.

Oh, no! Not him!

Chapter Eleven

Will saw Samantha's smile of welcome tighten into a polite mask. Had she made up her mind about him then? He had been hoping his help would be more welcome today and offer him another chance to prove himself to her.

Jamie had reported the number of coaches pulling up at her door. She might have plenty of staff to see to her family's basic needs, but someone was going to have to come up with entertainments to keep all her guests busy until the summer party next week. And anything he could do to assist her would in turn help to build trust between them, trust he badly needed to establish if she was to tell him anything about his brother's death and any other secrets.

He started to ask her pardon, but a discrete cough made him realize they had an audience. Turning, he saw that another gentleman had joined them.

He could not be an Everard. Instead of the lean, muscled bodies Will had expected in Samantha's cousins, this man was amply padded, from his beard-covered cheeks to the round belly straining his paisley waistcoat. His hair was a nondescript brown, his eyes a questionable gray. But the smile he bestowed on Samantha could only be called besotted.

"Lady Everard," he proclaimed, hurrying past as if Will was no more than a piece of furniture. "Dear lady, I am so very privileged to be invited to your home." He bowed over her hand and pressed a kiss against her knuckles. Will had to stifle an urge to yank the fellow back.

"Mr. Haygood," she said, and only the slight hitch in her voice betrayed her surprise as she pulled from his fervent grip. "How nice of you to join us."

Haygood warbled on, rhapsodizing about the journey from London ("worth every inconvenience to be with you"), the fells surrounding the valley ("like the cusp of God's hands"), the house ("an entirely enchanting enclave") and the daisies embroidered on Samantha's day dress ("smelling of the very depth of dew"). Will didn't think she heard a word of it. He could almost see the thoughts flying behind her dark eyes. Unless he missed his guess, she was in trouble.

He'd visited Dallsten Manor many times as a youth. The main corridor upstairs held five bedchambers, with a solarium in the south tower. He knew the Everards had repaired the north tower, so it was possible there was a bedchamber or two in it as well. Depending on the number of rooms needed for Samantha and her family, including their oldest children, the house was very likely full. She was no doubt calculating schemes as to which family member she would inconvenience to make room for this unexpected guest.

While he couldn't add another room to the manor, he could at least give her time to see her scheme through.

"Pardon me," Will interjected, causing Haygood to

stutter to a stop in the middle of praising the laces on her half boots. "I don't believe we've met."

"Of course," Samantha said with evident relief at the change in subject. "Forgive me. William Wentworth, Earl of Kendrick, may I present Mr. Prentice Haygood."

Haygood stuck out his hand. "Pleasure, my lord. Any friend of Lady Everard's is a friend of mine."

Will shook his hand, surprised by the firm grip in an otherwise inoffensive countenance.

"Mr. Haygood was a frequent visitor at Everard House this Season," Samantha seemed compelled to explain. "He is something of an historian and knows a great deal about the families of the ton."

Haygood waved the hand he had retrieved from Will's. "Just a hobby of mine. I find genealogy to be a fascinating subject. I hope to delve into yours while I'm here, Lady Everard. There's nothing like knowing one's origins to put life into perspective."

"I know quite enough about my origins," she countered. Her tone was so adamant that Will could only wonder at her vehemence.

Haygood took a step back. "I didn't mean to pry, my dear, I assure you! I have only your best interests at heart." He glanced over his shoulder toward the open door facing the drive. "Where shall I have my valet direct my things?"

Samantha's smile was clearly forced. "If you'll give me a few minutes, I'll make sure your room is ready. We're a bit at sixes and sevens today with so many arrivals."

"I'd be delighted to entertain Mr. Haygood for you," Will put in.

Her whole demeanor lightened. "Oh, Will, that's famous!"

Was he blushing again? Why did her pleasure so move him? "It's no trouble, I assure you. I believe my son is setting up a game of billiards, Haygood. You can join us."

It wasn't often he used his prestige as earl to his advantage, but this time he felt it was warranted to all but order the fellow about. To his surprise, Haygood hesitated.

"But I was hoping for some time alone with you, Lady Everard," he protested, blinking his gray eyes as if fighting emotions. "I have something very important I must ask you."

Samantha appeared entirely immune to his theatrics. "Oh, I'm certain there will be ample time later," she assured him, but Will heard her murmur "much later," under her breath.

She wanted to avoid the fellow. He had no trouble with that. But if she meant to include him in her efforts, she was fair and far off.

"Never fear, Haygood," he said, clapping the man on the padded shoulder of his coat. "We'll have you in your room with plenty of time to change for dinner. Which reminds me." He turned his look on Samantha. "What time did you want my son and me to return for dinner, Samantha?"

Haygood frowned, but Will wasn't sure whether it was his collusion with their hostess or his use of her given name that had concerned the man. Will thought Samantha might frown as well, but her eyes positively twinkled as if she knew his game and appreciated it.

"Six, Will," she said, emphasizing his given name as well. "We keep country hours here at Dallsten Manor. I shall see you all then."

* * *

So Will found himself in the game room of Dallsten Manor, standing beside the billiard table with Jamie and Prentice Haygood. The space must have been constructed while he had been abroad, for Will could not remember him and Gregory being shown such a room when they had visited the manor as children.

And they would certainly have enjoyed it. Small tables along the wainscoted walls were inlaid with chessboards and cribbage trails, the pieces, Will was sure, tucked away in little drawers built into the edge of each tabletop. A game of nine pins stood in the corner, the mahogany ball hanging from a brass chain, the lacquered pins gleaming in readiness.

In the center, surrounded by high padded benches for a rapt audience, stood a carved walnut billiard table, its verdant baize calling like a greening field. A long scoring board was affixed to one wall beside it. Jamie had already set the three balls into their proper positions and was examining a cue from the rack behind the table. Will introduced him to Haygood and offered to allow the gentleman to play with Jamie first.

Haygood demurred, chubby hands raised in front of his paisley waistcoat. "No, no! I wouldn't dream of intruding. Never was too terribly good at games and such. I'll be delighted to watch."

Jamie exchanged glances with Will, and he was fairly certain his son was unimpressed with Haygood. Will was more willing to give the fellow the benefit of the doubt.

"Perhaps you'd be so kind as to keep score, then," he said, going to choose a cue for himself. "What say, Jamie? Shall we keep it short and go to twenty-five points?"

"As you wish," Jamie agreed, positioning himself at the top of the table. "So long as you let me go first."

As Will grinned back at him, Haygood obligingly seated himself on one of the high benches, within easy reach of the scoring rack. But he had no sooner settled the tails of his brown coat than he renewed his rhapsodizing about their hostess.

"Lady Everard is the most marvelous woman of my acquaintance," he enthused as Jamie took his first shot, putting his ball neatly in the pocket after glancing it off the red ball in the center of the field. "How fortunate we are to be here in the very place of her birth."

Jamie hit his second shot and racked up another five points before straightening. "She wasn't born here. She was born in Carlisle. Her father bought Dallsten Manor when she was six."

Haygood did not bristle to have his mistake pointed out. He positively beamed at Jamie. "Ah, you know her so well. I envy you that."

"I consider her my closest friend." Jamie bent for his next shot and bounced his ball off the cushion to roll within inches of Will's. With a sigh, he stepped aside for his father.

"And why not?" Haygood agreed. "A woman of rare beauty and insight. Spirited, certainly, and eminently talented. Have you heard her play the pianoforte, Lord Kendrick?"

"I haven't had the pleasure," Will admitted, bending to take his shot as well. His son had left a scattered field, but he managed to put his ball into a pocket several times before having to surrender the table once more.

"I've heard her play," Jamie said. "She's brilliant."

"Oh, indeed, indeed," Haygood warbled as Jamie

leveled his cue for his turn. "Perhaps she'll favor us to-night. And dance? There isn't a lady lighter on her feet."

"That I can believe," Will replied, wishing yet again that he'd asked her to dance at Jamie's birthday party, before he'd known who she was or suspected she knew more about his brother's death.

"And ride," Haygood continued, gaze following Jamie has he positioned himself for a shot. "Well, I tell you, few gentlemen can match her."

"Now, that's the truth," Jamie agreed, sending his ball into a pocket for the third time. Will retrieved it and handed it to him. "She fences, too, did you know?" Jamie asked Haygood as he accepted the ball. "I beat her this week."

Will nearly cringed at the pride in his son's tone.

Haygood took it harder. His back stiffened, and his chin thrust out. "A tall tale to be sure, sir," he said, shaking a finger at Jamie.

Jamie hit his next shot cleanly. "It's not a Banbury tale. It's the truth. She fences well, but I fence better."

Haygood still looked unconvinced. "I am quite certain that if I were so fortunate as to join the lady for a match I would neither have the gall to defeat her nor the pride to brag about it afterwards."

Jamie straightened, fingers tightening on his cue.

Will stepped between them. "I think, gentlemen," he said, eying them each in turn, "that we are all in agreement that Lady Everard is a paragon."

Jamie relaxed with a nod and bent to take his next shot.

Haygood positively beamed. "Well said, Lord Kendrick, well said. I am the most fortunate of men, I know. It will be an excellent match."

Jamie's shot went wide, and the ball jumped across

the green baize table to roll to a stop against the opposite cushion.

Will felt as if his heart had taken a similar leap. So Haygood meant to offer for Samantha. He seemed confident of her response. Was this why she'd refused Jamie, pushed Will aside?

Immediately he dismissed the idea. Surely if she'd been intent on capturing Haygood's regard, she would have been far more welcoming on his arrival. And she would definitely have remembered inviting the fellow to her home in the first place!

Another possibility presented itself, and he tossed it aside as well. She did not seem the kind of woman who sought to engage the affections of every man who approached her, only to abandon them when they no longer amused her. He'd seen no sign of flirting with Jamie, or Haygood for that matter. She hadn't attracted undue attention at Jamie's party, where more than one gentleman would have looked her way had she beckoned, he was sure. And she'd showed no more than affection for her former suitor Toby Giles. In fact, the only man she'd showed the least partiality toward was Will.

He thought he must be grinning again, for Haygood went so far as to hop off his bench and wring Will's hand. "I can see you agree with me, my lord," he chattered. "Thank you for your encouragement. I intend to ask her at the first opportunity."

Will didn't have it in him to wish him luck as the fellow went to fetch a cue for himself to play against Jamie. Will was finding himself with another wish entirely, that he had the courage to ask the lady the same question. What was wrong with him? He never intended to marry. The flash of golden hair, the whiff of rose-scented perfume, and he was all aflutter? Ridiculous!

Jamie, however, obviously had a much harder time hearing that another man intended to marry Samantha. "She won't have you," he predicted. "I doubt she'll ever wed."

Something crossed behind Haygood's gray eyes, so fleeting it might have been a shadow from the lamp. "Sometimes all a lady requires is the right persuasion," he said. Then he bent to take his shot and put his ball neatly in the pocket.

Upstairs, Samantha also had no illusions as to why Prentice Haygood had followed her to Cumberland.

"What can he be thinking to show up like that?" she demanded as she and Imogene, Vaughn's wife, stole a few moments alone together before dinner. Of all her cousins' wives, Samantha liked Imogene the best with her chestnut curls worn close to her face and creamy jade-colored eyes. Adele would always be dear to her as the governess who'd raised her after her mother had died, and Claire held a special place in Samantha's affections for her efforts to guide her through Society. But Imogene was the closest in age, being merely three years older, and she was closer in temperament as well. The two had become good friends over the years.

Perhaps that's why Samantha had insisted that Imogene join her before dinner. She wasn't yet up to being alone in the room she had taken upon Mr. Haygood's unfortunate arrival. She hadn't wanted to inconvenience her cousins after they'd just arrived and unpacked, so she'd done the only thing possible. She'd given Haygood her own bedchamber and moved to her mother's.

The former Lady Everard's bedchamber hadn't been used since her untimely demise nearly twenty years ago. While the maids dusted and cleaned as needed, holland covers had still draped the canopied bed, wardrobe and pianoforte in the corner until now. Mrs. Linton hadn't questioned Samantha's decision, but the moisture pooling in the housekeeper's quicksilver eyes told Samantha she knew what that move meant to her mistress.

Imogene had no knowledge that Lady Everard had died in this very room. She cuddled into the elegant gold-trimmed armchair by the fire and wiggled her slippered toes before the heat warming the white marble hearth.

"You're certain you didn't invite Mr. Haygood?" she asked Samantha. "Things were a bit hectic before you headed north."

Samantha knew Imogene referred to the break-ins at Everard House. It had been unsettling to find her things pawed through, her guest rooms ravaged. And yet nothing had been taken. The thief had obviously been looking for something specific, for he'd struck three times before she'd had to travel to Cumberland for the party. That she'd been unable to determine his identity still rankled.

"I'm certain I'd remember," she said, pacing about the room, her green satin dressing gown whipping about her ankles. Sitting on the other chair facing the fire, the one meant for her father, felt wrong. And sleeping in the bed? She wasn't sure she could force herself to do that.

Don't let me make this more than I should, Father. It's only a bed.

Yea, though I walk through the valley of the shadow of death, I will fear no evil: for Thou art with me.

At the remembered verse she felt the burden slipping off her shoulders. But Imogene was watching her, as if unsure of her emotions.

"Well," she said, "I think showing up here was rather presumptuous of Mr. Haygood, to be sure."

Samantha nodded. "Unfortunately I didn't feel comfortable sending him away. He's simply too…loyal."

"I told you he would offer," Imogene replied, arms crossed over her own frothy white dressing gown. "He's followed you for much of the Season like a lost pup."

Samantha made a face. "And why? There are any number of other young ladies willing to encourage his attentions."

"Especially now it's known he will inherit his uncle's estates and titles," Imogene predicted. "Even with this sudden appearance, he seems rather sweet. Are you certain you cannot care for him?"

Samantha shook her head. "Quite certain."

Imogene rose to meet her in the center of the room, taking her hands and looking deep into her eyes. "Dearest, I adore you, and I'll stand by you no matter what. But your birthday is just over a week away. You know what that means."

Samantha pulled back her hands. "Everyone I care about knows what that means. But my mind is quite made up, Imogene. I won't marry, not even to save Dallsten Manor."

Imogene sighed. "I didn't believe you when you said that eight years ago at Richard and Claire's wedding. I suspect I must believe you now."

Samantha sagged. "I wish someone would."

"You cannot blame us for holding on to hope," Imogene replied, releasing her hands. "Adele, Claire and I are deliriously happy in our marriages. We want the same for you."

Samantha eyed her. "Can you tell me you and

Vaughn never fight? That you are in complete accordance with everything he does?"

Imogene giggled, jade eyes sparkling. "Fight? Never. Disagree strongly? Less often than you might have thought when we first married. And of course there are moments I wish to find his old blade and make my point." She took Samantha's hand and led her back toward the hearth. "But I have never regretted my decision to marry him. I knew he was the one God intended for me, and that has been proven true again and again."

Samantha's heart ached. "That is part of the problem, Imogene," she replied, stopping just short of the armchairs. "God seems to have another plan for me, for I've never felt that way about any of the men who pursued me. I'm sorry."

Imogene hugged her then. It never failed to amaze her that someone Imogene's size, still short and curvy even after having given birth to twins, could hug so fiercely. In the embrace Samantha felt her friend's care, her belief and her faith. When they released each other, tears sparkled in Imogene's eyes, and Samantha could feel answering tears in her own.

Imogene excused herself then and hurried off to change for dinner. Samantha's maid arrived to help her change as well. Life went on, and she somehow thought it should pause a pace. She'd confided that God had never sent her a man she could love as husband, but she feared the lack was not in her Lord. Somewhere along the road she'd lost the ability to believe in love. At times she felt rather mature about the matter. She was no longer a dewy-eyed debutante, pining after this fellow one week and that fellow the next.

Yet at the moment she felt as if she'd taken a wrong

turn, started down a crooked path. She could only hope the next few days would prove the truth of her plans, one way or the other.

Chapter Twelve

Despite Samantha's unsettled emotions, dinner proved to be a merry affair. Mrs. Linton prided herself on running an orderly household, and even though Samantha had encouraged her to keep things informal this first evening, the housekeeper had set the table with an embroidered damask cloth, the best china in pure white edged in gilt, and every piece of silver the house owned. The light from the candelabra glowed on the tureens of pea soup spiced with mint, the platters of dressed lamb and the bowls of steaming potatoes that made up the first course.

Even with all the children upstairs in the schoolroom, they sat down eleven to table, counting Mrs. Dallsten Walcott, Will, Jamie and Prentice Haygood. The gentlemen had dressed in tailored coats and cravats that ranged from elegant to austere, and the ladies were decked out in shiny lustring and soft lace.

The oddest thing about dinner was to have Vaughn at the head of the table as the highest-ranking member present. Two years ago, for services to the crown, he had been awarded the recreated Widmore marquessate, which had belonged to Imogene's late father. Though he was now known as Widmore in many circles, none of his family called him by his new title. The name held too many unpleasant memories for them. Imogene said she knew he would return honor to her family's former title.

As the second-highest ranking gentleman present, Will sat on his left across from Imogene. That put Samantha next to him and across from Jamie. She was just thankful Haygood ended up at the foot, across from Mrs. Dallsten Walcott, with Jerome, Adele, Richard and Claire in between.

Good thing Mrs. Linton's insistence on maintaining the rules of society only extended to the seating arrangements, for Samantha's family certainly didn't feel obliged to comply. Her cousins called jests and challenges up and down the table, and their wives joined in. Mrs. Dallsten Walcott took their boisterous camaraderie in stride for the most part, but Jamie didn't seem to know how to handle it, and Haygood, when Samantha managed to catch a glimpse of him, looked positively glassy eyed.

Not so Will. He dug into his food with gusto, laughed at all the jokes and joined the conversation freely.

"Planning to jump any fences while you're here?" he asked Vaughn at one point.

"Ha!" Richard leveled his silver fork at Vaughn from farther down the table, grin evident above his russet beard. Her second-oldest cousin had been a privateer before he'd turned merchant captain. He'd been gone from England for years before reacquainting himself with her sponsor Lady Claire Winthrop and marrying her. Samantha admired his quiet strength. It wasn't easy to upset Richard.

"You may have London fooled into thinking you're

the perfect marquess," he told Vaughn, "but you'll find it harder to live down your reputation here, my lad."

"I cannot think what you mean," Vaughn said archly, raising his chin so high the light caught on his platinum hair.

Will grinned. "I heard from my father you liked to jump your horse over any obstacle," he explained, then he glanced across the table at Jamie. "What was the story?"

"Every fence between here and Carlisle," Jamie said, obviously pleased to be included.

Vaughn picked up the crystal goblet before him, dark eyes scornful. "I am entirely beyond such things now."

Jamie's face fell.

Imogene nodded sagely, but Samantha saw the laughter in her friend's eyes. "Oh, my yes. I can't remember the last time he jumped a fence. But he set the record for curricle and pair to Brighton last month."

"Ho!" Jerome raised a glass in toast. "To new challenges."

"To new challenges," they all chorused with raised glasses while Vaughn gave it up and grinned.

"And what of you, Cousin?" he asked Samantha when they had all set down their glasses. "Any new challenges you've taken up recently?"

Imogene looked away, but the others were all watching Samantha, and she knew they hoped she'd confess to an engagement. Though she and Haygood seemed miles apart down the long table, they had to wonder why he was here. Even he was leaning forward as if intent on gazing at her. Now would be the perfect time for a clever quip, a funny tale. Unfortunately she suddenly felt more like crying than laughing.

"Not much challenges Lady Everard," Will said in

the silence. "She beat me in a fencing match just the other day."

Laughter returned to the table, and she could breathe again. "Only I lost to Jamie the very next match," she confessed with a smile to her friend.

"What a swordsman you must be, Lord Wentworth," Claire said on his right, her crystalline blue gaze warming with her praise.

"It was difficult facing a lady," he admitted, blushing.

"Don't be easy on her," Richard advised. "She'll take advantage of it."

"Well I like that!" Samantha declared. "Do you impugn my honor, Captain Everard?"

Richard held up his hands. "Never! I've no wish to meet you at dawn."

"A lady," Claire said, honey-blond-haired head high, "never rises so early." She nodded to Samantha. "Blades after tea, I think. Much more civilized."

"Come now," Haygood put in. "I heard this tale from Lord Wentworth earlier, and I still cannot credit it. Surely so delicate a flower as Lady Everard could not possibly wield a blade."

If she'd ever entertained the least notion of agreeing to Haygood's suit, that speech did it in. She had entirely too much experience dealing with people who wanted her to be something other than what she was. It never ended well.

"They are quizzing you, Mr. Haygood," Mrs. Dallsten Walcott said with a sniff. "You will find it a family trait."

Before Samantha could protest, Jerome, Adele, Claire and Richard all rushed to assure Mrs. Dallsten Walcott and Haygood with stories of Samantha's prowess.

Will leaned closer. "Small wonder you beat me. I had no idea I was taking my life in my hands."

He was teasing. She could see it in his smile, in the way his eyes crinkled at the corners. She felt her own heart lightening.

"Be warned then, my lord," she teased back. "Dealing too closely with me can be dangerous."

He inclined his head. "Perhaps you should be warned as well, then." His gaze met hers, and her cheeks heated at the warmth in it. "Like your cousin, I enjoy a challenge."

Will could not remember such an entertaining meal. Too often on the diplomatic circuit, dinners were difficult voyages constantly fighting undercurrents. Conversations held innuendos, looks hid treachery. The Everards did not seem to have anything to hide, and that surprised him.

It was the same after dinner. They all repaired to the withdrawing room, and each lady took a turn either playing at the piano or singing. Their husbands watched, with pleasure evident in their eyes and smiles. And when Samantha played, Will thought every man in the room nearly popped the buttons from his waistcoat each was so puffed with pride over knowing her.

Both Haygood and Jamie attempted to approach her when she finished, but she managed to elude them as she surrendered the instrument to Captain Everard's wife, who had already asked Will to call her Claire. Indeed all the Everards had insisted on a first-name basis, an unexpected honor. But Jamie and Haygood made quite the pair, staring soulfully after her until their gazes happened to collide. Then they hastily excused themselves and went to make conversation with others.

Will was tempted to rescue his son from what appeared to be a ringing lecture from Mrs. Dallsten Walcott, but Samantha had chosen to promenade, and she was drawing closer to his position by the windows overlooking the grounds. He could not give up the opportunity to talk to her.

"I fear your suitors have more determination than you have ways to avoid them," Will said as she neared. "I doubt you can evade them for long."

She stopped beside him. Up close he could see that she was not enjoying the evening as much as her family was. Though she smiled pleasantly enough, she held herself stiffly, as if every muscle had tightened in protest.

"And to whom are you referring, exactly?" she asked Will, golden brows arched.

Will lifted his chin to point to Haygood across the room. "Our poetic friend Mr. Haygood, for one. Am I right in assuming you'd prefer he not propose to you?"

She nodded, far too eagerly, then immediately dropped her gaze. "Forgive me. That was unkind. He's a dear friend, but I have no interest in marrying him."

That seemed a common refrain. Though he had expected as much, he was surprised at the relief that coursed through him.

"And what of Jamie and me?" Will asked. "Do you find us equally troublesome to your plans?"

She smiled, warmth softening the tension in her face. "No. In truth you both have been more help than you know. I hope you'll feel free to visit the manor often between now and the summer party."

It seemed his tactics were working. But he knew better than to press his advantage now. She wasn't ready to confide in him yet, and any attempt to openly encourage her was likely to be met by loyal opposition from her family. He merely had to wait. Surely over the course of the next few days he'd find an opportunity to question her again about his brother's death. And the more she saw him as a helpmate, the easier the questioning would go.

"It would be my pleasure to assist," Will assured her. "For now I'll gather up my son and Mrs. Dallsten Walcott and leave you with a few less heads to worry about tonight." He took her hand and bowed over it. He'd used the courtly gesture countless times to honor a lady. Yet the strength in her grip, the confidence in her touch was like nothing he'd ever felt. He only hoped his efforts to win her trust would be successful soon, so he could get the lovely Samantha Everard off his mind.

Thank God for good friends like Will! He at least noticed she was growing fatigued and acted to reduce the burden. She smiled after him as he took his leave from the others, collected Jamie and Mrs. Dallsten Walcott and withdrew. The room did not feel nearly as warm in his absence.

Prentice Haygood was another matter. No sooner had the Wentworths and her chaperone quit the room than her unwelcome houseguest headed in her direction. She tensed, trying to think of a way to fend him off, but Vaughn intercepted him.

"Mr. Haygood," he drawled, raising a quizzing glass to his eye and using it to effect. "I don't believe we've had the pleasure of meeting this Season. I find myself quite curious. Do share your background."

Haygood visibly squirmed, shoulders rolling in his brown coat, and immediately excused himself, pleading fatigue from his journey. Vaughn watched him hurry from the room. Behind her husband's back, Imogene winked at Samantha. Her friend had evidently told Vaughn about Samantha's feelings toward the fellow, and for once Samantha could not mind her cousin's interference.

Shortly after, Jerome and Adele headed off to the schoolroom to check on their children, and Richard declared that he and Claire were retiring. Vaughn also bid Samantha good-night with a bow.

Imogene, however, lagged behind, trailing Samantha toward the great stair.

"You sly goose!" she cried with a giggle. "Why didn't you tell me? You're in love with Lord Kendrick!"

"Hush!" Samantha grabbed her arm and drew her back behind the stairs to make sure none of the others heard them. "I am no such thing."

Imogene cocked her head, chestnut curls bouncing. "So you claim you have no feelings for the fellow."

Samantha dropped her hold. "I didn't say that."

"There seems to be a great deal you're not saying," Imogene pointed out. "But I noticed the looks flashing between the two of you at dinner, I heard snatches of your conversation. You cannot deny he held his own tonight, and that's saying a very great deal with our family."

Samantha couldn't deny it. Some of her suitors had held up well compared against Jerome or Richard. Few could match Vaughn. Will had gone toe-to-toe with her formidable cousins and had looked as if he'd enjoyed it. But she could not leave Imogene with the impression she cared for him. Samantha would never hear the end of it.

"What you saw was the beginnings of a friendship," she explained.

"Friendship?" From her tone to the curve of her coral-colored lips, Imogene put doubt into the word.

"Friendship," Samantha insisted. "It isn't surprising. I've been friends with his son for years. Why shouldn't I enjoy his company, too?"

"No reason at all," Imogene agreed, threading her arm through Samantha's and drawing her back to the stairs. "He's utterly charming and handsome, and he seems to share a number of interests with you."

Samantha was surprised her friend hadn't pushed the matter further, but she smiled and nodded as they started up the stairs, skirts rustling.

"He's kind as well," she told Imogene. "I feel as if he's looking out for me."

"And you wouldn't have to leave your beloved Dall-sten Manor," Imogene reminded her as they reached the top of the stairs. "You could even combine the estates."

Samantha pushed out her lower lip in thought. "I suppose we could. Though I'm not sure I like Kendrick Hall nearly as much as the manor."

"You could remodel," Imogene temporized as they turned the corner for the bedchambers. "You have more than enough in the legacy, once you marry."

Samantha pulled up short, suddenly realizing where the conversation had led her. "Wait…"

"Now, now," Imogene soothed, backing away from her as if she saw trouble coming. "I merely wish to point out how easily you consider a future with Lord Kendrick. All you need do is bring him around before your birthday and elope to Gretna Green, and all will be well."

"Imogene," Samantha started, but her friend had already turned her back and was hurrying off for her bedchamber with an airy wave.

Samantha shook her head. Marriage to Will? Ridiculous! Eloping to Gretna Green? Never! Wasn't that what had started her family's troubles to begin with?

Samantha turned to face the door to her mother's bedchamber. A lump rose in her throat, but she swallowed it. Raising her chin, she opened the door and marched in. Her maid had a lovely fire glowing in the grate, and the velvet curtains had been drawn over the night. Even the covers on the great bed had been turned down, beckoning her with the promise of restful slumber. She found the promise impossible to believe.

She undressed with the help of her maid then dismissed the woman for the night. Putting her back to the bed, she knelt on the rug before the hearth and watched the colors shifting in the heated coal.

Adele knew what had happened in this room, the tragic way Lady Everard's life had ended. Very likely she had shared the tale with Jerome. He could easily have told Richard and Vaughn. Samantha had been unaware of the secret until a few months ago, when Adele had come to visit her in London.

"I have something for you," she had said when the two of them were seated in the Everard House withdrawing room. Samantha had had it redecorated in the Egyptian style but had been surprised to find she wasn't overly fond of the gilded wall coverings and lion-footed furnishings.

Adele had held out the little wooden box that now rested in the wardrobe of this very room. "I probably should have given these to you years ago," her former governess said with a shake of her dark head. "But I was never sure the time was right."

Samantha accepted the box with fingers that seemed to be shaking. "What is it?"

"The last bits of your mother," Adele had said. "Treat them kindly."

She'd thought the advice a bit odd. How could she not treat anything her mother had left kindly? But going through the meager contents of the box after Adele left, Samantha could understand her hesitation. So little remained of a life that had brought joy to so many.

There was the miniature of her mother, very much the way Samantha remembered her. There were the ribbons her mother had worn in her hair the day she'd married. There was the marriage certificate linking her mother and father together forever. Cousin Richard said the signature of the officiating cleric must belong to one of the anvil priests, the men in Gretna Green who married English couples who had fled over the border to Scotland because their families protested their love. That paper was the only thing that proved Samantha was legitimately born and the rightful heir to the barony and the Everard legacy.

But as important as those fading lines were to her, the other document from her mother was more precious. Rosamunde Defaneuil had left a diary chronicling her married life. Samantha had stayed up one night reading it. What had started as eagerness to know more about the mother she'd lost had quickly turned to dismay and then sorrow. Marriage had transformed a vivacious, charming girl into a distraught, withdrawn woman who took the ultimate step to escape the prison she'd built for herself.

The pop and hiss of the coals was too loud in the bedchamber. Samantha drew her knees up under her nightgown and hugged them to her chest. Had her mother sat in that chair, stared at the glow? Had her tears wet this rug, the pillow on the great bed? Certainly her weight had bent the canopy as she'd hanged herself.

Samantha shuddered. Her mother's tempestuous emotions had destroyed her, left Samantha an orphan but for Adele and occasional visits from her father. How was she to know she would be any more successful in a marriage built on such emotions? She was her mother's daughter, finding joy easily, but falling into the dismals when left alone. Sometimes she thought her mother's moods were what had driven her father to London, what had kept him from acknowledging her and her mother to his friends and family. Could any man deal with such moods without tarnishing the love he had thought he felt? Could she?

Only with You, Lord.

She'd seen nothing in her mother's diary to indicate her mother had carried her worries and fears to the Lord in prayer. Samantha knew she had that source of help. But if she let her emotions rule her, could she make any kind of marriage? Sometimes she felt as if she had so many feelings inside they would gush out like water falling from the fells. Only it would not be a rainbow they formed but a flood to sweep away her future.

Surely self-control was the key, and that meant no hasty steps into marriage. Very likely it meant no marriage at all.

She rose and padded to the bed and pulled off the comforter. Then she wrapped it around her, huddled in her father's chair and watched until the glow faded from the coals.

Chapter Thirteen

"What do you think of the Everards, Father?" Jamie asked later that night in the Kendrick withdrawing room.

A part of Will had expected to dislike the Everard men on sight. From jumping fences to courting maidens, the stories of their antics were legendary in the valley. Instead he'd felt surprisingly at home.

"I like them," he admitted, stretching his legs toward the fire from where he and Jamie sat. "Your uncle and I were far enough apart in age, and we were never close, so at times I felt like an only child. It strikes me I could have done worse than to have one of these men as a brother or cousin."

Jamie nodded. "And Vaughn Everard isn't nearly as terrifying as I remembered. I can't see him killing Uncle." He leaned forward, and the light from the fire gave his face lines he hadn't yet earned. "You were next to Samantha all through dinner. Did you get a chance to ask?"

"One doesn't ask about murder in front of friends and family," Will cautioned, remembering the many years it had taken him to get the knack of move and countermove, all handled with velvet gloves. "And I'm not sure she trusts me enough to have that conversation yet."

Jamie leaned back and slapped the knees of his evening trousers. "Well, I say they're innocent. I'm sure you'll convince her to clear up the matter. I'll be off in the morning to help her. Will I see you there later?"

"Count on it," Will replied. Jamie might not appreciate Will hanging about, but Samantha had invited him. And he had work to do if he was to convince her to share what she knew about Gregory's death. Besides, just the thought of spending a day in the vibrant atmosphere he had experienced that evening raised his spirits.

Consequently he rose early and made sure there was no urgent estate business that needed his attention. His staff had never caught sight of the outrider Will had seen the other day, so he felt confident the fellow had moved on. He had Arrow saddled and rode across the fields to Dallsten Manor.

The day was clear and warm. The crisp scent Will attributed to the fells drifted on the breeze. The Everards had evidently decided to make the most of the good weather, for a number of them were out on the lawn in front of the manor. However two were conspicuously absent—Vaughn Everard and Prentice Haygood. Despite the marquess's claims to civility last night, Will could only hope he wasn't out somewhere challenging the unfortunate Mr. Haygood to a duel for daring to court his cousin.

Adele had her young daughter in her lap and was braiding buttercups into her hair. She waved to Will as a footman came up to take the reins so he could dismount. "Good morning, Lord Kendrick. I think we're in for pleasant weather for the party."

"And how could God send rain on such lovely ladies?" Will asked, bowing to them both. Her daughter giggled and snuggled closer to her mother. Adele offered him a smile.

Straightening, Will spotted Samantha, in a sprigged muslin gown as bright as the day. She had bent to help one of her cousin's children aim his ball toward the nearest wicket in what appeared to be a game of croquet. Jamie was standing along one side, arms crossed over the chest of his navy coat.

"You don't care to play?" Will asked, strolling up to his son.

Jamie snorted. "I was playing. She shot me down."

"*I* shot you down!" proclaimed the boy beside Samantha. Then he glanced at her. "Didn't I?"

"You certainly did, my lad," Samantha assured him with a pat on his shoulder. Then she smiled at Jamie and Will. "Lord Wentworth can't help that he's been away at school so long he's forgotten the very game he invented."

The boy's eyes widened, and he gazed at Jamie with obvious awe. With his thick black hair and deep blue eyes, the boy was likely Jerome Everard's son. "*You* invented smack ball?" he asked Jamie.

Jamie stood a little taller. "When I was younger than you."

Will hid a smile at his son's dismissive pride. "And how does one play this amazing game?" he asked.

"It's simple, my lord," Samantha offered, straightening. "It begins much like the game of croquet, only you earn points each time you smack your opponent's ball away from the goal. The person who reaches the far stake with the most points wins."

"And if your ball ends up in the water," Jamie added,

voice tinged with frustration, "you're immediately out."
He nodded toward the Dallsten Manor pond, where
Richard Everard was using a net to scoop out three
dripping colored balls while his wife watched with ill-
concealed amusement.

"I already smacked out my father, Uncle Vaughn and
Lord Wentworth," Jerome's son said proudly. "Now I
just have to reach the stake to win." He swung his mallet, and the ball knocked against the colored stick with
a whack. He beamed at Samantha.

She beamed back, all pride in him. Will remembered
his mother showing a similar pride in her sons before
illness had claimed her life while Will had been away
at Eton. He liked the fact that, even though Samantha
was obviously helping the boy, she let him take all the
credit for the win.

Will offered him his hand. "A great victory, sir. May
I request an introduction?"

"Justin Everard," he said, taking Will's hand.

"William Wentworth, Lord Kendrick," Will returned, shaking the boy's hand solemnly. "If you give
me a moment to arm myself against you, I'd like to play
this game my son invented."

Samantha grinned. "What do you say, Justin? Are
you willing to play against Lord Kendrick?"

"Certainly," Justin said magnanimously. "It's his
son's game, after all."

"Thank you," Will replied. "Perhaps if you'd be so
good as to retrieve the other balls from your uncle the
captain?"

Justin scampered off toward the pond.

"I'll fetch you a mallet, Father," Jamie offered, heading for the wheeled cart standing a few feet away.

"Busy already this morning," Will murmured to Samantha, shrugging out of his coat to give himself ease of motion to play. "What have you done with your other cousins and the devoted Mr. Haygood?"

"Who?" Samantha said, tearing her gaze away from his shoulders. "Oh, Mr. Haygood. He insisted on finding my origins and holed himself up in the muniment room. In truth I think he feels safest there. My cousins seem to intimidate him. Jerome and Vaughn are inspecting the site we intend to use for the party, as if I hadn't done so already." Her annoyance at her cousins was evident as she bent to snatch up a yellow ball and mallet for her own use.

Then Justin came dashing back and handed Will a red ball. Richard Everard strolled up and tossed Jamie's blue ball to him with a wink.

"Stay well ahead of her," he advised Jamie before returning to his wife's side where she'd sat next to Adele and her daughter to watch.

Justin, Jamie, Will and Samantha returned to the stake at one side of the lawn, and the boy invited the three of them to go first with such a generous air that Will had to stifle a smile. He quickly realized, however, that the gesture wasn't all kindness. It was evident that the last player had the advantage, being able to sight his opponents' balls much easier. When it came to Will's turn again, he angled his shot to keep the next wicket between his ball and the boy's.

Jamie, however, was clearly out for revenge. He managed to knock into either Will's or Justin's ball each round, racking up the points yet still ending up far enough away to make it difficult for them to retaliate. Will noticed he avoided hitting Samantha's ball. Samantha, on the other hand, hit whoever was available, from Will to Justin. Justin, however, felt the sting of

Jamie's skill, his frustration evident as his plays became more erratic.

Samantha must have noticed as well, for she edged up to Will. "I think your son needs a lesson in civility."

"Not every game is played civilly, my dear," Will countered, watching as Justin's ball missed Jamie's by a scant inch.

"And not every boy needs to learn that lesson at seven," she replied.

Will glanced at her. Her rosy lips were drawn in a tight line, and one booted foot tapped at the grass. She was clearly ready to defend Justin, no matter the cost.

"Or seventeen," he reminded her.

Her look softened, and she glanced to where Jamie was down on his knees in the grass, trying to spy the perfect angle to knock Justin down to the pond. The little boy was watching him, both hands clasped around his mallet, tension evident in every part of his small body.

"Oh, to be that young again," she murmured.

Will chuckled. "Said the aged crone."

She nudged him with her elbow. "Oh, I cannot claim *your* great number of years, my lord."

"Just for that, madam," he said, and smacked his ball up against hers, sending it careening across the lawn to land in front of the watching Everards.

"Now look what you've done!" Samantha cried with a laugh, hurrying after it even as her cousin's daughter picked it up and clutched it close. "Oh, come now, Addy. Give Auntie the ball, please?"

Love shining in her eyes, Addy held out the ball to Samantha.

Will smiled as Samantha curtsied to the little girl. What had he thought the moment he'd seen her? Sunshine had come to his home. Yet while she was capable of bringing joy to everyone who came across her, her own joy seemed tempered, muted. He wished he understood why.

Justin agreed that Samantha could play her ball from the edge of the lawn closest to the spectators, and she gave it a smack calculated to make it reach Will's. His ball cracked as hers hit it. "Well done," he acknowledged as she strolled up to him, mallet swung up on her shoulder.

"Thank you, my lord," she said, then jerked to a stop as Justin cried out. Jamie had just smacked his ball away from the final stake.

Will eyed his ball. He could hit Samantha again or take a longer shot to hit Jamie. But he thought he knew exactly the right move. He angled his shot and drew back the mallet. His ball raced across the lawn to stop short between Justin and the stake. Jamie groaned.

"You're mine, Lord Kendrick," the boy cried, and Will watched as his ball was deflected to one side and tumbled down the lawn to land with an ignominious plop in the pond.

Justin tapped his ball against the stake. "I believe I beat you, Lord Wentworth," he said to Jamie with great conviction.

Jamie bowed. "Indeed you did, sir. May I have your hand?"

The two shook hands. But Samantha's gaze was all for Will.

"You," she said, eyes as radiant as her smile, "are a rare find, William Wentworth, Earl of Kendrick. If you continue riding to the rescue, I shall owe you a very great favor indeed."

Though he knew the favor he should ask, he found

himself craving another one instead with her lips so sweetly curved. And that was enough to make him excuse himself from the next game to sit safely with the spectators.

The next three days proved to Samantha that Will was indeed a very handy fellow to have around. He and Jamie were at the manor from midmorning to late evening each day, lending a hand in whatever was happening. The activities at Dallsten Manor varied from games for the children to helping with preparations for the summer party, which was now only a few days away. Will consistently treated her cousins' children with respect and kindness, he made sure to involve Jamie in any activity, and while he was never intrusive, she knew he could be counted on for support when she needed it.

And she needed that support more than she'd expected. After her months of preparation, she'd thought she was ready for the summer party.

She'd reckoned without her family.

She shouldn't have been surprised that they each had an opinion. For as long as she'd known them, they'd never shirked in sharing their thoughts on anything she did.

"More flowers," Claire insisted after reviewing Samantha's plans to decorate the tree-ringed meadow where the party would be held.

"Kendrick Hall has a conservatory," Adele mused beside her.

"I'm sure Lord Kendrick would be amenable to supplying our needs," Mrs. Dallsten Walcott agreed.

Of course, Will was. And just when Samantha was ready to knock her former governess and sponsor's heads together over their insistence on incompatible decorating schemes, he intervened. "Perhaps those around the ring and those near the booths," he suggested.

The two women nodded sagely.

Will shot Samantha a conspiratorial grin that had her grinning back.

"We should have a horse race," Jerome had told Samantha only that morning. "You know how the villagers love a good contest."

She knew how much her cousins loved a good contest.

"I'll put up the prize," Imogene said with a wink to her husband.

"Allow me to suggest a course," Will said and laid out one guaranteed to please her cousins and every horse-mad fellow for miles without endangering the crops, their horses or her sanity.

"More fireworks," Vaughn had ordered a few moments ago, his twin sons bouncing up and down beside him.

"I believe," Will had interjected before Samantha could explain the trouble she'd had in locating such a large supply to begin with, "that you'll find the bonfire sufficiently interesting. I understand the flames frequently reach ten feet tall."

The children's eyes widened at that, and even Vaughn looked pleased.

The one person absent from the preparations was Prentice Haygood. While he occasionally took part in the games and was always present at meals, he continued to find her cousins daunting. Samantha noticed he went out of his way to avoid Vaughn in particular. Truth be told she was just as glad he did not attempt to seek her out. She truly didn't want to hurt his feelings by refusing his suit.

He apparently had not given up, but had merely changed his tactics. He had vowed to research her lineage as a present for her upcoming birthday and kept himself sequestered in the muniment room to pore over the estate records. She didn't argue, as it kept him safely occupied, but she feared he was doomed to disappointment. The manor's muniment room held records of the Dallsten family for hundreds of years. There was very little on the Everards. The most important papers, like her mother's marriage certificate, were safely upstairs.

But when she failed to catch sight of Haygood for most of the second day, she thought her duty as hostess demanded her to look in on him. Accordingly she left her cousins arguing over the placement of booths in the meadow and returned to the manor.

How busy the place was from what she remembered! As a child they had run short-staffed, except for the extra help brought in for the summer party her father had held each year. Now the manor swarmed with servants, all intent on making her visitors welcome.

Her cousins had brought their maids and valets plus the children's nurses. Those hired from the village for the party hurried about, learning their roles. Vendors met on a daily basis with Mrs. Linton, Mrs. Dallsten Walcott or one of the Everards. Even Samantha was stopped three times with questions between the entry hall and the nearby muniment room.

She started into the musty space and leaned against the nearest bookshelf for a moment to catch her breath, leaving the door open behind her. The room was small, with no windows and only the single door, the better to protect the precious pages from heat and light. The occasional sconce along the wall provided enough glow to navigate the room. Bookshelves lined the walls and marched in solemn rows down the center, with cupboards interspaced for smaller items. She always felt as if she'd entered a graveyard, knowing so much of the information spoke of people long dead.

Now she walked down the flagstones of the center aisle to the middle of the room, where she knew a worktable sat. Surely that's where she'd find Mr. Haygood. She kept her smile ready, but as she passed the last bookshelf, she found that the archivist's seat was empty. A lamp stood burning on one corner of the table, and open ledgers showed that someone had been studying the estate records from about eight years ago, when she'd first ascended to the title. But of her guest there was no sign.

"Mr. Haygood?" she called, glancing around. No bearded face peered from behind a bookcase and no chipper voice answered her call. In fact, the muniment room was silent, as if the generations of Dallstens chronicled in the papers around her were holding their breaths.

Except one. Somewhere close-at-hand, a body sucked in some of the dry air and coughed. Samantha turned her head toward the sound. "Mr. Haygood?"

Still nothing.

Gooseflesh pimpled her arms. Someone was here with her, someone who did not want to be found. It might have been a servant intent on a moment's break from the chaos of the manor and determined not to trouble her. Yet the silence felt heavy, vengeful.

The door shut with a thud.

Samantha jumped. Someone was trying to frighten her! She would not let them know they were doing a good job. She peered around the bookcase, but saw no one in the center aisle. The door seemed miles away.

"Mr. Haygood, if you are in here," she demanded, "I insist that you to show yourself."

The stillness mocked her.

She opened the drawer in the desk, felt around until her fingers closed on the folio knife. The little silver blade was used to cut open the leaves on new ledgers. Holding it in one hand, she crept along the aisle, gaze sweeping each row of bookshelves, breath jerking each time she saw the space empty. At last the door loomed before her, and she reached for the handle with her free hand.

Someone grabbed her shoulder and yanked her back into the room. Before she could cry out or use the knife, something heavy collided with her skull, and the world turned to blackness. The last thing she heard was the tinkle of the folio knife, hitting the stone floor a half second before she did.

Chapter Fourteen

"So what do you think, Lord Kendrick?" Mrs. Dallsten Walcott asked, holding up two swatches of fabric, "the lemon or the saffron for the tables?"

The two shades of yellow looked remarkably alike to him, but the gleam in her blue eyes told him the question was of immense importance to her. A quick glance confirmed that her daughter was too far away to save Will from having to answer the question. "I'm certain whichever you choose will be perfect," he assured her.

"Well, of course," she readily agreed, the fabric fluttering in the breeze where they stood on the meadow beside the manor. "But Lady Everard does not always agree with my advice." She batted her lashes at Will. "I did encourage her to accept your son. I want you to know that."

"How very kind of you," Will said, suddenly quite glad Samantha kept her own counsel. "I'm certain if you put your question to Lady Everard, she would be only too glad to share her opinion on this issue as well."

"Very likely," she said. Then she frowned and glanced around, lowering the fabric. "And where has that girl gone off to this afternoon?"

Will seized the opportunity. "I'll be delighted to find her for you. Excuse me." He hurried off before she could argue.

What an undertaking! He shook his head as he detoured around the workmen erecting the last of the booths. When he'd first been assigned to the embassy in Constantinople, he'd had to assist in the planning of any number of events like the annual party to celebrate King George's birthday. That had involved every member of the embassy staff, their families and any British subject who happened to be in the city at the time, with separate affairs for the local ruling class. The Everard summer party put the event to shame.

He hadn't attended the party the past two years since his father's death, but the other members of the gentry raved about the food, the music, the bonfire and the fireworks. Though the entire village was invited, everyone was on his or her best behavior, knowing that the couple completing the set in the dance was just as likely to be a titled lord and his wife as the local seamstress and her husband. For one night, as Samantha's father Arthur Everard had intended, everyone could just relax and enjoy themselves.

But it appeared Lord Everard's heir wasn't allowed to relax in the meantime! She had been everywhere the past few days, from directing the booth construction to planning the order of the dances. Her energy never failed, her determination never faltered. A shame Lord Wellington didn't have her in the Peninsula. He'd have beaten Napoleon long since!

Still, all that busyness had prevented an opportunity for a quiet chat. Now was as good a time as any to see if she was free. Someone had to have taken her direction.

Will first tried Vaughn, who with his impish twin

sons was attempting to advise the puppet master on a more exciting play for the children. They had not seen Samantha recently. He approached Adele, who was walking the perimeter of the meadow as if intent on making sure the space was sufficiently large, but she had no knowledge of her former charge either. He appealed to Jamie, who was closer to the house and attempting to marshal a fishing expedition for Jerome's two sons. Will wasn't surprised when his son had an answer.

"She retired to the manor about a quarter hour ago," he said, trying to coax a worm into a jar without touching the slimy creature. Will wasn't sure how well his son's reticence boded for their fishing plans, but he thanked Jamie and headed for Dallsten Manor.

The footman on duty near the front door offered to find her for him. Will refused. The staff already looked harried, and the party was still four days away. He had no desire to add to their burden. And he had every wish to find her alone so he could talk to her about his brother's death.

"If you'll just point out her direction," he told the footman, "I'll find her myself."

"She was going that way, my lord," the servant replied, indicating the rightmost corridor leading off the entry hall. "I believe she might have been making for the muniment room. It's to the right when you cross under the stairs and the first door on your left."

It took only a moment to find the room, but Will hesitated at the closed door. Much as he wanted a moment alone with Samantha, he knew the muniment room was unlikely to provide it. Prentice Haygood had stated his intentions of working there until he'd laid out Samantha's lineage. If she'd come here, she most likely meant to talk with him, and the man had made it plain he desperately wanted a word alone with her. Was he even now down on bended knee, gazing up into her deep brown eyes, pledging his undying devotion?

If he was, a part of Will was more than ready to barge in. The other part, his diplomatic side, cautioned restraint. Samantha would not thank him if she had decided to accept her swain's suit after all.

On the other hand, if she'd decided to send the fellow packing, she'd no doubt be delighted at the interruption.

Will raised a hand and knocked. "Lady Everard? Haygood? Are you there?"

No one answered.

Odd. Perhaps the footman had been mistaken, and the muniment room had not been Samantha's destination. Yet shouldn't Haygood have answered? Had something happened to the would-be scholar?

Will took hold of the latch and pushed open the door.

The sight over the threshold froze his blood. Samantha lay on her side, head cushioned from the stone floor by her arm. Her eyes were closed, her body unmoving. A few feet away Haygood lay in a similar fashion, arm outstretched as if he'd been reaching for her when he fell.

Will crouched beside Samantha, felt at her wrist and blew out a breath when her pulse tapped against his fingers. *Thank You, Lord!* Rising, he shouted out the door. "Help! Quickly! Your mistress has been hurt."

The cries and pounding feet answering his call told him he would soon have all the assistance he needed.

He knelt back at Samantha's side, gently touched her cheek. Her skin was like warm silk against his fingers.

"Samantha," he murmured, surprised by the choke in his voice, "can you hear me?"

Out of the corner of his eye Will saw the footman who had directed him skid to a stop in the doorway. "What's happened?"

"I don't know," Will replied. "I found them like this. See to Mr. Haygood, will you?"

The footman hurried to comply.

Beside Will, Samantha stirred. Her eyes opened, blinked, fixed on him, and relief washed over him as he saw recognition brighten her gaze.

"Well," she said, obviously surprised, and she levered herself up on her elbow. "What happened?"

"That's what we'd like to know," Will assured her, hand on her arm to steady her. He wanted to hug her close once more, cradle her in safety, but behind him he heard more exclamations as additional servants crowded the doorway.

Samantha put her other hand to her head as if the side pained her. "I came to the muniment room to look in on Mr. Haygood. I thought the room was empty until I heard someone breathing." She shuddered as if the memory chilled her, then winced. "When I tried to leave, someone struck me."

Anger surged inside him, but a groan to his left told him Haygood had woken as well.

"Lady Everard!" Haygood cried, crawling toward her on hands and knees. "Please, tell me you are all right!"

"I think so," she answered. "Although my head is pounding."

Will wanted to pound the person who had done this. Who would have dared to strike her? Was it some sort of accident or did someone intend to harm her? Was that why he'd seen an outrider following her before her relatives came, to ensure her protection? Was she not safe in her own home, surrounded by family?

"And what of you, Haygood?" he demanded. "What explanation do you have for all this?"

Her suitor blanched. "You cannot think that I would…that I could…" He held out a hand beseechingly toward Samantha. "Dear Lady Everard, you know that I would never harm you!"

"Of course you wouldn't, Mr. Haygood," she assured him.

Will wasn't so certain. "Then I suggest you explain yourself, sir. How did we come to find you here like this?"

Haygood sucked in his chubby cheeks. "Of course. Anything to help. I had stepped out to…pluck a rose, by your leave."

"A rose?" Will interrupted. "What rose?"

Haygood turned as red as the flower.

Samantha touched Will's arm, drawing his attention to her. "I believe he means the necessary," she murmured.

Haygood tugged at his rumpled cravat. "Yes, just so, thank you. When I returned, I found Lady Everard lying on the floor. Of course I bent to help her, and someone struck me from behind." He touched the back of his head and grimaced.

"A thief," one of the servants offered from the doorway, and murmurs of agreement rippled through the group.

"In the muniment room?" Will questioned. "What would he want in here?"

"You might be surprised." Samantha attempted to rise and Will helped her up, arm around her waist. He would never understand how someone so determined could weigh so little.

"Easy," he cautioned her. As he helped her take a

step, his foot hit something. He heard the object skitter away across the stone.

Before he could look to see what it was, Haygood scrambled to his feet as well.

"Yes, please, Lady Everard," he begged. "You mustn't exert yourself after such a trial." He glanced around at the people in the doorway. "Does anyone have any vinaigrette?"

Will couldn't help wondering whether he wanted some of the strong smelling salts for Samantha or himself.

Samantha would have none of it. "I assure you, I'm fine," she insisted, though she stayed close to Will as she gazed at her assembled staff.

"Search the house," she ordered them. "I want to know if anything is missing. Chevers, speak to each member of my family, make sure no one else was accosted. Warren, alert the nursery."

"Right away, Lady Everard," the two footmen cried before dashing off.

She held out a hand to Haygood, who clung to it. "My deepest apologies, Mr. Haygood. I regret that you should have been injured in my home. Mrs. Linton, if you'd be so good as to send for the physician and Mr. Haygood's valet to attend him."

"No need," he insisted, gaze fervent. "I'm more concerned about you."

So was Will. He could feel her trembling against him. Was she more injured than she'd claimed? Terrified by this intrusion to her home? Everything in him shouted to protect her, to keep her safe.

But when she spoke, he realized it wasn't pain or fear that moved her. It was anger.

"I said I'm fine," she snapped, pulling away from

Will as if to prove it. "Thank you both for your concern. But this incident requires immediate investigation. I will allow no one to threaten my family. Thank you, but I will take matters from here."

What arrogance, what gall! Samantha trembled with the very knowledge of it. Someone had invaded her home, again! Some horrid person had used her father's marvelous summer party as an excuse for villainy. It was monstrous!

"Go to the stables," she ordered the remaining staff who were trailing after her as she strode from the muniment room. "See if there's a stray horse. He'd want to get away quickly." She stopped to eye the young man they'd hired from the village as an extra footman. "Find the gamekeeper and have him look through the woods as well."

"Yes, your ladyship," he cried before hurrying off with the others.

One more man stood ready to assist, and she wasn't surprised to find Will beside her. Haygood had suffered Mrs. Linton to lead him upstairs, still protesting that he didn't need the services of a physician.

"You should lie down," Will said.

She glared at him. "I'm no exotic bloom raised in your conservatory, my lord. I grew up in this climate, and I assure you I know how to thrive in it."

He inclined his head, keeping his distance as if he feared she had a fencing foil hidden behind her. "I'm certain you're up to the challenge. But you insisted that a physician see to Haygood. Your injury would seem to require similar care."

The dull ache in her head agreed with him. Her

anger did not. *Be with me now, Father. You know what I must do.*

"I'm fine," she told Will. "If you wish to be of assistance, ride for the physician yourself. I'm sure Mr. Haygood will thank you for it in the end."

Instead he closed the distance to her side. "Haygood can wait. I'm more concerned about you. Look at me."

She bristled at the order but met him gaze for gaze. He studied her, jaw tense, eyes searching.

"Your pupils look fine," he reported as if he were the physician. "No sign of a concussion. Does your head hurt?"

"Nothing I cannot manage," Samantha replied. Indeed the hardest things to manage at the moment were the emotions surging through her, and having him regard her that way was not helping. She attempted to turn away from him, but he angled his body to block her path.

"Then help me determine who did this," he said. "You're certain you saw nothing? A sleeve? A boot as you fell?"

"What are you doing?" Samantha demanded, fingers clamping to the soft muslin of her gown. "This is my home, Lord Kendrick. This is my problem. I am perfectly capable of solving it."

"Perhaps not," he replied, "or I wouldn't have found you on the floor. Where was your bodyguard?"

The question penetrated the red mist that seemed to have enveloped her, and her hands fell. "Bodyguard? What are you talking about?"

He glanced around the entry hall as if expecting to find a burly servant lurking in a corner. "When you left Kendrick Hall last Monday, I saw an outrider following you. Was he not a servant or hired man?"

"No," she assured him, stomach tightening. "No. It seems someone has been watching me even here." She ought to feel chilled by the prospect, she knew, but her anger had the upper hand, and she wanted to lash out, demand satisfaction. If only she knew who owed it to her!

"Forgive me," he said. "I should have mentioned it before now. I simply thought you had the protection you needed."

He thought she needed protection? Now her heart was pounding harder than her head. Did he consider her so feeble or dimwitted that she could not care for herself? Was that why he continued to offer assistance?

Something inside her snapped. All the emotions she'd kept bottled up came streaming out. She could feel them in the way her body tensed, hear them in the sharp words. "I have never hired a bodyguard, my lord. I never saw the need for protection, as you put it. Neither do I need the services of a nanny or nurse."

"I didn't mean to imply that you did," he said, but his usual calm voice seemed to have deserted him. In fact he looked nearly as angry as she felt, his eyes narrowed, his hands fisted. It seemed even a diplomat found dealing with her emotions trying.

"But if the man following you was not in your employ," he said, "then someone may wish you ill. He could easily have been the one to accost you just now. Let me help you discover who it is."

More help. Always help. What, had she no gumption, no imagination to learn the nature of her enemy? Did he see her as so incapable?

Every part of her shook with the emotions welling up. She stepped next to him, raised her chin and pressed her hands against the green tweed of his waistcoat.

"Let me make this perfectly clear, my lord," she said, punching out each word like a thrust of her sword. "My affairs are my own. I don't need help from you, your son, any of my cousins or their wives. I don't need another hero in my life. I'm surrounded by them!"

As if to prove it the front door banged open, and Jerome, Richard and Vaughn crowded into the entry hall. She dropped her hands and stepped back from Will to meet their onslaught.

"What's this about a thief?" Jerome demanded, dark head high as if ready to fight.

"If he's hurt you, I promise he'll pay," Vaughn declared, face hardened with purpose.

"Count on us to help," Richard agreed, hands held tight at his sides.

Samantha's look to Will was pointed. But he didn't argue, didn't attempt to further the fight, with her or her cousins. He stood there, head high, a rock.

But not one she was ready to lean on.

She turned to her cousins. "I'm fine," she assured them. "I have staff searching the house for intruders and missing items, and I've sent the footmen to search the stables and alert the gamekeeper to watch the woods. If there's a stranger among us, we'll find him."

She could see the protests building in their eyes, their stiffening shoulders. No! She was not going to listen to another word of remonstrance. She could handle her own affairs. It was time they all learned that.

She pushed past them to the door. "Excuse me. I must finish the preparations if we're to have a party in a few days, and I refuse to be cowed by someone who hasn't the backbone to look me in the eye when raising his hand for a blow."

Chapter Fifteen

Stubborn, valiant woman! Will watched as Samantha swept out the door, her cousins right behind, voices raised in protest and demand. Only one failed to follow, standing there with his hands behind his dun-tail coat.

Jerome Everard eyed Will across the space. "You found her, I take it."

Will wasn't sure whether to expect a challenge or a barrage of questions, but he stood taller. "I did."

The oldest of the Everard cousins nodded. "Thank you. She can usually take care of herself, but someone got the better of her this time. I'm glad you were there to help." He turned for the door.

"So am I," Will murmured. Indeed, he could not remember feeling so determined. He was fairly certain her anger stemmed from frustration and fear. His did. Seeing her there on the floor had made him feel as helpless as when he'd watched Peg take her last breath, newborn babe in her arms.

Samantha did not want his help to uncover the villain who had struck her, but he could not see a lady harmed. Besides, identifying her assailant would convince her she could trust him. Then he'd have the answers he sought.

Help me, Lord. Let the truth come out, in both cases.

He paused on his way to the door. She had said she needed no hero. Indeed, she persistently saw his offers of help as an insult to her capabilities when he meant them as courtesies. Perhaps instead of solving the problems for her he should partner with her on the investigation.

He had no doubt she knew things he would never consider, and he had experience she could not have gained. And the more she saw him working on her behalf, the more she would trust him. But when he approached her he needed a peace offering, and he thought he knew just where to find it, in the muniment room.

As he entered the room, he saw nothing out of order. All the books and papers were lined up neatly on the shelves. He found where Haygood had been reviewing some estate records related to the summer party. Will wasn't sure how the information was connected to the Everard lineage. Perhaps Haygood sought to help Samantha prepare now by studying previous parties. Will had another way to help the lady. He got down on his hands and knees and peered under the lips of the bookcases near the door until he spotted the only thing he might have kicked.

He fished out the folio knife, and his fingers tightened on the silver. Had the culprit been using this for its intended purpose, or had he planned to use it as a weapon? If so, why strike Samantha and Haygood? Or had Will found them before the villain could do more harm? Palming the knife, he went to find Samantha.

She stood in the center of the meadow, but with her servants dashing about and her cousins stalking about, she looked as if she waited in the eye of the storm. Her arms were crossed over her chest, he thought perhaps in an attempt to hold her emotions in. He put on his most charming smile and approached cautiously.

"Allow me to apologize," he said. "You are an intelligent, talented peeress, and I never meant to imply that you were anything less than capable."

She lowered her arms, but she didn't smile. "And I apologize. I suspect I have been patronized one time too many."

"And struck on the head," Will pointed out.

She grimaced. "That, too. Oh, but I'd like to know who would dare!"

Will closed the gap between them. "So would I. These are our people, our place. If there's a danger, we must put a stop to it."

He thought she might protest his assumption they were in this together, but she nodded, eyes narrowing. "You're right. This villain has brought the fight to Evendale, but he will find that we are more than a match for him."

"And the more knowledge we have, the easier it will be to apprehend him," Will assured her.

She cocked her head as if trying to see the problem from that angle. Her three cousins, and her for that matter, seemed to prefer to act first and ask questions later. Will had come to appreciate the opposite approach.

"What do you suggest?" she asked warily.

Will offered her the folio knife. "Let us pool our insights and our talents. I found this just now, under the lip of a bookcase in the muniment room."

At last she smiled. "So that's where it went. I must have dropped it when I fell."

He had thought he'd learned to keep a stoic face during negotiations, but he had evidently lost the skill for her laugh bubbled up, pushing back the darkness of the past hour. "Don't look so shocked, Will. I told you I can take care of myself."

"Forgive my presumption," he managed, handing her the knife with a bow.

She took it with another laugh. "So where do we go from here?"

"I suggest," Will said, straightening, "that we attempt to determine who was in the manor just now."

"I have servants searching," she reminded him, toying with the silver handle of the knife in a way that would have raised his concerns for his safety had she been anyone else.

"What I planned was a bit more subtle," he said, offering her his arm. Looking once more bemused, she put her hand on his, and they set off.

The other members of her family and staff had been alerted to the possible danger, but each was willing to talk to Will, particularly with Samantha at his side. After depositing the knife in the muniment room, they looked for possible witnesses. As it turned out, at the time of the attack, Imogene had been in the rear garden supervising her twin sons as they prepared to go fishing with Jamie. She had noticed no one enter the manor by the kitchen door. Of course, given the attention her boisterous sons required, Will could forgive her if she had missed seeing someone.

The two gardeners trimming hedges at the side of the manor were more certain that no one had entered by the tower door near them. The footman on duty at the front door would surely have seen and stopped any stranger attempting to enter that way. So, it was highly likely that whoever had struck Samantha and Haygood had been in the manor ahead of them.

"That still leaves too many people," Will told Samantha as they returned to the house.

"Not really," she countered. She'd been so intent on Will's questions that he could only hope she approved of his approach. "There are only two ways to the muniment room, from the entry hall and down the south tower stairs." She squeezed his arm. "Let's ask Chevers who came through the hall." She fairly pulled him inside.

The footman answered her questions readily enough, as if used to his mistress's odd whims. "Lord Kendrick, yourself, Mr. Haygood, and Lord Widmore passed, your ladyship," he said. Then he glanced at Will contritely as if afraid he'd given something away. "And of course the captain's lady was upstairs."

As Samantha thanked the footman, Will frowned in thought. Suspecting Vaughn Everard was easy. The man's role in Gregory's death was still a mystery, and though Vaughn assured everyone he had outgrown his wild ways, his own wife indicated otherwise. Yet by all accounts, he adored Samantha. Why strike her? He had every right to be in the muniment room if he chose. Why would he need to hide his presence, to the point of battering two people?

Claire made as little sense. She had been Samantha's sponsor for her Season, Will knew from Jamie. She had stayed in the house previously, so if she'd had cause to steal anything she could have taken it years ago. Certainly Samantha and all her family trusted the woman.

Samantha had evidently reached the same conclusion. "None of them is the culprit," she insisted as they moved away from the footman. "We're looking for a stranger, perhaps the man you saw following me. I'm certain of it."

Will wished he could be so certain. "We have one more witness," he reminded her, "but I doubt Haygood is up to questioning."

"Let's find out," she said and led the way up the stairs.

Samantha's suitor was sitting up in the bedchamber he had been given, an outrageously feminine room in pink and white that Will's mother would have adored. Haygood looked far less comfortable, even reclining against the gilded white headboard of the bed. Adele sat beside him, placing a cool compress on his brow, and her mother Mrs. Dallsten Walcott stood next to her, carrying on a helpful dialogue.

"And asparagus," she was insisting as Will and Samantha entered the room. "I have heard it is most efficacious in cases of the megrims. It must be ground up and sprinkled in tea."

Haygood choked and turned the movement into a cough. "Most kind of you, but I assure you, I'm fine."

"I'm glad to hear you say that," Will said, moving with Samantha up to the bed. "I imagine it was a nasty surprise coming upon Lady Everard that way."

At the sight of Samantha, Haygood struggled to sit taller. "Oh, my dear, that you should see me like this!" He pulled back from Adele's ministrations with a wince. "Do tell me you are feeling better."

"I'm fine," she promised him. "Lord Kendrick has some questions for you about our attack. I'm sure you can help discover the culprit."

He wilted against the pillow, eyes widening. "Anything for you."

Will refused to encourage him. "Can you remember

anything more about the scene? Did you hear anything, catch the scent of cologne, perfume?"

Adele was frowning at Will as if she wasn't sure what he was about, but Mrs. Dallsten Walcott clapped her hands.

"Oh, well done, my lord. We shall uncover the culprit." She affixed Haygood with a stern eye. "What do you remember, sir? Search the depths of your mind."

Haygood swallowed against his squashed cravat as if he doubted his mind had sufficient depth to search. "Nothing! I swear! One moment I was bending over Lady Everard, the next waking up on the floor. I beg you all to just leave me alone!" He burst into tears and covered his face in his hands.

Samantha raised her brows, and Mrs. Dallsten Walcott looked ready to remonstrate, but her daughter rose, forestalling all conversation.

"I believe we should do as Mr. Haygood asks," she said, so firmly that Will had no choice but to quit the room, Samantha beside him and Mrs. Dallsten Walcott right behind. As soon as the door shut, however, Adele stopped in the corridor.

"What are you about, Samantha?" she asked.

"Merely trying to catch our villain," Samantha replied. "Lord Kendrick is very good at solving difficulties. He's had years of experience, haven't you, my lord?"

He felt as if he'd gained two inches in height as he gazed down at Adele's narrowed eyes. "Indeed."

Her lips tightened, but he could not be sure whether she was fighting laughter or a tart response. He hadn't had a moment to converse privately with her before now, but he remembered her friendship when he was growing up. The Dallsten Walcotts and the Wentworths had been close in those days, so close many had considered a match between his brother and her likely. Then her father had died, leaving a mountain of debt, and Gregory, as was typical, had turned his sights elsewhere.

Looking at her now, the epitome of elegance from her carefully coiffed dark brown hair to the lace edging her pale muslin gown, he had one more reason to suspect his older brother's character and intelligence had been impaired.

She turned to Samantha. "I'm very glad to hear you have availed yourself of his skills. I'm certain Lord Kendrick will be a match…for the villain."

As if she meant to protect Will, Samantha stepped between him and Adele. "Let me take those for you, Adele. I'm sure Jerome must be wondering where you are."

Perhaps Samantha had the makings of a diplomat after all. Adele smiled as she handed her the bowl and towel, then excused herself. But as she passed Will, he would have sworn she winked at him.

When Adele had started down the corridor, Mrs. Dallsten Walcott touched Will's arm. "My daughter is right. You are a very clever fellow, Lord Kendrick." She gave a nod of approval. "Tell me, do you believe this story of a thief?"

He had wondered about the motivation, but it suddenly struck him that he could be looking at the very person. Jamie had said the lady was pilfering from Dallsten Manor. Will had thought Samantha was aware of the problem, but what if she wasn't? What if the lady had seen fit to hide her deeds by the strategic use of a blow to the head? She might be elderly, but he'd seen no sign of her strength failing. And she certainly had as much determination as Samantha. What was more, no servant had mentioned her whereabouts during the past few hours.

He rubbed his chin with one hand even as he drew Samantha closer with the other. "I have been considering the matter."

Samantha frowned at him, but her chaperone leaned forward as if to impart a secret. "It's rubbish. Nothing is missing. I know. No, sir, this person had another reason to accost Lady Everard and Mr. Haygood." Her eyes narrowed. "Have you considered your son?"

Will blinked, but Samantha rose immediately to the defensive, stiffening beside him.

"Jamie?" she scoffed. "What possible reason could he have?"

Mrs. Dallsten Walcott shook her finger at Samantha. "He is in love with you, and he must have seen that Mr. Haygood has a similar obsession. What better way to rid himself of his rival than to discredit him in your eyes for a fool and a weakling, unable to protect you?"

It might have made sense, had she been talking about any other man except his son. "Lord Wentworth adores Lady Everard," Will said. "He would never strike her."

Samantha nodded so adamantly that she set the water in the porcelain bowl to sloshing.

"Perhaps," Mrs. Dallsten Walcott said, turning toward the stairs. "But stranger things have been done in the name of love."

"Ignore her," Samantha advised as her chaperone flounced away. "It cannot have been Jamie."

"Agreed," Will replied. "Though she is right that we should not rule out anyone unless we have proof."

"I'll accept the proof of my heart in this case," Samantha said, heading for the stairs herself. "No one in my family would have struck me, and neither would Jamie or Prentice Haygood."

"I notice you do not include me," he said, moving to take her burden from her. That she accepted his help in carrying the basin told him he was making headway in earning her trust.

"That goes without saying," she said, lifting her skirts to start down the stairs. "From nearly the moment I arrived you have been my friend. Thank you."

"It is my pleasure," he said, casting her a glance. The furrow between her eyes had faded. She descended with the usual bounce in her step. But after what she'd been through, he could not feel comfortable pressuring her for information about his brother now.

"What next?" she asked as they reached the bottom of the stair and she waved to the footman to come take the towel and basin.

Will watched the fellow hurry away with the items. "You might send someone to the village inn, see if any strangers have arrived in the past week."

She nodded. "Excellent suggestion. I should have thought of that. And we can ask around the village as well. It's generally fairly easy to spot a stranger in Evendale. Mrs. Dallsten Walcott is right—you are a clever fellow."

Will chuckled. "I don't think of it as clever so much as self-preservation."

"I imagine that trait came in handy in the diplomatic corps." She shifted on her feet as if she longed to pace, to run, and her skirts brushed his boots. "Jamie and I were sure some task of international significance kept you away, you know. You were chasing bandits in Corsica, fighting Barbary pirates, saving Egyptian antiquities from the French. You were quite the dashing hero."

"A hero neither of you now need," Will felt compelled to point out.

"Jamie needs you," she temporized, but her usual direct gaze danced away from his. "He must. I needed my father when I was seventeen. Unfortunately he was already gone."

Will touched her hand, and her gaze returned to his. "I'm sorry he wasn't there when you needed him."

"I had Adele," she replied, but she didn't move away from his touch. "And then my cousins and Claire and Imogene. But there comes a time when we must take responsibility for our own actions. Unfortunately I'm finding that difficult. You've seen how my family tends to swaddle me."

He had, and he felt her rebellion each time. "They will learn," he predicted.

"I can hope. But I shouldn't complain. I know they care about me. My besetting sin is letting my emotions rule me. I like to think I'm moving beyond that, most days."

Was that why her light dimmed at times? Was she consciously trying to snuff it out? But what a waste! Didn't she know how much the rest of the world craved such joy? Indeed, if he remembered his Bible verses correctly, joy and love were signs of spiritual maturity.

"I hope," he murmured, "that you will allow yourself to feel the joy you bring to others."

Her eyes widened, drawing him in. He was suddenly aware how close she stood, how near her lips. She gazed up at him, a dimple appearing near the side of her mouth.

"You are very kind to me, Will," she said. "I'm glad you're my friend."

Suddenly friendship seemed a pale and lifeless thing

next to what he wanted from this woman. He could imagine days together, riding, laughing, working to improve their holdings, helping others in the valley take advantage of these new industries that were cropping up all over England. She would be the fire he had wished for; he could be the steadying force she wanted. He could envision growing old together. The hope was like spring water, wetting his thirsty heart.

He forced himself to drop his hand and step back. "I should go see about Jamie," he said. "And I'll give more thought about how to catch your thief."

She snorted. "It's not a thief, Will. I recognize the pattern. Everard House was broken into several times when I was either out or busy entertaining. A staff member would find a window unlatched, mud on a carpet no one had crossed. My personal things were moved about and not by me or my maid."

She shuddered, and Will moved closer again to run a hand up her arm.

"It was an unsettling feeling," she confessed. "I thought I'd left the problem behind in London. Apparently I was wrong." She put her hand on his. "But we'll get to the bottom of it, Will. I know it."

Her touch brought a comfort he hadn't realized he'd been seeking. He took her hand, bowed over it.

"I'm certain you're right," he said. "I shall see you in the morning. If you need anything before then, you have only to send word."

As he straightened, he knew she'd never call for him. Indeed, he was beginning to realize he was the one who needed assistance, from her.

Samantha didn't want to send Will home. Her entire family stood ready to help her, but his presence was more comforting, less judgmental. Still, she saw him to the door, waited until his horse was brought around. He kept the conversation light, as if he knew she could take no more right then. She smiled as he bowed over her hand again and couldn't help her sigh of appreciation as he left.

"A very prepossessing gentleman," Claire said.

Samantha turned to find her former sponsor descending the grand stair. Samantha had once dreamed of coming into Claire's grace when she reached her majority. Though some of the lady's languid movements came from a need to cushion an old leg injury, Claire was ever polished and contained. She had mastered the art of temperate behavior. She didn't leap, didn't raise her voice, rarely fell into the dismals. Samantha may have found her own style, but she'd long ago resigned herself to the fact that there was only one Claire.

"Yes, Lord Kendrick is a good friend," Samantha agreed, going to meet her at the foot of the stair.

"A friendship with a gentleman can never be overvalued," Claire maintained as the two made their way toward the withdrawing room. "I've cherished a number of friends over the years. None more than Richard, of course."

"I'm glad you and my cousin have become friends," Samantha told her. "I know he missed you terribly when he thought you were lost to him."

Her face softened, as if she'd missed him, too. The two had fallen in love young when Richard was still an impoverished second son, and Claire had chosen the supposedly safer path of marrying a wealthy viscount instead while Richard was away at sea seeking his fortune. Only when Samantha had needed a sponsor for her Season had Richard encountered the then-widowed Claire again.

"As my husband, Richard is my best, truest, friend," she said now, pausing in the doorway of the withdrawing room. "But he and I were friends when we first met as well. I could talk to him about anything. It is a trait I still value."

She preceded Samantha into the room, but Samantha found her mind too full for her body to move. She'd held off suitors, including Jamie, with the fact that they were merely friends. How odd to think of friendship as the vehicle to marriage.

Certainly her mother and father had not been friends. Besides Claire and Richard, her other cousins and their wives had not known each other long enough to have formed an abiding friendship before marrying.

Yet, did friendship need years to mature? Most of the friendships she'd made in London had been formed in a few weeks. Certainly she considered Will a friend, and she'd known him a little more than a week.

Was their friendship strong enough to endure her family secrets, her unbridled emotions? If not, could she call it a friendship at all?

And if it was strong enough, what did that mean to her carefully laid plans?

Chapter Sixteen

Neither her staff nor her cousins found any evidence of a break-in, and no one in the village had noticed a stranger nearby. Samantha couldn't say she was surprised. As she'd told Will, the pattern was too like her last few weeks in London. Someone was intent on rifling through her possessions, growing bolder each time, following her even to the fells of Cumberland. She only wished she'd seen the horseman Will had mentioned, for very likely he was the culprit!

But what was he looking for? Why did he think she possessed it? Or was there some other reason he seemed intent on tormenting her?

"I've asked all the staff to be on the alert," Jerome told her when she met her cousins in the library before dinner. She'd noticed they tended to congregate in that room, just as the ladies seemed to prefer the withdrawing room. The tall oak bookcases and gilt-edged tomes promised the wisdom of the ages. The well-padded armchairs offered rest. And the Oriental rug in the center of the room said that the owner had a sense of adventure as well. At times she thought she still smelled her father's cologne, years after he'd left Dallsten Manor forever.

So she sat in his favorite chair, the tall-backed arm-chair by the fire and regarded her cousins. Jerome was seated behind the desk, even though that was no longer his place with her having the title. Richard sat opposite her, long legs pointed toward the hearth. Vaughn was pacing across the carpet.

"A shame we learned nothing from the London break-ins," she told Jerome.

Richard's snort answered for him. "Whoever is doing this is too good at hiding himself."

"Agreed," Jerome said. "The constables are aware of the matter and promised to keep an eye on the house while we're away."

"And that obviously won't matter," Richard added, "as the culprit has followed us here."

Jerome spread his hands. "We don't know that. It could be a coincidence. With the summer party nearly here, anyone passing through the valley might expect to be able to enter the manor without being questioned. Someone could be taking advantage of our vulnerability."

Samantha wasn't the only one who winced at the word. "I would prefer not to live in a fortified castle in order to feel secure," she said.

"Nor should you have to," Jerome assured her. "We will get to the bottom of this, I promise."

She forced herself not to bristle. "You needn't feel obliged. Lord Kendrick and I made inquiries this afternoon. I believe he can learn the truth."

Jerome and Richard exchanged glances. She hated when they did that. It was a sure sign they knew more than she did and were trying to shield her.

"But you will want to focus on the summer party,"

Jerome reminded her. "I apologize for not being more help to you before now. I can see it is a daunting task."

"Whatever you need," Richard put in, "consider it done."

Only because being busy with the party kept her safely occupied elsewhere, she was sure. She thanked them for their trouble, but assured them she had the matter in hand.

She couldn't help noticing, however, that Vaughn had not so much as paused in his pacing through the entire conversation. As her other two cousins went to collect their wives for dinner, Samantha stopped him in the library doorway.

"What do you know about all this?" she asked.

Vaughn raised his platinum brows. "Why do you single me out?"

"Because you said nothing when you are generally the first to offer an opinion," she replied. "Is this something you and the Carpenter's Club are investigating?"

At the name of the select London club he patronized, Vaughn stiffened. "If it is, I would not be at liberty to discuss the matter. Leave be, Samantha. Things will sort themselves out shortly."

He seemed to think she would be satisfied with his answer. And that alone told her something was up.

She didn't dare question him over dinner. He would never admit to skullduggery before witnesses. And as they ate he certainly gave no indication that his conscience tweaked him, joking with the rest of the family as he usually did. Oh, but it was maddening to think Vaughn knew the truth and refused to share it with her!

She tried to corner him again after dinner, but he neatly avoided her, scooping up Imogene and hurrying her off to the schoolroom with some tale about seeing to their sons. Breakfast was no better; he was up and out riding before she even reached the table, and hours earlier than he'd risen the other days he'd been in residence. She tried waiting at the stables for him, but a groom returned the horse saying that Lord Widmore was out on the meadow, inspecting the booths.

Samantha stalked out to the meadow in pursuit. However, Vaughn kept himself surrounded by his sons, his wife or, astonishingly, Prentice Haygood, none of whom she wanted to witness her conversation with her cousin. Oh, but Vaughn could be wily when he chose! Surely he knew he could not avoid her the entire time he was at Dallsten Manor. Unfortunately she wasn't willing to wait him out.

She wished she had Will's gift for diplomacy. He could have found a way through her cousin's defenses, and very likely Vaughn would not notice until it was too late to hide his secrets. The more she thought about it, the more she liked the idea. When Will arrived today, she'd ask him to approach Vaughn. He could speak to her cousin on her behalf, find out what was going on, one man to another. And then he could tell her everything.

She was out on the meadow, trying to convince Jerome and Richard to leave the workmen alone, when Will and Jamie rode up. Excusing herself, she hurried to greet them.

"I need your help," she said to Will as soon as she'd sent Jamie off to deposit the horses in the stables. She linked arms with him and began a slow promenade about the meadow. Her cousins, their wives and Mrs. Dallsten Walcott were eying her with varying degrees of speculation, but she ignored them.

"I'd be delighted to be of assistance," he said, and she could hear the curiosity in his voice.

Samantha squeezed his arm. "So you have said, many times. And I appreciate it even if I have not always expressed it properly."

"Indeed," Will said, facing forward, mouth twitching. "I believe the exact words were 'I don't need another hero in my life.'"

Samantha wrinkled her nose. "Yes, well, I don't, actually, but I do need some assistance in something I lack on occasion. Diplomacy."

"I see," he said, laughter dancing in his voice. "And you think that I, being a former diplomat, might be able to help."

"I'm sure of it." She nodded to where Vaughn was lifting one of his sons down from a tree. "Vaughn knows something about this business yesterday."

He didn't miss a step, but she felt the tension in his arm. "You suspect he struck you after all?"

"Oh, heavens no! Vaughn would never hurt me! But he's hiding something. I can tell. I was hoping he might be willing to confide in you."

He cast her a glance from the corner of his eye. "So you'd like me to confront the man who might have killed my brother. In the name of diplomacy, of course."

Samantha jerked to a stop. "Oh, Will. How thoughtless of me. Of course not! And Vaughn didn't kill your brother. I know that for a fact."

Will disengaged. "A fact, may I point out, that you refuse to share with me."

There she went again—acting without thinking things through! Was there any wonder she suspected she'd make a terrible wife? "I'm so sorry. Never mind.

I'll find another way to learn the truth. You needn't trouble yourself."

She pulled away from him, but he caught her hand. "Samantha," he started, when voices rose from the other side of the meadow.

"Oh, what now?" Samantha murmured.

Her cousins were swiftly approaching, with Jamie, Haygood and Jerome's son close behind. They all came to stand in a ring surrounding her and Will.

"I believe we should test the course for the race," Jerome said to Samantha, and she knew by the light in his blue eyes that the statement was not a request. "We need to be certain it will accommodate our plans for the party."

As Will had been the one to lay out the course, she glanced his way.

"I'd be delighted to show you the course, Everard," he said.

"Simply looking at it won't tell him anything," Jamie put in, then blushed as all gazes shifted to him. "By your leave, Father."

"Very well," Will said. "A few volunteers could test it."

"I'll volunteer," Jamie said.

"I'll race Lord Wentworth," Justin piped up, then he glanced at his father. "May I, Papa?"

Jerome put his hand on his son's shoulder. "A generous offer, but you've already beaten him twice at smack ball. Perhaps we should give someone else a chance."

"I'll race," Vaughn said with studied nonchalance that fooled no one, Samantha was sure.

"Count me in," Richard added. "Can't let his lordship have all the fun. But there ought to be a prize."

"Other than the delight of besting you?" Vaughn quipped.

Richard waved a hand. "You do that entirely too often as it is."

"I know," Claire offered, strolling closer from where she and Adele had been measuring the space they intended to drape in bunting. "What if the winner were to receive a kiss from the lady of his choice?"

"That's no prize," Justin scoffed, making a face.

Samantha hid a smile as Vaughn patted his head. "Depends on the lady, my lad." His gaze sought out Imogene, who blushed.

Haygood cleared his throat. "I do believe I'll join you, if someone could supply me with a horse."

Oh, no! Samantha was fairly certain whose kiss he'd claim if he won. She edged closer to Richard.

"Make sure he gets old Treacle," she murmured, remembering the slowest horse in the stables.

"Done," Richard murmured back.

With the gentlemen agreed, they all repaired to the stables to have their respective horses saddled. Samantha joined Adele, Mrs. Dallsten Walcott, Claire, Imogene, Vaughn's sons and Justin at the stone fence along the stretch of road that would serve as the racetrack for the party. The traffic was generally light on the country lane, but a servant was dispatched to either end to prevent wagons or carriages from colliding with the riders.

The racers cantered down the drive from the stables and took up their positions in a line across the road. Jerome, on a mare as black as his hair, was the farthest away, his look determined as he patted the horse's neck. Vaughn's mouth was turned up in one corner, his gaze on the finish line a quarter mile away. Jamie's horse was prancing with its rider's excitement; Richard's stood as calm as he was.

Haygood, closest to her, was so pale she thought he might be ill. Her conscience tweaked her. He could not know his horse stood no chance of throwing him. It also stood no chance of winning. Samantha put both hands on the top of the fence and pressed herself close.

"You don't have to do this, you know," she said to Haygood. "You were injured only yesterday. Use that as your excuse. I will still consider you my friend."

His smile flashed a moment before disappearing under a frown. "Nonsense. I'm a gentleman of my word."

The pride was so heavy she knew nothing she could say would dissuade him. Samantha pulled back with a nod. "Very well, then. Do your best."

Vaughn's horse stamped its feet impatiently. "Start us off, Cousin," he ordered Samantha, eyes narrowed on the distance.

Mrs. Dallsten Walcott hurried forward and pressed her lace-edged handkerchief into Samantha's grip. "Good luck," she said, but Samantha rather thought her chaperone was speaking to her instead of the gentlemen.

Samantha crossed to the side of the road a little ahead of them, where they could all see her, and raised the handkerchief. "When I release this," she said, "fly. Three—two—one…" She dropped the cloth.

The horses shot forward. And one flew past her.

She recognized the dappled gray horse, the bottle-green coat on the rider. Will had entered the lists. He pounded past Haygood, left Jamie in the dust. Samantha ran back to the fence to get a better look as the lane turned toward Kendrick Hall. His horse's neck was stretched, its feet a blur. He tore past Richard, overtook Jerome in the blink of an eye and began to close on Vaughn.

"Come on, come on." Samantha didn't realize the encouragement had come from her mouth until Claire glanced her way with a smile. Very likely her cousin's wife thought she was cheering for Vaughn. Likely she should have been.

But she found herself holding her breath as Will edged past her cousin and flashed through the finish.

"Well done!" Imogene cried, clapping, and the other women followed suit. Justin and the twins were jumping up and down and waving their hands as the riders ambled back in their direction.

"I believe," Vaughn told Samantha as he passed her, "that this track is suitable for a race."

"And I believe," Imogene added with a grin to Samantha, "that the winner is owed a kiss!"

Samantha thought her heart must be pounding harder than the horses' hooves as Will rode past the fence to the cheers of the boys and drew up near Samantha. A servant came forward to take the reins. He threw his leg over the horse and slid from the saddle.

Her mouth was dry, and she licked her lips as he approached.

"I've come to claim my reward," he said.

Her smile felt tight. "Of course." She held out her hand, noticed it was trembling and stiffened her fingers.

He glanced at her hand quizzically, then pulled her into his arms.

In the eight years since she'd come out, more than one gentleman had stolen a kiss. She'd laughed them off, ordered them to desist and in one case threatened to find her sword or call her cousins. Somehow she didn't think Will would be so easily dissuaded.

And she found she had no interest in dissuading him. The warmth of his embrace, the firm pressure of his lips, made her feel as if her blood had turned to bubbles lighter than air. It wasn't his horse that could fly but her! Her emotions tumbled over each other, threatening to sweep her away.

No! Never that!

Samantha pushed her hands against his chest, forced him to break the kiss.

"Congratulations, Lord Kendrick," she made herself say. "I believe that is sufficient reward."

He stared at her as if he'd never truly seen her until that moment. She knew the others were staring as well.

"Excuse me," she said, face heating, and hurried for the house. She was running away again, but somehow she thought at that moment it was the best choice.

Will stared after Samantha. She was moving so quickly her skirts were a swirl of cream about her legs, her golden head bowed. The kiss had affected her more than she wanted any of them to know. He understood. He felt the same way.

He'd kissed other women. His wife Peg had been particularly enthusiastic. In his diplomatic duties chaste kisses on a hand or one or both cheeks were commonplace. None of those kisses compared to kissing Samantha. They were a tallow candle against the blazing light of a crystal chandelier.

What had he done?

He knew why he'd raced. He liked to race, especially with opponents like the Everards, who could challenge him. And the sight of Prentice Haygood lining up, so determined to win, had brought out Will's chivalrous side. Surely Will's kiss was to be preferred to his.

He simply never dreamed her kiss would be preferable to all others.

With knowing smiles, the women were gathering up the boys and starting for the house. Most of his opponents were heading for the stables. For the first time he focused on Vaughn Everard's horse as it moved away from him. He hadn't even noticed the beast as he'd raced, so intent had he been on winning. Now he saw that it was a powerful roan, exactly like the horse of Samantha's outrider.

Surely Vaughn Everard had not borrowed the horse. He was a man used to driving his own carriage, and it seemed, riding his own mounts. But he apparently hadn't arrived at Dallsten Manor until the day after Will had seen the horse.

Before he could follow the man and ask, Haygood drew his horse up beside Will.

"I am very disappointed in you, my lord," he said, face tight and hands tighter on the reins. "I shared my intentions toward Lady Everard with you. I thought you understood."

"I meant no disrespect," Will assured him.

But Haygood pointed a finger at him as if he wished it were a loaded pistol. "I trust you will comport yourself as a gentleman for the remainder of my sojourn here. I should hate to have to call you out."

He turned and rode back toward the stables, and the plodding steps of his mare did not belie the stiff set of his shoulders. Jamie took up his place at Will's side, face equally stiff.

"I suppose you wish to berate me as well," Will said.

Jamie's mouth worked as if he could not bring himself to utter the words aloud, and Will waited for the condemnation.

"You've fallen in love with her, too," Jamie accused.

Had he? After years of guarding his heart, of telling himself he was better off alone, had he tumbled into love with a woman he'd known a little more than a week? True, he'd heard stories of her for the past eight years, and even before that through his father's and Jamie's letters. But was this love, the kind of love on which to base a marriage?

It couldn't be. Samantha was an amazing woman, but he wasn't ready to be a husband again.

"I cannot claim love," he told Jamie. "She is bright and beautiful, and even a blind man would fall for her charm."

"As well as a man not so blind," Jamie replied. "I think the others will expect a declaration after that demonstration."

Will ran his hand back through his hair. "I will have to beg her pardon, and her cousins' as well."

"That," Jamie said, turning his horse, "would be a mistake. We already lost Uncle. I should hate to lose you, too. I doubt Mr. Haygood's ability to put you under. I'm not so sure about the Everards."

Knowing a conversation with Vaughn Everard would have to wait, Will went to remount Arrow. "I won't accept a challenge. I did nothing to impugn the lady's honor."

"No, only steal her heart."

Will stiffened in the saddle. "She doesn't love me, Jamie. Trust me on that."

"I wouldn't be so sure," Jamie replied. "What I want to know is what you intend to do about the matter."

His son's gaze was so stormy Will wondered if he shouldn't expect a challenge from that quarter as well. Jamie had to be smarting over the fact that Will had just kissed the woman he loved, in front of her entire family. He had to convince his son that he had no plans to make Samantha Everard his wife.

"What I intend to do," he told Jamie, pulling Arrow in beside his horse, "is go home. See to my horse and my estate. Remember who I am."

Jamie nodded, and his shoulders came down. "An excellent plan. Remember exactly who you are—the Earl of Kendrick. Our family has safeguarded this valley for generations, or so Grandfather always said."

The weight of Will's responsibilities settled over him. "Your grandfather was right. I won't forget."

"Good," Jamie said, taking up his place beside Will as they started across the fields. "Because it strikes me you could be just what Samantha needs. I think you should marry her, Father. Tomorrow."

Chapter Seventeen

Will was so surprised by Jamie's statement that he reined in Arrow. "What?"

Jamie turned his horse to meet Will's gaze. Will had never seen his son so serious. His dark brows were down, his body centered over the saddle.

"I think you should marry Samantha," he repeated. "It solves all our problems."

Will felt as if the ground was sliding away beneath him. His hands tightened on the reins as he started forward again. "Marriage can easily cause more problems than it solves," he advised, nearly grimacing at how pessimistic he sounded.

"Not in this case," Jamie assured him. "I am not at liberty to offer details, but marriage is exactly what Samantha needs right now. And so do we."

"We?" Will frowned at him. "Since when is marriage a threesome, sir?"

Jamie rolled his eyes. "That's not what I meant. I know about the estate, Father. I've looked at the ledgers. We need an influx of cash, and Samantha can provide that."

Will reined in once more, forcing Jamie to do the

same. "Tell me you didn't offer to marry her because of her fortune."

Jamie could not quite meet his gaze. "Not entirely because of the fortune," he said. "Make no mistake," he hurried on when Will opened his mouth to protest. "I think I've loved Samantha Everard since the day Miss Walcott brought her to Kendrick Hall to visit Grandfather and she slipped me the last biscuit from the tea tray. But she doesn't love me, not as a woman should love a man. From what I just saw, she appears to have offered that love to you."

Will shook his head as the horses headed for home. "It was a kiss, Jamie. Nothing more."

"A kiss that caused her to tremble," Jamie countered. "A kiss that made her dash away to seek her composure."

Will barked a laugh. "You see those things as signs of love. They could as easily be signs of disgust."

"If you had disgusted her, you'd be facing her blade," Jamie promised. "Or the blade of one of her cousins. No one chastised you but Mr. Haygood, and even he saw what we all saw. You have feelings for her, and she returns them."

Did she have feelings for him? He supposed it was possible. He had been insistent in his attentions, and she may have taken those attentions as more than friendship, despite his protests. But if Samantha Everard held him in her affections, there were only two respectable outcomes for those feelings—friendship or marriage. Jamie apparently had decided friendship was not enough. But Will refused to offer marriage for money.

"It matters not," he insisted. "Neither of us has any intention of marrying."

Jamie frowned and drew his horse closer. "Why not? She's beautiful and charming. You said so yourself."

"I'm too old for her," Will tried.

Jamie made a face. "Well, I grant you ten years is a little much."

Will told himself not to argue. If he managed to dissuade his son from this line of thinking, then pretending to a few gray hairs was worth it. "Entirely too much."

Jamie held up a finger. "But Uncle was even older than you are, and he was accounted a viable suitor."

"And look where his suit led him," Will pointed out.

Jamie dropped his hand and rested it on the pommel of his saddle. "We agreed the Everards are likely innocent. So, Uncle was murdered for another reason. You cannot use that as an excuse not to pursue her."

Will chucked to Arrow, who started to trot, and Jamie came alongside to keep up. "I don't need to pursue anyone," he told his son. "I have no need for a wife. I have an heir."

"That's not the only reason to wed," Jamie all but scolded. "Did you marry Mother because you wanted an heir?"

How could he be having this conversation with his son? Will focused on avoiding the grazing sheep ahead of them. "That is an entirely different situation."

"Not where I sit," Jamie declared. "You married Mother without thinking twice, from what I've heard. Why are you so hesitant now?"

Will urged Arrow faster, but Jamie increased his pace as well, shooting him a look that told Will he could not avoid him.

"I was only the second son in those days," Will explained. "Who I married was less important than who your uncle married. Besides, your mother and I were wildly in love."

Jamie pushed his horse forward and wheeled it in front of Arrow, forcing the gelding to stutter to a stop. "So that's it. You're still grieving Mother."

Something tugged at Will's throat, and he knew it wasn't his cravat. "If I am, it is only her due."

"It's been seventeen years, Father," Jamie said, voice kind. "She would want you to be happy."

Pain shoved up from deep inside him. For once, he gave it voice.

"As happy as she was to leave us behind?" Will challenged. "As happy as your uncle was to be snuffed out just when his candle burned brightest? As happy as your grandfather to die with so many things unfinished?"

Jamie paled. "By your leave, Father, that's not what I meant."

It might not have been what Jamie had meant, but it was what had been. "This conversation is over," Will said. "I've lost entirely too many people to want to add one more to the list."

He clamped his heels to Arrow's flanks and sent the horse charging forward. Jamie pulled his mount aside in time to avoid a collision. Will caught a glimpse of him, mouth opened in an *O* of surprise, face pale under his midnight hair. He knew he'd wounded the boy, but he couldn't seem to help himself. For once, he felt as if his own wounds were on display.

And he didn't like the feeling.

He urged the horse on, flying across the fields and into the forest beyond. The trees flashed past on either side, rich with their summer green. Shadow and sunlight striped the graveled riding path; birds shot into the boughs at his passing.

He kept riding. Jamie did not follow.

His losses were like a whip, driving him on. He'd been beaten once in Constantinople when he'd strayed out of the areas frequented by his fellow countrymen. His eye had been black for a week. He'd gone without food for nearly as long once while trying to protect Egyptian antiquities from a marauding French troop. He thought his belly might drop off his body, his tongue rot in his mouth.

Those physical pains were nothing to the pain inside him now.

So many lost, Father. I have never understood why You had to take Peg. I was the one who pushed for the marriage. Why punish her?

And Gregory. He'd trained for the position of earl. He wanted it! I never envied him. I saw the responsibilities he'd have to shoulder. Why take him and leave them to me?

And our father. With losing wife, daughter-in-law and son, he never had a moment's peace. Why? Was he unworthy in Your sight? What more could he have done?

What more can I do?

In the world ye shall have tribulation: but be of good cheer; I have overcome the world.

He wanted to overcome—these feelings, his past. But always something seemed to pull him back. Was it the memory of Peg or something else?

Alone at the edge of the tree line, the fells rising before him, Will dismounted and stood stroking Arrow's lathered muzzle. His horse dropped its head and rubbed it against Will's arm. It was an easy thing to calm a horse. That at least he'd been trained to do. Raising Jamie, saving the estate, those were far more complicated.

But not as complicated as his feelings for Samantha. What had he been thinking to kiss her? He'd planned to keep it chaste. A quick peck on her hand or her cheek. It was one more pebble on his side of the scales, showing he was a gentleman she could trust with her secrets.

But apparently not with her feelings. She'd held out her hand. A gentleman would have taken it, pressed a kiss against her knuckles, released her with a bow. He'd taken one look at those rosy lips and known he had to taste them.

Fool! He'd given Jamie false hope of a marriage that could solve their financial problems. He could well have destroyed the trust he'd worked so hard to establish with Samantha.

There was only one thing for it. He would have to apologize. Immediately.

Samantha was struggling nearly as much. She'd tried to hole up in her mother's bedchamber. Surely her family would understand her need for quiet for once! In the past two days, she'd been struck over the head and kissed senseless. Any lady might be expected to retreat under such circumstances.

But retreating, she found, was not nearly as satisfying as it sounded. She couldn't sit, on the chairs or the bed. She couldn't seem to be still. She paced from the hearth to the wardrobe and back, her movements loud in the stillness. Her thoughts seemed to chase her at every turn. And all she could think about was that kiss!

What had Will been about? Had he joined the race with the sole intention of winning and claiming his reward? Why, when he'd protested over and over that all he wanted was a friendship?

And when he'd kissed her, had he felt the enormity of it, like a mountain rising from the depths of a clear lake? Impossible to ignore, magnificent in every aspect, mirrored in her very soul.

If he'd felt what she'd felt, what would he do next? Would he offer for her? Oh, how could she bear to refuse him?

Yet how could she forget the reason for her refusal when it was staring her in the face? She stopped at the foot of her mother's bed. She'd prayed herself to sleep each night, trying not to focus on the canopy above her. She knew exactly where to look and reached up to finger the fabric now. Mrs. Linton had had her late husband put cloth over the iron frame, but Samantha could see the bow where her mother's body had swung.

She dropped her hand, feeling as if her fingers had caught fire. Her mother had chosen death rather than a marriage where the passion that had fueled it had burned out. She had allowed her emotions to override her reason. Samantha would not, could not follow a similar path. A kiss, even a kiss as wondrous as the one William had given her, could not compare.

Father, help me. I know temptations are supposed to come, and that You will always give us a way out from under them. But I don't see the way. My heart leans toward Will—his strength, his kindness, even the insufferable way he keeps wanting to rescue me. But these feelings have come so quickly, just as my mother's came for my father and his for her. How can I know these feelings will last? How do I dare take a chance on them?

The emotions underlying her prayer were jumbled,

confused. She certainly couldn't trust them. Surely the best approach was to stay the course she had laid out.

But just as she steeled her resolve once more, someone tapped at her door. Raising her chin, she swept to the panel, prepared to tell her cousins, their wives or even their darling children that when it came to the matter of William Wentworth, Earl of Kendrick, she had nothing to say to them.

Chevers, her footman, bobbed his head as she opened the door. "Begging your pardon, your ladyship, but Lord Kendrick is downstairs, wishing a word. He wouldn't take no for an answer."

Her heart turned over in her chest. He was here to offer. He'd seen how the kiss had affected her, and he knew that he had to respond for propriety's sake. And she knew what her response must be.

Feet leaden, she followed Chevers back to the entry hall. Will stood on the parquet floor, head bowed as if weighty matters consumed him. His gaze came up to meet hers the moment she started down the stairs, and she nearly missed her step. Oh, this would never do! She had to stay strong. Raising her chin, she descended to his side and held out her hand.

As if he took her cue, he bowed over her fingers just as formally as meeting a duchess. Perhaps it was best that way. That's how the ton responded to acquaintances—with formality, with propriety. She'd never mastered the art, preferring to speak from the heart. But where he was concerned, her heart was not her best lead.

"Is there something you need of me, Lord Kendrick?" she asked as Chevers went to take up his place beside the front door again.

"Only to apologize," Will said, straightening. His

hands hung heavy beside his chamois trousers. "My behavior earlier today was inappropriate."

Now why did those words cause a pain inside her? She knew he was right. He shouldn't have kissed her that way in front of her family, as if holding her fulfilled every dream. The smartest thing she could do now was finish this.

"Apology accepted," she said. "Thank you for coming." She turned for the stair.

He caught her arm. "That's all you have to say to me?"

What could she say that wouldn't get them both into more trouble? "On that matter, yes, Lord Kendrick," she replied with her best smile. "Will you and James be back to join us for dinner?"

He glanced around the space, then nodded toward the open door of the library. "I think there's more to the matter than that. We must talk."

Not in the library. She was fairly sure at least one of her cousins was in their favorite lair. And not the withdrawing room. She could hear the faint strains of the pianoforte from here, telling her Claire or Adele or both were there. Even in a house the size of Dallsten Manor, there were limited places to have a private conversation with all her family in residence.

"Chevers," she called. "Will you fetch my pelisse? Lord Kendrick and I will take a walk around the grounds. If any of my family comes seeking me, tell them I'll be back shortly."

Will released her with a nod.

A few moments later they were walking down the lawn toward the pond. She couldn't call it a stroll. She could feel the tension in his arm under hers even through his wool coat, see it in the way his booted feet struck the grass.

Samantha was thankful to find the pond deserted. The glassy surface reflected the blue of the summer sky, the green of the shore around it.

"You didn't have to apologize," she said as they began the circuit of the water, moving along the rocky path. "I know it was just a kiss."

He paused beside their rowboat, pulled up among the rushes at one side of the pond. "Apparently not to those who saw it. Haygood and Jamie have already berated me for accosting you."

Her cheeks were heating. "You didn't accost me. You won the race fairly, and you claimed your prize."

She thought he smiled, but he bent to retrieve a stone from the path before she could be sure. "The prize you offered was a kiss to your hand. I took more."

Perhaps even her heart. But she couldn't tell him that. "I didn't protest."

"No, you didn't. But I never gave you a chance." He slung the stone into the pond. To Samantha's surprise, it bounced across the water three times before sinking.

"How did you do that?" she demanded.

Will's gaze swung from the water to her. "Did none of your cousins ever teach you to skip a rock?"

"Not one," she said, thoroughly annoyed with them. "I don't know what they were thinking. Show me how to do it."

He started laughing. "Madam, I brought you out here to explain my actions."

Samantha waved a hand. "You did. I accepted your apology. Can we move on?"

He cocked his head. "Is it that simple for you?"

"Nothing about our friendship is simple," she replied.

"But that doesn't mean I intend to wallow in it. You have chosen not to marry. I have chosen not to marry. Let's leave it at that." She bent and picked up a stone. "Now, show me."

Will shook his head. "You are an amazing woman, Samantha Everard. Very well. We will remain friends."

For some reason the answer disappointed her nearly as much as her cousins' lack of teaching on the fine art of rock skipping.

"You truly wish to learn to skip a rock, at this very moment?" he asked.

In answer she merely pushed the rock toward him and raised her brows. He could not know how badly she needed a distraction.

He laughed again. "All right. How could I claim myself a gentleman and refuse you?" He glanced around, then leaned down to pick up a rock. "To begin with, you need a certain kind of stone. See here, how it's relatively flat?"

Samantha peered at the smooth oblong stone. "Oh, yes." The scent of Will's cologne washed over her, clean and crisp with a hint of the exotic, the perfect combination for her diplomat-adventurer. She had to stop herself from drinking in the scent like water.

Will angled the rock in his hand. He had long fingers, strong fingers. She remembered waking to the feel of them, tender, on her cheek when she'd been struck. She forced herself to focus on his words.

"Hold the stone between your thumb and fingers and release it with your wrist. Like this." He flicked the stone at the water. It leaped four times before sinking.

"Wonderful!" Samantha cried. She cast about until she found a rock similar to what Will had described and picked it up. Aiming at the water, she let it fly. It sank immediately.

She stepped away from the pond. "What did I do wrong?"

"I'm not sure," Will admitted. "Let's try again."

He turned to look for a stone, and she did likewise. She could feel him nearby, hear the crunch of his beautiful boots against the path. Perhaps it would be enough to take comfort and pleasure from his company. She didn't need to hold his strong hand as they walked, know the touch of his lips against hers. They could be friends, just as he said.

They regrouped, and Will demonstrated his throwing technique again. Samantha watched his fingers cup the rock, his arm move with the motion of throwing. She shook her head as the rock ricocheted off the surface three times.

"I'm certain that's exactly what I did," she exclaimed.

"Here," Will said. He stood behind her, wrapped an arm about her and cradled her hand in his. "Hold your hand thus. Do you feel the difference?"

Oh, but did she feel the difference. Her heart had sped, her cheeks were heating again, and the rock suddenly weighed ten stone. "I think so," she managed.

She could feel his body behind hers as he drew back her arm.

"Ready?" he asked.

She would never be ready—to let him go, to let go of her feelings. But if she wanted to be free of the past, she had to do both.

"Yes," she said. And she threw the rock toward the pond.

It arced across the water, touching once, twice, three

times, before dropping beneath the surface in ever-widening circles.

"Well done," Will said, stepping back. "You seem to have the hang of it now."

Perhaps. But she was afraid she would never get the hang of being friends with him.

Chapter Eighteen

Samantha waved Will goodbye and trudged back up the drive to the manor, thoughts as heavy as her steps. He was such a wonderful man, kind, considerate, willing to play along with her mad whims. Yet how could she trust her feelings, knowing how quickly they had come?

She had reached the foot of the grand stair when the knocker slammed down on the front door. She turned with a sigh to find Chevers eyeing her.

"Go ahead," she said. "We might as well answer it."

With a smile of understanding, he turned to do his duty.

Jamie spilled into the entryway, hat askew and eyes stormy. Samantha's heart slammed into her ribs. Something had happened to Will. His horse had tripped in a marmot hole and thrown him. Her cousins had challenged him to a duel. She couldn't know how he had been hurt, she only knew that he had, and that she had to help him. She flew to Jamie's side.

"What's happened?" she demanded. "Where is he? How bad is it? Oh, why aren't you speaking!"

Jamie stepped back from her. "What are you talking about?"

She took in his rumpled cravat, the pallor of his face. He was hurting more than she was.

"Oh, Jamie," she murmured. "What do you need from me?"

He drew in a shaky breath. "A few moments of your time. Alone."

"Of course." She nodded to the footman. "Lord Wentworth and I will be in the library, Chevers. Please wait outside the door."

She led Jamie to the library and glanced inside the room, quite ready to evict her cousins if needed. But the room was empty for once. She entered, leaving the door open for propriety's sake. Motioning her friend toward a chair by the fire, she went to take the opposite one.

Jamie sat, but stiffly, fists knotted on the buckskin of his trousers. "I had to talk to you."

She nodded encouragement. "What's happened? Has your father been hurt?"

"Hurt?" He frowned, then shook his head. "No, no, not in the way you mean." He edged forward on his seat as if intent on making his case. "Samantha, my father is in love with you."

Her hopes leaped like a startled grouse, but she shot them down. She had decided to ignore these feelings—she certainly wasn't about to confess them to Jamie!

"I'm terribly sorry," she said. "I didn't encourage him."

Jamie gaped at her. "Why not?"

He sounded like he wanted her to return his father's affections. But that made no sense! She shook her head. "Forgive me. I seem to be rather confused at the moment. Your father is fine—no fall from his horse, no mishap on the way home?"

Jamie shrugged. "Nothing, unless you find riding off in a temper disturbing. I did. That's not like him."

She thought she understood. "It's all right, Jamie. He was here just now, apologizing. We settled things between us."

His face scrunched up until he looked ages older. "The only way to settle things between the two of you is for you to marry him."

Samantha raised her chin. "You presume too much."

"Do I? You care for him. I know it. I saw how you reacted to his kiss."

"It was nothing," Samantha insisted. "I wish you wouldn't refine on it."

"And I wish you would," Jamie declared, leaning back so solidly the chair rocked on its hardwood legs.

Samantha threw up her hands. "I cannot understand you. Are you saying you think I *should* encourage your father?"

"Certainly," Jamie said hotly. "He's not bad looking, and he's an earl."

"And you think those should be my criteria for a husband?" She felt her temper rising even as her back stiffened. "I'll have you know that I have been courted by men more handsome who were dukes. I was less impressed with them than I am with your father."

"So why not marry him?" Jamie demanded. "It would solve your problem!"

"And possibly cause any number of other problems," Samantha assured him. "No, thank you."

Jamie surged to his feet. "Why are you so stubborn?"

Samantha rose to meet him. "Well, if that isn't the pot calling the kettle black!"

Jamie drew in a breath as if realizing he'd pressed too hard. "Perhaps I am stubborn," he admitted. "When I see an injustice, I feel compelled to right it. I got that from my father."

"And as I told your father," Samantha replied, forcing herself to return to her seat, "while I appreciate your intentions, I don't need your help."

"If you don't," Jamie challenged, "he does."

Samantha's concerns rose once more. "What do you mean? What's wrong with your father?"

Jamie sat and leaned closer again, lowering his voice as if he didn't even trust her footman with the news.

"He doesn't like to talk about it," he murmured, "but I can see the problem in the estate books. Kendrick Hall is failing. There's not enough farmland to support the rising costs. If things get any worse, we may have to sell."

Something twisted inside her. "Sell? How can you sell? Isn't the estate entailed?" She knew entails were a way to keep properties safe for the next generation.

His face tightened. "The entail was broken when my uncle died, and Grandfather never had a chance to reinstate it."

So yet again the former Lord Wentworth's death brought pain. "You'd lose the estate, your home?" she pressed.

"Everything but the London house," Jamie confirmed, dealing her hopes a death blow. "With the proceeds, Father and I could live there."

The situation was so like hers it brought tears to her eyes. "Oh, Jamie! I'm so sorry. I wish I could help."

He fell onto his knees before her, took both her hands in his, eyes as beseeching as when he'd offered for her.

"You can help, don't you see?" he begged, gaze

searching hers as if he could find assurance. "If you marry Father before your birthday, you get to keep Dallsten Manor and you could help us keep Kendrick Hall. We all win."

She could see how he'd come to that conclusion. There were many things to commend such a match. She'd be a countess as well as a baroness in her own right. As Imogene had pointed out, Samantha would never have to leave her beloved Cumberland again. With access to the legacy Will would have the money he needed to maintain his estate, perhaps make improvements that would allow it to bring a profit again.

Was that why he was kind to her? Had he been hoping for just such a match? She felt as if her heart shriveled at the thought. But no, surely not Will! Why protest her friendship with Jamie when she'd first arrived if he was intent on getting his hands on her inheritance? Her marriage to his son would have brought him just as much access to the funds. Oh, but she would never understand men!

And they could not know what they asked by suggesting she join her family to theirs. How could she bring the true Everard legacy—the secrets, the emotional upheaval—to her marriage? That burden crushed any monetary benefit or change in position or prestige. And she'd never much cared about position or prestige anyway.

"I'm sorry," she repeated. "I can't marry your father, Jamie. I told you—I doubt I'll marry anyone."

"But why?" Jamie asked, giving her hands a squeeze. "Are you so determined to hang on to your independence?"

"It's not that," she promised.

"Then do you think Father would squander your inheritance?" He released her hands to gesture with his own. "He's an excellent manager. He didn't cause these problems with the estate, and he's done all he can to solve them."

"I'm sure he has," Samantha said. "I would trust him with the legacy."

"But not your heart," Jamie guessed.

Not her heart. That she must keep hidden, along with the secrets it defended, the emotions that all too often guided it.

Samantha smiled at him, but wished she actually felt happy with her decision. "It's for the best, Jamie. Your father deserves a woman who will truly love him."

"So you keep saying," Jamie replied, rising. "But it seems to me that if two people love each other, they should be together."

"The world isn't that simple, I fear," Samantha told him, remembering when she'd thought otherwise.

"And it isn't as complicated as you're making it," Jamie said before heading for the door. "For someone who claims to enjoy adventure, you've put quite a hedge around yourself. I just hope you don't end up finding that by shutting everyone else out, you've boxed yourself in."

Will also assured himself it was all for the best. Surely he and Samantha could build a companionable friendship. He would not refine on that kiss, the sweetness of her, the way she melted against him, the feel of her in his arms. He was a gentleman, an earl, with responsibilities to consume him.

For some reason those responsibilities felt hollow.

Instead he found himself unaccountably eager for services the next morning. He told himself that such devotion was commendable, but the church seemed brighter, his prayers more heartfelt with Samantha sitting in front of him. Had he reached out his hand, he could have touched her golden hair. Had he whispered of love, she would have heard him.

He refused to whisper in church!

Determined to be proper, he sought her out in the churchyard afterward, but she kept slipping away from him. He'd approach the group where she was conversing, and she'd excuse herself. He loitered beside her carriage, and she prolonged her discussions or chased her cousin's children across the lawn. And when the sun popped into view at precisely half past eleven, her feet did not so much as turn to seek her waterfall.

The other Everards had no trouble greeting him. Each of the gentlemen and their wives took pains to talk with him, encourage him to join them on various outings and in activities. He tried to question Vaughn Everard about his horse, but the fellow fended him off with witty jokes. Besides, Will was more concerned about Samantha. She didn't come near him. He felt as if he'd lost the best part of himself.

His focus had been on gaining her trust to learn the truth about his brother. Now he was more interested in the cares that burdened her. He'd thought his apology yesterday had cleared the air between them, but he'd obviously been wrong. What else could he do to restore their friendship?

He decided to ask his son's advice as they headed for home in the carriage. "Do you know why Lady Everard is avoiding me?" he asked.

Jamie shifted as if the padded leather seat had grown too hard. "For the same reason you avoided her, I warrant. But I am resigned that you are both fools determined to make yourselves miserable."

"How highly you hold me in esteem," Will quipped.

Jamie shrugged, hunching in his navy coat. "You are my father. I have a duty to you. That doesn't mean I have to agree with everything you do or say."

"No, indeed," Will assured him. "But may I remind you I earned my years honestly? I have some pretense toward knowledge."

Jamie's face was tight. "And may I remind you that you were my age when you first knew love?"

"What Samantha Everard and I feel for each other isn't love," Will insisted, his voice sounding gruff even to him.

"So you say. But it seems you've forgotten that emotion in the intervening years."

The chastisement stung, yet Will could not argue with his son. Indeed the revelation stilled his tongue for the remainder of the ride home. Had he forgotten the stirrings of that tender emotion? He tried to remember his time with Peg—how it had felt. But the circumstances were so different. He was so different.

His brother had been the one to point out Peggy Demesne to him one day as they rode through the village. Will had just finished schooling at Eton—much like Jamie—and Gregory, a few years ahead of him, liked to flaunt his town bronze.

"Now there's a tasty morsel," his brother had said with a nod toward the village mill. Peg had been standing by the side of the pond with her father, helping him remove plants that had sprouted in the water and could hinder the mill's working. "Perhaps I could learn to enjoy flour. I wager a few of the lads around here do."

Will had been uncomfortable with his brother's insinuation, but he'd said nothing. Gregory had been the older brother, the heir. Everyone from their father to the lowliest chambermaid acquiesced to his wishes. Will knew their father would never countenance a marriage between his brother and the daughter of a miller. But he had a feeling his brother had something other than marriage in mind.

"I saw her first," he'd said when he'd actually only noticed her at Gregory's direction. "We have an understanding."

Gregory had scoffed. "Well, then, I wish you and your future brats well." He galloped ahead, his laughter floating back to Will on the breeze.

And Will had stopped to talk to Peg. Talk had led to walks across the green, holding hands behind the church, kisses stolen at the garden gate. He knew he was expected to choose a bride from among his own class, a lady who understood Society's dictates, someone who could enrich their family. But back then he had felt tongue-tied among those ladies. Like Gregory, they seemed to laugh at his intentions, his dreams to enter the diplomatic corps and see the world.

Peg had made him feel smarter and stronger than even his brother. With her his character seemed more noble, his ambitions worthwhile. Peg saw him as the leader. He was the most important person in her world, whereas he often felt like the least important person at Kendrick Hall.

Was that all it was, Father? Did I love her because I first felt truly a man in her presence?

But he had no doubts who he was now. His experience in the diplomatic corps, seeing places and cultures so different from the sheltered village where he'd grown up and the school he'd attended, had made him a better man, a stronger man. He knew what the Lord wanted of him—to take his responsibilities more seriously than his brother had, to see Jamie to manhood, to manage the estate and care for its people. A wife wasn't necessary to any of that.

Who can find a woman of valor? For her price is far above rubies. The heart of her husband doth safely trust in her, so that he shall have no lack of gain.

He knew the verse. He could not argue that Samantha was a woman of valor; he simply wasn't sure his heart was ready to trust again.

He managed to chivvy Jamie into a better frame of mind with a game of skittles his son won handily, and they spent the day in relative peace. But Samantha Everard was still on Will's mind when he woke the next morning. He could not like the tension between them. Their lands marched side by side. Surely it was in the best interest of the community for them to be civil to each other. He owed it to his neighbors to try to apologize once more.

Accordingly, after breakfast and a talk with his estate manager, he rode Arrow over to Dallsten Manor and asked after Samantha. The footman Chevers was so used to Will's presence that he directed him behind the house to the kitchen gardens as if Will were a member of the family.

The garden behind the house held graveled paths marching through beds of fragrant herbs and vegetables in raised boxes. He spotted the tops of carrots waving in the breeze and the thick leaves of rhubarb. He grimaced at the gaping holes here and there, evidence of where his son and the Everard twins had gone digging for worms.

Samantha was standing at the crossroads of several

paths, surrounded by lavender and chives, the purple blossoms bringing out the blue in her striped cambric gown. Her wide-brimmed straw hat shadowed her eyes, so it was hard to tell her expression. But she was gazing down at Prentice Haygood, who knelt in the gravel at her feet, greatcoat puddled about him, and held her hand, face upturned.

"And thus it would give me the greatest honor if you would consent to be my bride," he finished as Will pulled up beside a trellis of sweet peas.

Not again.

Something inside him leaped like a lion. He wanted to stride forward, push between the two, haul Prentice Haygood to his feet by his wilted cravat and order him from the grounds for his presumption. But Will sincerely doubted Samantha would appreciate such a barbaric response. He held himself perfectly still, unwilling to interrupt, unable to leave. Still he felt his body protest.

Why must he stand silent while other men kept proposing to the woman he loved?

The sentiment struck him squarely in the face. He was in love with Samantha Everard. He hadn't asked for it, had fought any suggestion of it. But he could no longer deny it. He didn't want her to leave Evendale after the summer party. He wasn't content to wait for her to return for an occasional visit. Friendship felt puny, insignificant, totally unsatisfactory.

Lord, is this what You want? Is this what You've been trying to tell me?

The rightness of it settled in his soul, as comfortable as a padded chair by the fire on a rainy day. Jamie had been right. Will needed to let Peg go, once and for all, and open his heart to the chance of love again.

But loving Samantha Everard came at a price, particularly to his consequence. He could not be certain she returned his feelings. She could easily fend him off as she had Jamie. Yet if she agreed, what a reward—spending his days alongside her, showing her the worlds he'd come to know, learning the secrets of her heart.

He didn't want her marrying anyone but him, which meant that he'd have to propose to her himself.

Chapter Nineteen

Not again! Samantha stared down into Prentice Haygood's earnest face and forced herself not to cringe. Surely he deserved better than that.

The problem was, she was not feeling at all the thing. Like a Paisley shawl that had come unbound, the edges of her life seemed to be unraveling, the vibrant pattern disappearing into nothing. It didn't help that she had had a difficult night.

She'd dreamed her mother was crying, sitting in the armchair across from Samantha by the fire and sobbing disconsolately as she used to do when Samantha's father would leave for London. Samantha had tried to cheer her, but her mother had only sobbed the harder, face buried in her fingers.

"I'm alone! So alone!"

"You're not alone, Mama," Samantha had protested, kneeling at her feet and trying to take her mother's cold hands away from her face. "You have me!"

The hands had fallen, revealing her mother's face, eyes blazing brighter than the fire. "And who do you have?" her mother had challenged. "You're throwing away your chance at love!"

Even in the morning the dream still shook Samantha. She'd been so sure she was making the right decision. What if she was wrong? What if marriage, a good, solid marriage, was possible for her? What if she was throwing away the Everard legacy, everything her grandfather, father and cousins had worked to build, for nothing?

The house had felt too confining, so she'd repaired to the garden. Mrs. Linton was baking meat pies today, and a few sprigs of fresh basil would be just the thing. Basket hooked over one arm, she'd wandered through the herbs, inhaling their dusky scents. And then Prentice Haygood had found her.

She'd dreaded his purpose even before he'd knelt in front of her. His heartfelt speech only raised her pity. He was so meek, so self-effacing. He'd never be happy in her family. Even if she had been willing to contemplate marriage, she could not agree to his proposal merely to save the legacy.

"I'm so very sorry, Mr. Haygood," she said. "But I don't return your affections. You deserve better in a wife."

The smile disappeared from his chubby face as if she'd wiped his joy away with a washcloth. He climbed heavily to his feet. "And you deserve better than to lose everything you hold dear because of pride. I found your father's will."

Of course. She should have realized there'd be a copy in the muniment room. Seeking information about the Everard family, he'd probably found the will all too easily.

"Then you know what happens the day after the summer party," she replied.

He took her hand, but she pulled back before he

could cradle it close. He drew himself up as if she'd wounded him.

"I know," he said, voice turned cautious. "But if you run away with me today to Gretna Green, you won't have to deal with any of it."

His answer was easy and completely wrong. "So it would seem," she acknowledged. "But the answer is still no, Mr. Haygood."

She thought he would protest, perhaps lament her hard heart. Instead he took a step closer and narrowed his eyes, his gaze drilling into her. "Do you know who I am?"

What was wrong with him? Did he honestly think the fact that he'd soon come into his uncle's title meant anything to her? That the influence he might wield was any danger to her family's legacy?

She held her ground. "You are a guest in my home who is dangerously close to wearing out his welcome."

He grabbed her arms, fingers digging into her flesh, eyes manic. "I won't let you do this. Marriage would be preferable, but if you insist on refusing…"

"She'll simply be proving how wise she is," Will said, striding out from behind the colorful sweet peas. "Take your hands off her. Now."

She staggered as Haygood released her, but she caught her balance. With a nod to Will as he came to a stop beside her, she said, "Thank you, Lord Kendrick, for your kindness. I'm certain Mr. Haygood was about to apologize." She couldn't manage a smile as she glanced at her suitor.

Haygood's jaw was equally tight as he snapped a bow. "Of course. Please ascribe my behavior to my vast disappointment. I am your servant as always, Lady Everard." He pushed past Will for the house.

Samantha blew out a breath. "I must be losing my touch. They usually take my refusal so much better."

"No one could take a refusal from you with any grace," Will countered. "Are you certain you're all right?"

Samantha nodded, drawing in another deep breath of the scented air and vowing to put the incident behind her. "Fine. Did you have need of me?"

"I begin to think so," he replied, removing the top hat from his head. "I know this is poor timing considering what just happened, but as I'm never sure when I'm going to find you in the middle of a proposal, I thought I'd better put in my bid before it's too late."

She could not have understood him. "I beg your pardon?"

His smile turned up at one corner. "I very much fear I'm about to offer you marriage, my dear."

Samantha stared at him. The breeze was threading through his dark wavy hair like tender fingers, and he leaned toward her as if with every intention of making his case. Oh, she couldn't go through this now, not when she was so unsure of her way!

"Lord Kendrick," she started, "Will, I…"

"Please," he said, holding up one hand, "hear me out. I realize we were only formally introduced a little more than a week ago, but I feel as if I've known you much of my life."

Perhaps she could fend him off. She didn't want to hurt him. Already the pain was building inside her at the thought of refusing him.

"I feel the same way," she replied. "Jamie and your father told me so many stories about you and read me your letters. I feel as if you're an old friend."

If he heard her emphasis on the word *friend,* he didn't

show it. "And I heard stories—from my father, Mrs. Dallsten Walcott and Jamie, stories that could not prepare me for your beauty and charm."

"Well, they couldn't have been very good stories then," she teased over the thundering of her heart. "Truly, Will, there's no need for this."

He cocked his head. "Can you tell me that honestly, especially considering our kiss?"

Her face was heating, and she ducked her head and fiddled with the handle on the basket to keep him from seeing her reddening cheeks. "You won the race. I kissed you. That's all there is to it."

"You felt nothing?"

She swallowed. It was wrong to lie, but how could she tell him the truth? A lady simply did not admit to a gentleman that his kiss had sent her over the moon and back.

"What I felt has no bearing on this discussion," she said with a sufficiently prim tone that Mrs. Dallsten Walcott would have been proud of her.

"Then you find me objectionable," he persisted.

Her head came up. He was standing there, hat in one hand, waiting patiently. For once she wished he was not such a diplomat and would simply let things go!

"Of course I don't find you objectionable," she said. "But I don't intend to marry. I wish everyone would accept that."

"I suppose I must believe you, as I've seen you turn down two candidates in the past fortnight." He ran his free hand back through his hair. "But I find it harder to accept when it's me you're refusing. Will you at least tell me why?"

How could she admit her concerns? In the light of his devotion, they seemed petty. Yet her father had been just as devoted, the stories said, and he had been unable to withstand the ebb and flow of her mother's emotions.

"I have my reasons," she said. "And I'm afraid they are sufficient to prevent me from changing my mind. Forgive me." Tears were starting, and she brushed past him, intent on escaping. But he caught her shoulder and held her gently.

"Forgive me," he murmured. "I never meant to hurt you."

"Oh, Will." For a moment she allowed herself to rest against him, head on his chest, arms warming her. She was squashing her hat and his, and very likely her basket was poking his ribs, but she couldn't care. This was what a true marriage was intended to be—two people, sheltering each other from life's blows, rejoicing in the good times.

In sickness and in health, forsaking all others.

She'd heard that statement so many times as friends and family had married over the years. Could those words really be meant for her?

She raised her head. His face was still, sorrowful, as if he realized he would not hold her like this again. He bent and pressed a kiss against her forehead, and she knew it was farewell. The pain inside her pushed its way up, blocked her breath, spilled her tears. Each step she took away from him felt like a thousand miles.

She couldn't return to the house, answer the questions her cousins would raise at the sight of her tears. She had to get away from her past, give herself a moment to mourn the loss of her future.

"Excuse me," she managed. "I think I'd like to be alone. Please tell the others I'll return by luncheon."

She hurried for the riding path that led into the woods—anything to erase the memory of his tender touch.

Will stood alone in the garden, hat in his hand. Why was it always his lot to watch Samantha walk away? She cared about him—the look on her face, the gentleness of her touch, the warmth of her wit all testified as much. He had fought the attraction because of his past. Having lost so many, he'd refused to take the chance of loving another. But Samantha Everard had pried open his locked heart, letting in the light. What kept her own heart guarded?

He wanted to go after her, beg her to see reason, threaten to carry her off to Gretna Green, but he thought he might be the last person she wanted to see at the moment. He wasn't surprised, however, to notice another movement along the riding path. Prentice Haygood was following Samantha. Perhaps he too sought to press his case, comfort her. But Will didn't like it.

He took a step forward and heard his name called.

"Kendrick—a word with you."

He turned to find Vaughn Everard striding from the house, tailored cerulean coat hugging his lean body. From the set of his jaw, Will didn't think he'd be easily avoided. He inclined his head and slipped his top hat back into place.

"Lord Widmore," he greeted him. "How can I help you?"

"I'm here to offer my help," Vaughn said, stopping before him. He wore no hat; Will could easily believe that platinum hair gave back the light it took in from the sun. His dark eyes were half lidded, as if he didn't wish Will to have a glimpse of his thoughts. "You seemed determined to talk to me yesterday," he said. "I assume it was about your brother's death."

Here it was, the opportunity to learn the truth at last. Will could not believe it would be that easy. "And will you grant me answers now, after all these years?"

Vaughn bowed, arm outstretched like a courtier of old. "Perhaps if you'd walk with me, I could explain." He straightened and motioned toward the path that edged the woods. As the direction would parallel the one Samantha and Haygood had taken, Will accepted the offer and fell into step beside him.

"I believe you know your brother dueled with me the day he was killed," Vaughn said, long legs eating up the graveled track so swiftly the tassels on his polished boots were swinging.

"So the authorities told my father," Will replied, pacing him. "They said you were exonerated. But no one has ever named the murderer, nor, as far as I know, brought him to justice."

"Allow me to set your mind at rest. Your brother's murderer was accused of treason and spent the rest of his life incarcerated. He died a few years ago."

Will jerked to a stop. "Why were we never told? What has treason to do with murder?"

Vaughn stopped as well, his tassels stilling their swing. "Do you remember when we all thought Napoleon meant to invade?"

Will shook his head. "I wasn't in England then. I was fighting the French on the diplomatic front, in Constantinople."

Vaughn nodded in acceptance. "It was a frantic time in government," he replied, gaze going out toward the wood. "Move, countermove, all our lives hanging precariously in the balance. Decisions were made that satisfied no one. A group of Englishmen led by a high-ranking member of Parliament decided a revolution was in order, in England."

Will took a step back. "In England? Were they mad?"

Vaughn's eyes glittered as if he were a little mad himself. "Some thought so. But they cast a compelling vision—an England where privilege and power were available to all men, a place of peace and prosperity again. They very nearly handed the country over to Napoleon, but their plans were discovered and ultimately foiled."

"I don't understand," Will insisted, spreading his feet on the path. "But what has this to do with my brother?"

"Hear me out," Vaughn replied, adjusting his own stance. Will suddenly realized anyone watching them would think they meant to come to blows any moment. Where were his diplomacy skills? He forced his fists to relax.

"Your brother knew the leader," Vaughn continued, "and the leader deemed him a danger. He is the one who struck the fatal blows after my duel with your brother."

Will eyed him. "You have proof, I assume."

Vaughn spread his hands. "Alas, we have only the leader's testimony to prove he killed your brother. No one saw him, and he left no evidence behind that would incriminate him."

"In point of fact," Will said, "he did a good job of incriminating you."

Vaughn inclined his head. "So the magistrates originally thought. But they were willing to change their minds. I hope you are as well."

It was a wild tale, treason and treachery and crowns at risk. Another man might have questioned it further, demanded redress. But Will had seen too much of such skullduggery in foreign circles. What was to say that it couldn't happen in England? And the story certainly explained why the authorities had been unable to share the truth with his father at the time.

"Why tell me now?" Will asked. "Why not a few years ago when we knew the fear of invasion was over?"

Vaughn brushed a stray leaf from his trousers. "All those involved were sworn to secrecy, on penalty of treason. We didn't want the group to know the location of their leader for fear his men would reassemble and attempt a rescue. As I mentioned, the leader has now passed on and is no longer a threat to the crown."

"You said he died several years ago," Will countered. "You could have come to me then, explained all this."

"I could have," he admitted. "But I'd rather hoped you'd put it behind you. Only when you were so intent on questioning me yesterday did I suspect the death still rankled." He held out his hand. "Forgive me for not speaking sooner."

Will glanced at the long-fingered hand, a hand, if the stories were true, that had wounded more than one man. But it seemed it was not the hand that had killed his brother. He reached out and clasped it. "Thank you for telling me. Now I understand why Samantha could not explain. I only hope you won't have to bear the consequences for breaking your vow of silence."

Vaughn's smile tipped up at one corner as he drew back his hand. "I can reasonably say I'm safe. For the past seven years, I've worked with a group of gentlemen in the Carpenter's Club intent on doing their Christian duty. It's brought me to the attention of the Regent and the Prime Minister, in a good way."

"Hence your elevation to marquess."

His smile broadened. "Precisely. And it's something

my wife had wanted for a long time. The title would have gone into abeyance otherwise. Nevertheless Lord Liverpool's government allows me a certain latitude, so long as its cause is served."

He sobered suddenly and took a step closer. "You've been the king's man in the diplomatic corps. Tell me, William Wentworth, Earl of Kendrick, are you willing to help the Empire again?"

Will frowned at his intensity. "I remain His Majesty's obedient servant. What did you have in mind?"

"We have reason to believe the story I just told you has not quite reached its conclusion, and I could use your help to tidy up some loose ends."

Will felt his head come up, the blood pumping through his veins. Here was a chance to right his brother's death, to make a difference for England again. Hadn't he been looking for a diversion? It seemed to have found him instead.

"I'm your man," he replied. "What would you have me do?"

Vaughn's mouth quirked. "Nothing too onerous or dangerous, I promise you."

Will's disappointment must have shown on his face, for Vaughn barked a laugh and clapped him on the shoulder. "Good man. Let me tell you the situation as we see it. Back in 1805, when the leader was captured, we collected many of his followers, but some remained only rumors. Those we've managed to track down over the years. One suspected accomplice fled to the Continent, and we lost all trace of him. However, we have reason to think he recently returned to England. We believe he is the one stalking my cousin."

"The thief!" Will realized, pulling away even as he felt himself stiffening again, this time for a fight.

"Indeed," Vaughn agreed. "When he struck first in London, we weren't sure of his motives or even who was behind it. We managed to convince Samantha to head north to safety while we attempted to solve the mystery."

"But you weren't happy," Will guessed. "You suspected she might be in danger. That's why you followed her."

Vaughn raised his brows. "I assure you this mystery held all my attentions."

"Enough so that I saw you and that roan of yours here in Evendale before your family arrived."

He blew out a breath. "How very clumsy of me. But you're right. I was here to keep an eye on her, until I realized you were doing a much better job of it."

Will could not agree. "Yet still the miscreant struck. Did you learn why? What has she to do with any of this in the first place?"

"Her father, my uncle, was second in command of the group for a time," Vaughn explained, and Will thought his tension was rising again as well. "I believe he found faith and attempted to change the leader's mind. He was killed for his trouble. However, any number of plans were made right here, in Dallsten Manor, under the cover of this summer party. It's possible our last follower thinks to find some incriminating evidence of his involvement and destroy it before anyone is the wiser."

"It sounds as if you know who you're looking for," Will said, watching him. "Is it one of the staff? Someone staying in the area?"

Vaughn eyed him, and Will could see the calculation behind those deep brown eyes. He didn't want Will knowing any more than necessary. That much was clear from the way he'd carefully withheld the leader's name. He wasn't sure whether to trust Will now.

"I can't help if I don't know the truth," Will said. "And I want to help. This man was part of a plot against England that cost me my brother. I'd like to see him brought to justice."

Vaughn was silent a moment longer, then squared his shoulders as if making a decision. "Very well, Lord Kendrick. But I want your word you will do nothing without consulting me first."

Though it rankled, Will nodded. "You have my word. Who do you suspect as your traitor?"

"My cousin's most devoted suitor," he said. "Prentice Haygood."

Chapter Twenty

Sunlight slanted through the oaks; the leaves chattered in the breeze. The day was warm, the air resinous with the scent from the pine trees a long-lost Dallsten had planted. Normally she would have strolled along the path, watching for red squirrels scampering up the bark, for roe deer leaping away through the green.

But the farther along the path Samantha walked, the more her feet slowed. She wasn't physically tired, but she felt as if she carried the weight of the fells on the shoulders of her cambric gown. She seemed to be hurting everyone around her, when all she wanted was to end the cycle of blame and hurt.

Tears stung her cheeks.

Oh, Lord, You carried a much bigger burden. Won't You help me carry this one?

For my yoke is easy, and my burden is light.

That verse again? She'd always struggled with it. Growing up in privilege should have made her burden light indeed, yet it always seemed worry lurked behind her. Why was her father so often gone? Didn't he love her and her mother? Why was her mother so sad? Now that she understood the whole story of their courtship and marriage, she had some answers, but the burden had shifted to her. She was equal parts of her mother and father. What hope did she have for a good marriage?

Ahead, an opening in the trees filled the space with light. She stopped in the golden air and lifted her face to the warmth.

I know Your promises, Lord. But the yoke doesn't seem light now. As Baroness Everard, I feel responsible for so many things—Dallsten Manor, the legacy, the well-being of my cousins and their families. And if I marry, I'll have a responsibility to my husband and children as well. I can't do it alone.

But she wasn't alone.

Here in her forest, with the light shining from above, she could believe the Lord was right here with her. She took a deep breath, steepled her fingers and pressed them to her lips in promise.

Thank You, Lord. I will lean on You when my strength fails me.

The tears kept falling, but they felt cleansing and cool. She wiped them away with her fingers before lowering her hands. What a watering pot she'd become! She'd never had to carry a handkerchief before returning to Dallsten Manor!

With a laugh, she shook the tears from her fingers and stood taller. She could do this. She was meant to do this. She'd return to the house, carry on with her plan. She would not let her family, or Will, sway her.

Even if just the thought of Will made her sway on her feet.

Something, perhaps a twig, snapped behind her, and she knew that she had company. Time to take up her role. Putting on a bright smile, she turned, expecting to see Jamie or one of her cousins out for a walk or ride.

Instead Prentice Haygood stood on the path, hands deep in the folds of his greatcoat. He offered her a tremulous smile.

"I thought perhaps I could convince you to reconsider," he said.

She could not be angry with him, seeing him standing there so penitently. The sunlight made a halo on his mousey hair, as if to affirm his innocence.

"How sweet," she said. "You have been a loyal friend, Mr. Haygood. But I'm afraid my mind is quite made up. Please do not pursue the matter further."

He approached her slowly, each step so hesitant she thought he was sure she'd bolt. "But I must pursue the matter. It's the best course to my happiness, I am assured."

What had she done to make him so determined? She'd never encouraged more than a friendship! "And I am equally assured that I would make you singularly miserable," Samantha insisted. "If you continue with this course, I will have to ask you to leave."

He stopped two feet away from her, gray eyes flickering over her face as if he searched for the truth in it. "You're absolutely certain."

A sigh escaped her. "Yes, Mr. Haygood, absolutely certain. This isn't some maidenly restraint you see. I fear it's quite fierce determination, a besetting sin you will be glad to have avoided in a wife."

His hands had come out to worry now, turning over and over each other like two fat puppies in play. She found the gesture far less charming. "Is there nothing I can say to dissuade you from this course?" he begged, taking another step closer. "I assure you I will be a devoted husband."

"And I assure you I will make a wretched wife."

"Pity," he said, then his hands shot out and wrapped around her throat.

Samantha gasped in pain and shock. She pushed back from him, but his grip was like a vise, squeezing, crushing. The air in her lungs fought for release. All uncertainty, all hesitancy had vanished from his chubby face, leaving him grim, hard. She had no doubt he meant to kill her. He thought because she was a woman, it would be easy.

She might be a woman, but she was also an Everard. And she did not intend to go into that dark night without a fight.

She swung up both hands, rammed her thumbs into his eyes and brought the heel of one half boot down on his instep with all the strength she had. With a roar of pain, he released her, stumbling back. Air rushed into her lungs, clear, pure.

She didn't give herself, or him, a moment to recover. She gathered her skirts in her hands and ran, darting off the path and into the trees.

"You can't escape!" he shouted after her. "I will find you."

Not while she drew breath, and oh that breath tasted sweet right now. She wanted to run, she wanted to fly up the fells behind the forest. But she knew from experience that the green grass springing up at the base of the trees hid gnarled roots, moss-crusted rocks. She had to be careful if she was to reach safety.

She could hear him behind her, blundering along, cursing at the branches that must reach for his coat, his face. A thud and a string of oaths told her one of the rocks had found its prey.

But the forest was her friend. She'd grown up in these woods. Though trees had fallen and new ones grown to replace them, this was still her home. She scrambled over stumps, wove her way among the saplings. She lost her hat, her basket, but never did she lose her way or her purpose.

The occasional pine gave way to oak and birch, and she knew that Kendrick Hall was a good mile away. That meant Dallsten Manor lay a similar distance behind her. Had she felt safe cutting across the path again, she might make her way to the right and the fields beyond. Only the empty fells rose on her left; they would offer no rescue. Indeed she was far enough away from anyone who might help that no one would hear her if she called.

But their location also meant that Haygood couldn't block all routes to escape. She just had to keep moving, reach Kendrick Hall, and she was safe.

Something whizzed past her cheek, and the bark of the tree ahead of her exploded even as she heard the roar of a pistol.

Haygood was armed.

Heart hammering, she ducked behind a massive oak and put her back against it. The bark bit into her fingers as she fought for breath once more. Pistols only had a single shot before they had to be reloaded. She had a few precious seconds to lose him before he fired again.

Lord, please, protect me. Show me how to get away.

She listened, but the only sound was the breeze moving through the branches. Prentice Haygood was stalking her, like a gamekeeper intent on a fox. She had to be more clever.

She'd played in these woods as a child, running with Jamie in a game of catch-me-who-can. Then, Adele or a Kendrick groom or footman had kept watch. There was no one watching over her now except her Heavenly Father. She'd fenced with Vaughn along the path when he'd first come to Dallsten Manor, using trees and rocks to their advantage. Now she didn't have her blade to defend herself.

But she could still play the game, still use the forest for help. She had to. This time, she was playing for much greater stakes—her life.

On the path beside the forest Will's heart was hammering nearly as hard, at Vaughn's revelation.

"Haygood is your traitor?" Will cried. "It can't be. He just proposed to your cousin. He claimed to love her."

Vaughn frowned, rubbing his chin with one hand. "It's possible he does love her. She tends to have that effect on a fellow."

Will included. But now was no time to declare his undying devotion. His concern was all for Samantha.

"Then you don't think he'll hurt her," he challenged.

Vaughn's smile was confident. "Not with all of us to protect her."

Will could not be so certain. When he'd interrupted Haygood and Samantha, he'd thought the man looked too intense, like a watch too tightly wound. It was possible he merely took her rejection hard. But given Vaughn's tale it was just as likely more was afoot.

"He followed her a few minutes ago, into the woods," Will reported. "I cannot like it. I'm going after them."

Vaughn inclined his head. "A wise precaution, though I'm certain my cousin can hold her own."

As if to belie his words, from the forest to their left, a shot rang out.

Will jerked even as Vaughn's hand darted to his side as if reaching for a blade. Will started for the trees.

"If I'm not back in a quarter hour," he flung over his shoulder, "send reinforcements."

"You have ten minutes," Vaughn called. "Then I bring an army."

Will dashed into the woods, but as soon as the trees closed around him, he slowed. The shot could have come from the Dallsten Manor gamekeeper or even the Kendrick Hall gamekeeper considering how close they had walked to his estate. One of the other Everards or Jamie might have taken out a gun for a go. But given that Samantha's life could hang in the balance, Will refused to take chances.

He located the main riding path through the forest easily enough. He'd ridden this way—first as a youth and then as the Earl of Kendrick. He knew its turns, its rises and falls, the places where tree roots made footing uneven. He was familiar with the bird calls that echoed at dawn and dusk, the scent of pine and damp oak. Now every sense was focused on picking out the aberrant, the unusual—the headlong flight of a terrified woman and the pursuit of her attacker.

But the forest was too quiet, as if Will was its lone denizen. He knew that couldn't be right. Foxes made their dens here; marmots roamed the fells. They too cowered away from the predator.

Will smiled. No, Samantha would never cower. And silence could be her friend rather than her enemy. Right now it was his friend as well.

He stole along the path, his gaze ever moving, ears attuned to the rustle of bushes, the snap of a branch or twig. Through the treetops, he could see that the sun had reached its zenith, the shadows short in every direction, giving no clue as to east or west, north or south.

Haygood could easily miss his direction. But Will knew these lands too well to mistake his way.

Haygood must be behind her, which meant Samantha's best choice was to make for the hall. For a moment he had a vision of her lying on the shadowed grasses, golden tresses marred with blood. No! He would not allow it. He could not lose her.

Father, protect her!

Fear stabbed at him. He'd whispered the same prayer for Peg, and she'd been taken from him. This is what it meant to open his heart again, loss and fear and anxiety. Some part of him demanded to know whether the effort to love was worth the cost.

Where Samantha was concerned, he had no more doubts.

Ahead to his right he caught a flash of blue, and his breath caught. Too large to be one of the flowers that sprang up among the trees, too low to be a bird's wing. He started to call out and immediately thought better of it. No reason to startle her or give away her position. No reason to alert Haygood she had help. He turned off the path, climbed over a fallen tree and followed.

That he had sighted Samantha was soon apparent. There was no mistaking sunlight gleaming on her hair or the flutter of her cambric skirt. But where was Haygood?

Will paused long enough to glance around. They had crossed onto his land; he sighted the cleft just ahead where the stream trickled down from the fells through mossy rocks and thick fern rising to Will's waist. Behind and to either side, nothing moved, and Will could see no sign of a white cravat, a pale face.

Had the man given up? Or had Will been wrong in his assessment? But if he had been wrong, why was

Samantha fleeing through the trees instead of walking along the path?

Whatever was happening, he needed to bring this chase to an end. Even a woman of Samantha's stamina must be tiring. Glancing ahead, he realized he'd lost sight of her and puffed out a sigh. Well, she'd have to find some way to cross that stream. He merely had to wait along the banks, perhaps take a chance and call to her.

He started forward once more, ducking under a low-hanging branch. He rose just in time to find another branch swinging at him. It hit him square in the upper chest, slamming into him. He stumbled back with a gasp of breath that hurt.

Samantha came hurtling out of the wood, dead tree limb in both hands, raised as if to strike. She met his gaze and skidded to stop. Her brown eyes were huge, her hair tumbled down around her shoulders in a cape of gold, and a stripe of green marred her fair cheek.

"Oh, Will," she cried. The branch fell from her fingers, and she launched herself into his arms.

Will caught her, held her close, thanksgiving eclipsing any pain from his stinging chest. She trembled against him, arms wrapped around his waist, face buried in his cravat. Relief merged into a tenderness that shook him, and he could only stand there, eyes closed, breathing in the scent of roses.

Thank You, Lord!

She pulled back first, leaving him chilled.

"I'm so sorry!" she said, face anguished. "I meant that for Haygood. Are you hurt?"

Will shrugged and winced as his ribs protested. "Nothing that won't mend. If I'd been shorter, though, you would have taken my head off."

"That was the general idea," she said with charming disregard for her former suitor's health. She bent and retrieved her branch. "He shot at me, Will! He has gone completely mad, all because I refused to marry him!"

"It seems it wasn't just your refusal that sent him around the bend," Will replied. He glanced about, but still could find no sign of her assailant. Haygood could be anywhere—hiding beside a tree, crouching behind a rock. By now he had to have reloaded. Was he taking aim?

The thought chilled him further, and he found himself reaching for Samantha's arm, drawing her against him once more. She blinked in surprise, but at his gesture or his words, he wasn't sure.

"What shall we do?" she asked.

"We will see you home," Will replied, determination building. "I have a great deal to tell you about your so-called suitor, but it will have to wait until you're safely back at the manor."

"You forget," she said, pulling away from him. "Haygood is between us and my home. We should head for Kendrick Hall instead. Far more people there."

Will grinned. "There will be far more people in the woods shortly. Your cousin Vaughn gave me ten minutes to find you before turning out the guard. By the location of the sun, I'd say they'll be here any moment."

He thought she would smile as well, but she did not look comforted. "Do they know he is armed?"

"We heard the shot," Will explained. "They'll be prepared."

She took a breath as if he had relieved a concern. "Good. Then you and I need only stay out of sight until he's captured."

She wanted to hide? His bold Samantha? The move

was so unlike her that Will looked closer. Her gown was speckled with leaves, the hem torn and frayed. Her bare arms were crossed with angry red welts where branches must have lashed her. But worse were the purpling bands around her neck, four along the sides and one in the center.

Anger was a poker in Will's side. Haygood had tried to strangle her! Small wonder she shrank from facing him. How dare Haygood treat her this way!

Will put his hand on her arm. "You are safe with me. I promise he will not hurt you again."

Her lips trembled, as if she could not find the words. He could not find the will to resist her. He bent and kissed her, once, softly, a seal on his promise.

A seal he found difficult to break.

When he straightened, her smile said she'd felt the same. "We need to get out of sight," she reminded him.

If she worried for her life, Will was the last one to begrudge her a little peace. "Very well," he said. "There's an old gamekeeper's cottage not far from here."

She brightened. "The troll's lair! I remember. Jamie and I used to play there. It's perfect!"

"Perhaps not as perfect as you'd like," Will warned. "While we wait, we'll have time for me to ask you questions you may not want to answer."

She raised her chin, her former spirit reasserting itself. "Then you should know that I'll do the same. Lead the way."

Chapter Twenty-One

Samantha knew she should not take such comfort in Will loping along beside her as they cut through the woods. She had planned her life for independence, beholden to no one, responsible for too many, always in conflict with her tempestuous emotions. But she had to admit to a certain pleasure when he took her hand and helped her over a fallen tree, and she didn't protest when her hand remained in his for the rest of their walk.

It simply felt…right.

They quickly reached the gamekeeper's cottage at the back of the woods, less than a mile from Kendrick Hall. The cottage was a one-room building of undressed stone with a plank roof crusted with moss. The place was so heavy and shadowed, she still thought it a fitting home for a troll.

Will, it seemed, had no such illusions. He shoved against the door, and it swung open on hinges that protested. He grimaced as if he knew he might have just given away their location.

As he ushered Samantha through the door, she glanced behind, but nothing larger than a leaf was moving in the woods. She could only hope her cousins and servants were just beyond the range of sight and hearing and would capture Haygood before he found her and Will.

The tiny cottage felt like the bolt-hole it was. The stone walls had been paneled in rough wood, speckled with hooks and shelves that had once held the implements of the gamekeeper's trade. A worktable stained dark red in places stood in the center, with a bench on either side. A single window on the south side let in light filtered through the trees.

"Oh, this is perfect," Samantha said, following Will inside and closing the door behind her. "Doesn't it just look like the trolls lived here?" She pointed to the table. "That's where they carved up their victims."

Will chuckled. "Jamie said he never saw our gamekeeper the same way after your story. I can't blame him. I was terrified by Mr. Michaelson when I was a lad and certain he captured more than foxes in those traps he liked to lay out."

Samantha wandered to the empty hearth, where a cast-iron grate stood ready for a log from the forest and an iron poker leaned against the stone, waiting to stoke the flames. "How long should we wait, do you think?" she asked.

"Knowing your cousins, a quarter hour at most." He strolled closer. "Just long enough to settle our differences."

Samantha turned to meet his gaze. In the dim light behind him, she found it hard to be sure of the look on his face—eager to know her secrets? Determined to make her change her mind?

"Differences?" she tried teasing. "I wasn't aware we were at odds, my lord."

She was certain his mouth quirked. "Funny. I thought

you found something objectionable about me. After all, you refused my proposal."

At once she could not look at him and dropped her gaze to the hearth again. "I had my reasons. And I must ask you not to repeat your proposal. I've had quite enough for one day."

Even though she wasn't looking at him, she could hear the humor in his warm voice. "Very well. I'll wait at least until tomorrow."

The giggle came out more easily than she'd expected. "Very gentlemanly of you."

Out of the corner of her eye she could see him spread his hands. "I do my best. Will you answer me another question, then?"

"I'll try," she said, poking at a loose stone in the hearth with her boot. She waited for him to speak again—asking about Haygood, about her reasons for not marrying, about her understanding with his brother. Perhaps they had some differences to settle after all!

"Do you love me?" he asked.

If he had shot her with an arrow at such a close range she could not have felt the wound more deeply. Everything about her rebelled at answering. Her shoulders tightened even as her hands fisted at her sides. The dusty air in the cottage seemed to be caught in her lungs.

"That is a highly impertinent question," she managed.

"I was under the impression you Everards value impertinence," he replied, voice calm and reasoned. "And you didn't answer me."

How could she answer? Did she love him? She loved how he guided Jamie, with a kind and deft touch that usually spared the young man's consequence. She loved how well he rode and fenced, head high, smile on his lips, as if enjoying every moment. She loved how he treated her with respect, something she'd come to expect in her family but something she'd occasionally missed in other gentlemen of her class. She loved the way he humbly worshipped. She loved the sound of his laugh and the touch of his hand. Was all that really love? A love strong enough to withstand her family legacy?

"I don't know," she told the hearth. "I'm not sure I know what the love between a man and a woman should be."

She could feel him standing there, still a comforting presence even with his questions.

"You surprise me," he murmured. "Surely you've seen love. Look at your cousins and their wives."

"I have," she assured him, daring to glance up at him. He was watching her, and she could see that his dark brows were down in a frown, as if he were truly trying to understand.

"They seem content in each other's company, happy," she admitted, "and the attraction between each pair cannot be denied."

His hand slipped over hers, warmed her, and she felt as if the connection ran all the way to her heart. "Then what do you think is lacking between the two of us?" he murmured.

She made herself pull away. "A future, I fear, my lord."

He angled his head to meet her gaze, eyes narrowed so that she could no longer see the deep green in the shadows. "Do you think I would be unfaithful? What basis have I given you?"

"None," she promised. "I imagine you would honor your vows just as I would. My mother and father honored their vows from what I can tell. They were highly attracted to each other. For a short while, they were happy. And then they were miserable."

He straightened. "Why? What changed?"

"Nothing," she assured him. "Don't you see? It was all an illusion, an attraction based on the fire of emotion that grew as dark as this hearth." She kicked at a stone to prove her point. "It really wasn't love."

He crossed his arms over his chest. "And you think me equally blinded by your beauty."

"I am not that vain, Will. But more than one fellow has been prompted to propose because he found me, or the Everard legacy, attractive."

His arms fell to his sides. "I am no fortune hunter."

She didn't want to see him in that light. She never wanted to see a fellow as so mercenary. But she'd learned well from her mistakes. She took a step closer to him, daring to inhale the spicy scent that clung to him like his foreign past.

"Even you could be tempted, Will. Jamie told me about Kendrick Hall. If you don't marry well, you could lose it."

He drew himself up. "I don't need to marry for money. I have a plan, and it will bear fruit in time."

"Then you wouldn't mind waiting to marry me, say for a year?"

Now she watched him, looking for any sign of deception. His eyes remained narrowed, his brow furrowed, but his color seemed to be rising, as if she'd discovered something he wanted hidden.

Oh, Father, please, not him! You know my feelings better than I know them. You know how tempted I am to accept his proposal. But I will refuse him if he plans to capture the legacy instead of my heart!

"If that pleases you, of course I'll wait," he said. "Though I cannot imagine either of us would be any happier waiting than marrying by license in the next month."

"A month?" Samantha felt as if she could draw breath. "You'd wait an entire month?"

His frown deepened. "Certainly. I imagine even a lady of your talents needs some time to prepare. And we must have the banns read or I'd have to ride to London and return with a special license. All that takes time."

"There's Gretna Green," she said, refusing to take her eyes off him.

He shrugged. "Gretna Green is not nearly as romantic as the stories make it out to be. I'd prefer you to have the wedding you deserve, with our friends and family around us."

He could not know how his words warmed her, yet still she could not trust them.

"A lovely picture. Would you still choose to paint it if you knew I'd lose everything?"

"What are you talking about?" he demanded.

"You see," Samantha explained, "if I'm not married before my twenty-fifth birthday, three days from now, my father's will dictates that everything not entailed be given to charity. That will include the bulk of the funds invested in the Exchange, all our ships except my cousin Richard's, even Dallsten Manor. I'll have sufficient funds to live, and of course my cousins keep their inheritances, but everything else will be given away or tied up for my heir."

He shook his head, and her heart sank. "What was your father thinking?" he said.

"Oh, my father knew me too well," she replied and hoped the bitterness wasn't as evident as it felt. "He was afraid I'd be too much like him, refusing to wed until late in life, chasing after independence, becoming too headstrong. He thought to offer me an incentive I couldn't refuse. That's where he went wrong. I do refuse it. I won't marry, to please him or anyone else."

"I can't believe this," Will protested. "You refuse me, you refuse all your other suitors, to spite your father? Are you willing to let your past rob you of a future?"

He didn't understand. She had to make him understand. "I'm not trying to spite my father. I'm trying to avoid the path my father and mother took. I refuse to end up like her, allowing my emotions to rule me, to drive me to do the unspeakable."

No! She'd almost said it aloud! She snapped shut her lips and stared at the grate. Unfortunately it was hard to see it through the tears that were as determined to come as she was to stop them.

"So that's the issue," he said softly. "I knew something was troubling you. Tell me. What did your mother do when she became unhappy in her marriage? Did she take her frustrations out of you? Run away from him?"

"Neither." She swallowed. Did she dare trust him? He was the Earl of Kendrick; the churchyard came under his keep. If it became widely known that her mother had committed suicide, he could insist that she be exhumed, move her out of hallowed ground. The action would blacken her mother's name, bring up stories that were best left buried as well.

Yet now that she knew him better, she knew he would do nothing to hurt her, or her mother.

"What then?" he pressed.

"She took her own life." Just saying the words made her shudder, and he reached out as if to embrace her. She pushed him away.

"Do you understand now, Will?" she challenged. "That's what can come of a marriage based solely on passions—tragedy and pain and children left to carry burdens too heavy for them. Do you fault me for trying to keep the past from repeating itself?"

His face was sad. "Never. But emotion can as easily be light as darkness. Indeed, in this world, you cannot have one without the other. I learned that lesson, to my sorrow. Despite my brother's jeers, my father's council, I married Peggy Demesne in a bright cloud of joy. She died bearing my child, and I was so young and heartbroken I left him, for years, trying to forget."

"Oh, Will," she said. "But you came back. You're here helping Jamie now. He loves you."

"And I love him. But I never forgot the pain of losing my first love, never even contemplated falling in love again. Until I met you."

He opened his arms, inviting her in. How could she refuse? She no longer knew the right answer to his proposal, was no longer sure of her way. But right here, right now, she wanted to comfort him, feel herself comforted.

She entered his embrace, slipped her arms about his waist, rested her head against his chest. Warmth slid over her, loosened stiff muscles, made breathing easier. He held her, simply, reverently, and for a moment, that was all that mattered.

"I love you, Samantha Everard," he murmured against her temple. "Please think about my offer. It's taken me seventeen years and three continents to find the courage to make it."

How odd that he, who had faced down Barbary pirates and nearly stopped a war, should need courage to propose to her. Is that what she lacked? How could that be? She was an Everard. Her family had fought off murderous servants, devious French spies and a madman intent on ruling England. How could a little thing like marriage seem so terrifying?

Yet she was terrified, terrified of losing herself, of losing her life, of leaving behind a motherless child. She'd thought she was doing all this so nobly, but it was fear that held her back. Why hadn't she seen that before?

Did her cousins know? No, they would have scolded her, helped her overcome it had they realized. Had her father known when he'd penned his will so many years ago now? She'd never understood his choices, in marrying on a whim, in leaving her for months at a time, in bringing men here to Dallsten Manor to plot treason under cover of the summer party. She could still see those men, streaming through the front door of Dallsten Manor, faces alight with pleasure. She'd thought it was the party that so moved them. Now she knew better.

Even as the picture of her father's men faded, one face stood out among the crowd. Samantha gasped and pulled back, staring up at Will, aghast.

"Will! I remembered! Prentice Haygood used to come to the summer party with my father. He was much thinner then, and clean shaven, but I'd swear it was him."

"Very good, my dear," Haygood said, pushing open the door with the barrel of his pistol. "I knew you were too clever for your own good, and mine."

Will took one look at Haygood in the doorway and shoved Samantha behind him, mind reeling. Vaughn and the other Everards and their servants had to be close. All Will had to do was make Haygood leave or keep him talking for a few minutes, and Samantha would be safe.

"If you hope to escape," Will said, "go now. The Everards are onto you."

"Well, that's news to me," Samantha muttered behind him. He felt her move and swung both arms back to cage her in.

"But do they have proof?" Haygood ventured closer. His brow glistened with sweat, and Will could see it trickling through the beard on his flabby cheeks. "I've tried to find it, but to no avail. Can they bring me before the magistrates?"

"If my cousins don't, I will," Samantha declared.

Will grabbed one of her hands and squeezed it, hoping she understood that her best choice lay in silence. The less Haygood focused on her, the better.

"I'd flee for the Continent if I were you," Will offered. "I won't stop you."

By the way Samantha shifted behind him, he thought she would have preferred he had.

"What do you think I did eight years ago?" Haygood replied, edging into the room as if he suspected Will of hiding a weapon instead of an irate woman behind him. "When the Everards captured Lord Widmore, I knew I had no option but to run."

Lord Widmore? Then the mysterious lord who had started all this was Imogene's father, the man who had held the title before it had been re-created for Vaughn Everard. Small wonder Samantha's cousin chose not to name the fellow. It was one more reason for Samantha to keep silent on the matter, too. She'd been protecting her friend Imogene.

"Then you know how to survive there," Will encouraged Haygood. He nodded toward the door. "If you leave now, you might have enough of a head start to evade them."

"What are you doing?" Samantha whispered against his back.

"Trust me," he whispered back.

"It won't do," Haygood insisted. "Italy can be an expensive place, particularly for someone of my tastes." He stopped a few feet from Will, eying him, pistol at the ready.

"You won't find money here," Will assured him, keeping himself between the gun and Samantha.

"Nor did I intend to," Haygood said. "I'll have funds aplenty once my uncle obligingly dies. But I can't inherit if I'm branded a traitor."

"So you changed your looks," Samantha piped up, peering around Will despite his efforts. "Attempted to persuade me you were a good friend. Why not just stay away?"

"Because I didn't know if you remembered! I had to be certain there was nothing to incriminate me, in London or here."

"You!" she cried, and Will felt her drawing herself up. "You robbed the London house!"

"I took nothing!" he protested.

"Because there was nothing to take! And there was nothing here either, yet that didn't stop you from hitting me over the head, and to no purpose. You'd told me you were in the muniment room. I wouldn't have suspected anything had I found you there."

He grimaced. "I panicked. I thought you'd come to unmask me in private."

"If I had come to unmask you," Samantha informed him, "I would have brought the constable."

He raised his pistol, and Will stiffened, pushing Samantha behind him once more.

"All the more reason to finish you off now," Haygood said, inspecting the gun as if to make sure it was properly primed, "before your devoted cousins show up. It's all your fault, you know. If you had married me, you'd have had reason to keep quiet, for the scandal would have affected you, too. But if you die, your cousin Jerome Everard inherits. He'll never sell Dallsten Manor. If the secret is there, it will molder away, unnoticed. And I'll be safe."

He nodded to Will as he drew a second small pistol from his greatcoat. "I'll have to kill you, too, Kendrick. Terribly sorry. You were a good sport, at least at first."

Will's mind clicked through options with lightning speed. One pistol he might have avoided. Two were more likely to be successful in hitting him or Samantha or both.

"On my word," he murmured to Samantha, as Haygood inspected the second pistol, "run for the door. I'll hold him as long as I can." He squeezed Samantha's hand, felt the strength, the promise as she squeezed back. He knew what he intended to do was right. It was something he only wished he could have done years ago, when Peg and his brother had lain in harm's way.

Thank you, Lord, for giving me the opportunity I lacked those years ago. Please honor my sacrifice and protect Samantha.

"Now!" he shouted and leaped across the space at Haygood.

Chapter Twenty-Two

"**W**ill!" Samantha cried, but the pistol roared, and he fell.

Her heart fell with him. What had she done? She'd tried so hard to prevent pain. Had she caused bloodshed instead? The despair of it threatened to overwhelm her.

No! She raised her head, squared her shoulders. She hadn't pointed that pistol. She hadn't plotted against England. She and Will were innocent. But that didn't mean she was helpless.

She seized the fireplace poker and advanced on Haygood. "Drop that pistol and move away from him."

Haygood's hand shook, and his face glowed a ghastly white in the dim light, but he managed to point his unspent gun at her. "I fear not, Lady Everard. It is my life or yours."

"They will find you," she predicted, taking another step. A little closer and she should be able to knock the gun out of his hand. The poker weighed heavily in her grip, far more than her blade and not nearly so balanced. But with Will's life at stake, she thought she could wield a battle-ax. A shame the gamekeeper hadn't thought to leave one behind!

"They won't know to look for me," he insisted. "With you both dead and hidden in this hovel, they will think it was a lover's quarrel."

The story had enough holes to march a regiment through. As if even Haygood understood that, his hand shook so hard she was certain he could easily fail to hit a fatal target if he fired.

"And Lord Kendrick put a ball in his own chest?" she pointed out. "Not likely."

From outside came the sound of horses and the calls of men intent on their search. Haygood glanced at the door.

Please, Lord, protect Will and guide my hand!

Samantha lunged, poker extended. Haygood cried out as metal struck his hand, and the pistol fell to the floor, spitting its deadly ball into the wood with a roar like its twin.

Haygood stumbled back, turned to run.

Samantha didn't pursue him. "Vaughn, Richard, Jerome!" she shouted. "In here!" Then she threw herself down beside Will.

His body lay still, and she feared what she would find. Was life even now seeping away? Gut clenching, she touched his shoulder and felt it rise with a breath.

Thank You, Lord!

She bent and turned him ever so gently. His face was bloodless, his eyes closed. Under him the floor was redder than the table nearby. A wave of nausea threatened. She swallowed it down.

Cradling his head and shoulders in her lap, she pressed her fingers against the tide flowing from his upper chest. She felt his heart pounding and prayed that it would keep pumping.

"Will," she murmured. "Can you hear me?"

His eyes opened, and his gaze, dimmed with pain, met hers.

"Is it bad?" she asked.

He managed a smile she was sure was all bravado. "I'll survive."

"You'd better," she warned.

With the crack of a boot heel on wood, the door was smashed open, and her cousins swarmed into the room.

Haygood held up his hands. "I surrender!"

Jerome put a sword to his throat as if taking no chances. Richard's gaze was sweeping the room as if to make sure no other assailants lay waiting. She could see their servants crowding in the doorway, eyes wide, faces determined.

Vaughn rushed to Samantha's side. "Are you all right?"

"Fine," she assured him. "Lord Kendrick saved my life."

"And took the worst of it, it seems," Richard said, crouching beside them. He looked Will over, reached out a hand, then stopped. "May I, my lord?"

Will nodded, his head moving against Samantha. So weakly! Fear reached clawed fingers for her, and she fought it back. She pulled away her hand, refused to look at the warm stickiness she felt clinging to it.

Richard probed at the gaping wound. She knew each time Will stiffened, every tightening of his lips, every contraction of his muscles. She took his hand and squeezed hard.

"How is he?" Jerome asked, coming to join them. Samantha glanced up long enough to see that Haygood had been removed. She could only imagine some of the servants had been dispatched to return him to Dallsten Manor or the magistrate's office in the village.

"He needs a physician," Richard reported. He pulled out a handkerchief and held it to the wound. "Soon."

Pain shot through Samantha. "You'll be fine, Will. I know it."

Her cousins exchanged glances, but Will merely smiled at her.

Vaughn unwound his cravat and tossed it to Richard. "Use this to bind the wound. Can you get him to Kendrick Hall while I ride for the physician?"

"Done," Richard said.

She ought to protest. They were leaving her out again, taking matters into their own hands as if she were still a child. But at the moment she was willing to let them. Her greatest concern was Will.

"I'm coming with you," she told Richard. She was merely thankful that her cousins knew her well enough not to argue.

With Jerome on one side and Richard on the other, they managed to get Will to his feet and out the door to the horses.

"I can ride," he assured them, but they put him up in front of Richard as if he were an untried child instead of a bruising rider. Samantha was glad her cousins had thought to bring her horse, sidesaddle in place. She had to hitch up her skirts a bit to mount, but she would have managed worse to remain at Will's side.

Vaughn didn't even wait until they were settled before tearing down the path for the village. The remaining servants were sent to alert the residents of Dallsten Manor, and Jerome accompanied Richard and Samantha to Kendrick Hall.

She had ridden this path so many times, but never with such a heavy heart. She wished Will was sitting in front of her, his head leaning back onto her shoulder, her arms holding him steady. Instead the best she could do was keep her horse close to Richard's, her hand ready to reach out if needed.

Will swayed in the saddle, a far cry from his usual confident self. His face remained white, and she could see blood soaking through Vaughn's cravat. Though he said nothing to her, his lips moved as if he were uttering a prayer.

She felt a similar prayer welling from her heart. *Lord, please save him. Don't take him away from Jamie, away from me!*

Trust in the Lord with all thine heart; and lean not unto thine own understanding. In all thy ways acknowledge Him, and He shall direct thy paths.

That's what she needed now, to trust and to follow the path before her. She raised her head and rode.

The moment they were in sight of the stables, Jerome galloped ahead, calling for help. Before Will's horse had even stopped moving his staff had gathered. They had him off the horse and into the house in a very short time, settling him upstairs in his bedchamber. A fresh bandage was in place, his valet and Jamie in attendance. A helpful maid had washed Samantha's hand of Will's precious blood, offered to find her a room where she could lie down with a cold compress.

She had never lain down with a cold compress in her life.

So she'd retired to the entirely too formal, thoroughly unsatisfactory, withdrawing room to wait.

"Care to explain what happened?" Jerome asked as he and Richard waited with her.

She glanced at her two oldest cousins sitting so calmly as if having no care that their travel dirt might smudge the white upholstery of the chairs. Though they were brothers, they did not resemble each other in temperament or looks. Dark-haired Jerome was cool cunning; red-headed Richard was patient calculation. They had each borne the pain of loss before finding the women they now loved and called wife. Still, she did not think they could possibly understand the things going through her mind right then. She barely understood herself!

"Haygood attempted to kill me," she reported as she stood near the hearth. "Twice." She pulled down at the neck of her gown to emphasize the bruises she could see in the mirror over the marble fireplace. By the darkening of her cousins' gazes, she was certain Haygood was much safer away from Kendrick Hall.

"I stopped him the first time," she continued, returning her gown to its proper place. "Lord Kendrick stopped him the second time by putting himself in front of me. I hit the miscreant before he could make another attempt."

"Well done," Richard put in.

She shrugged off his praise, turning to his brother. "Haygood was at the summer party, Jerome. He was one of the traitors who followed the former Lord Widmore."

Jerome and Richard exchanged glances, and she realized what they were going to say before they said it.

"You knew!" She advanced at her cousins, fingers clenched at her sides. "You knew, and you never told me!"

Jerome held up his hands as if in surrender. "We were only trying to protect you."

"And a jolly good job you did, to be sure." She glared at them both, and they each found something else to admire about the withdrawing room.

Samantha dropped her hands. "When will you learn that I'm not a child to be cosseted?"

Jerome rose. "I no longer see you as a child, Samantha. But you cannot ask me to stop trying to protect you."

Richard stood as well. "That is a gentleman's duty to those he loves."

With them on either side so tall and righteous, she should probably back down, but the emotions of the day were still pushing at her, and she simply could not let things stand.

"And is it not a lady's as well?" she demanded. "Would you expect Adele to sit calmly while you were in danger, Jerome?"

"Certainly not," he started, "but…"

"And you, Richard," Samantha persisted, "do you imagine Claire waiting at home while you sailed off having adventures?"

Richard's mouth turned up. "She hated it the first time. I don't think she'd allow it the second."

"Then why," she finished, "do you think I would be any more willing?"

They exchanged glances again, and she wanted to shove between them, demand they look at her instead. But she stood, watching them, daring them with her gaze and her high chin to continue this odious habit of attempting to limit her life.

"Perhaps it's because we learned of you so late," Jerome tried, charming smile, complete with dimples, popping into place.

"You are like a sister to us," Richard reminded her, gaze more solemn.

"And you are like the brothers I never had," Samantha agreed. "But you don't see me trying to order you around or protect you from every little mishap."

"No," Richard replied. "You only tried to pair us up with our wives."

Samantha grinned at him. "And I succeeded rather well."

"That you did, infant," Vaughn declared, striding into the room. "The physician has been retrieved and is conferring with Lord Kendrick as we speak. What have I missed?"

"A scolding," Richard muttered, returning to his seat.

"A course correction," Samantha replied. "Isn't that what you call it when your vessel drifts? You three are seriously off course if you think I cannot take care of myself."

"Now, then, infant," Vaughn started, moving deeper into the room.

Samantha stopped him with a look. "And no more of that. I wasn't even an infant when you met me. I certainly cannot be called one now."

Vaughn snapped a nod. "Very well, your ladyship, the Baroness Everard." He swept her a deep bow.

"Cousin Samantha will do," she informed him. "I suppose you knew about Haygood as well."

He straightened and eyed her. "Something other than he is a miserable worm?"

"Give it up," Richard advised. "She remembered him."

"Ah." Vaughn went to take up Samantha's former place by the hearth. "Yes, I knew. We've been watching for him to return from the Continent for eight years."

"And you never said a word to me," she accused, following him.

"There are some things you do not need to know, inf... Cousin," Vaughn returned.

"When those things could affect my happiness, and my life, I disagree. There have been far too many secrets in this family. Nothing good ever came of them."

They could not argue with her about that. She could see it by the way their gazes dropped.

"Go home," she told the three of them. "Tell your wives what happened. I will return as soon as I know that Lord Kendrick is well."

She thought they might protest, but they had apparently taken her request to heart, for they bowed over her hand, promised her their devotion and left. She could only hope this would mark a new beginning in their family.

And so she waited, and her thoughts closed in on her.

She hated waiting. She'd waited months between visits by her father; she'd waited years to go to London for her Season; she'd waited all her life to find someone like Will. She could no longer deny that what she felt was love. She wished she was the one lying in that bed, anything to spare him pain, save his life.

Greater love hath no man than this, that a man lay down his life for his friends.

How had she been so blind? Will had too many responsibilities and too much honor to merely throw away his life. Jamie needed his father's strength; Will knew that. Kendrick Hall might fall but for Will's guidance. With all that at stake he had put himself in the path of a bullet, risked his life, to save her, a woman who had given him no hope of returning his love, no reason to expect she would even stay in this valley.

That was love.

That was the patient, kind, self-sacrifice the Bible

spoke of. That was the love she'd always dreamed might exist, the love her father and mother had never found. That was the love on which to build a marriage, a family, a future.

"Oh, Will," she murmured to the ceiling, "forgive me."

She only prayed she'd have a chance to tell him in person.

Will swam to consciousness as the physician was rebandaging his shoulder. The searing pain had been reduced to a dull ache. Glancing around, he found he was in his bedchamber, the familiar blue damask bed hangings on either side of him, his walnut wardrobe and dressing table nearby. He didn't remember reaching the room, only Samantha holding his hand and promising all would be well.

She appeared to be correct, as the physician hurried to assure him. "Missed the bone and your lung," the man reported, packing up the instruments he'd apparently used to remove the bullet. "You'll be sore for some time, and we'll need to monitor the use of your right arm, but you should survive so long as infection does not set in." With that cheery thought he left instructions with Will's valet, then promised to see Will the next day.

Will was more aware of Jamie hovering in the background. As soon as the physician had vacated the spindle-backed chair that had been drawn up to the bed, Jamie took it.

"You gave me quite a scare, Father," he said, fumbling with his already crushed cravat. His eyes were too large in his face, reminding Will of the day he'd first seen his son again.

"So you're not ready to have a go at being earl just yet," Will teased, hoping to reassure both of them.

Jamie smiled, but his color remained pale. "No, sir." He glanced over his shoulder as the valet let the physician out, then refocused on Will. "Mr. Haygood is in the village jail, by the way. Lord Widmore plans to return him to London after the summer party to stand trial for treason."

Then Samantha was safe. Will relaxed against his pillow. "Good. And I know the truth about your uncle's death. I'll be glad to tell you the details, if you tell me something first. Where is Samantha?"

Jamie's smile hitched up. "Downstairs, wearing out the new carpet in the withdrawing room. I gather you two have come to an understanding."

"Not yet," Will warned. "But I realize what's kept her from accepting marriage, and I believe I can overcome her reservations. Before I do, I must ask you—would you have any trouble accepting her as my wife?"

"None," Jamie promised, and so quickly Will had to believe him. Then his son made a face. "But I won't be calling her Mother. That would be entirely too odd."

"Agreed," Will said with a smile. "With her permission, you may continue to call her Samantha in private and use your ladyship or the countess in public. Assuming she'll have me, of course."

Jamie rose. "Oh, she'll have you. You don't threaten everyone you love with murder if they fail to take good care of a certain gentleman unless you have marriage in mind."

"You never know," Will said with a laugh cut short by a throb from his shoulder. "She is an Everard, after all."

Jamie had reached the door. "Then you'll just have to ask her," he said. "I'll bring her back shortly."

Will watched as the door shut. Indeed he found it ridiculously hard to take his eyes off the portal as the moments ticked by. His valet asked after Will's injury, and Will waved him away with his other hand.

Could he convince Samantha that he loved her? Was his promise that he would be beside her through thick and thin enough to let her know she needn't fear the darker side of her emotions? Was there anything he could do or say that would make his second proposal more successful than his first?

The door opened, and Samantha flew into the room. Will braced himself, but she checked her headlong flight just short of the bed and stood beside him, eyes teary, chest heaving.

"Oh, Will," she said. "I'm so sorry!"

"I did tell her the physician's assessment," Jamie assured Will, following her to the bed.

She held up one hand as if to stop him. "I'd already quizzed the man in any event. And I have a great many things to apologize to your father for, if you please."

Jamie raised his brows and began to back away. "Perhaps I should wait in the corridor."

"No need," she said, gaze fixed on Will. "I'd actually like a witness to what I have to say."

"Samantha," Will started, but she had gone down on both knees, so that her face was level with his. Those dark brown eyes were more solemn than he'd ever seen them. The scent of roses drifted over him, sweet.

"I know this is highly unusual," she murmured. "But then, both of us have lived unusual lives." She reached out and took his free hand, her grip strong. "My darling Will, you proposed to me earlier today, and I, in my pigheaded stupidity, refused."

"You aren't stupid," Will corrected her with a smile.

She laughed. "I notice you didn't take exception to the pigheaded part."

Will knew better than to attempt a shrug. "I'm not stupid either."

She sobered. "Indeed you aren't. You are brave and kind and thoughtful, and you have proven that you love me," she sucked in a breath, "more than life, it seems. How could I fail to love such a man? So this time I will ask you. Will you marry me?"

The room was silent, and Will thought Jamie and his valet were holding their breaths. Yet all he could see was Samantha. Her rosy lips were trembling, her face puckered as if she had put all she had into a fervent wish for his acceptance. What man could have refused?

He pulled his hand from hers and touched her cheek.

"My lady, you honor me. I would be the luckiest man alive to be your husband."

She threw her arms around his neck, kissed him with all she was. His shoulder protested. He ignored it. What was a little pain to knowing he would spend the rest of his life with this marvelous woman?

Chapter Twenty-Three

The Dallsten Manor summer party was in full swing. From the carriageway, Samantha could smell the ox roasting on the spit, hear the squeals from the children on the whirligig. Villagers cavorted around the lawn, laughing, calling to friends. Flags flew from every corner of the manor.

She watched with a smile as Justin hit his uncle Richard's ball and tumbled it down the slope into the pond to the cheers of the dozen other children who had joined in his game of smack ball.

"He's getting entirely too good at that," Jamie complained on her right.

He was dressed to join in the fun, in a tweed jacket and chamois trousers. Her travel pelisse with its black military braid seemed far too somber. But the gown of yellow silk packed in her valise was perfect for how she meant to spend her afternoon.

"And I'm glad he's enjoying himself," Samantha countered. "I hope everyone takes as much joy from the day."

"Everyone but Prentice Haygood," Jamie agreed.

"He's still cooling his heels in jail and looking forward to a talk with the War Office."

"Who should be considerably less busy after the news we heard yesterday," Samantha replied.

"Good for Wellington," Jamie agreed. "A decisive victory in Vitoria! I can't believe Napoleon is nearly beaten at last. We've been fighting him for most of my life!"

"Indeed, we have," Will said from the interior of the carriage as his valet climbed down from settling him. "Are you certain you don't want to stay for the celebrations, Samantha? You did promise me a dance."

She'd wanted to dance at the summer party most of her life, even before they'd heard the news about the Battle of Vitoria. This place, these people were part of her. Leaving them would have been a great tragedy. She saw that now.

Leaving Will would have been worse. She knew they were meant to be together. She had convinced him to elope with her to Gretna Green today. That way Dallsten Manor and the legacy would be safe for their children. And she could help ease the burden he carried in worrying about his estate.

The physician had not been pleased with their decision to travel only two days after Will had been shot, but he could not argue that Will was well enough for the journey. Samantha thought Will looked rather handsome in his navy coat, one arm in a crimson sling like some wounded general returning from battle.

She hadn't been sure what her family would think of their plans, but they'd all encouraged her when she'd admitted her and Will's intentions at a late dinner last night. Richard and Jerome had assured her Will was a great fellow; Adele and Claire had promised her happiness lay ahead. Imogene had squealed for joy, clapping her hands and offering a toast.

"I knew you were a clever girl," Mrs. Dallsten Walcott had proclaimed with a superior sniff as she set down her glass. "We'll have the Countess of Kendrick in our family at last."

From the head of the table Vaughn had leveled his silver fork at her as if extending a blade. "If you have any difficulty with the fellow, come see me. I'll be delighted to teach him a thing or two."

Samantha had winked at Imogene. "You forget. I've already beaten him in a fencing match. I don't think we'll need your sword or consequence to settle any difficulties we might have."

She still could not believe those difficulties would not come. But she knew now that she and Will shared a love that could overcome obstacles. She had to put her faith in him and in God.

And now her bags were packed and stowed atop the carriage with Will's. Richard and Claire were journeying with them to act as witnesses so there would be no doubt that this marriage was legitimate and blessed by her family. All she had to do was climb aboard.

She glanced back at the house where she'd grown up, the people who'd known her since she was a child. They were lined up before the door, her cousins, her servants, her neighbors, all smiles, all ready for her to take this next step in her life.

She was ready as well. *Thank You, Lord!*

"Let's go," she said, and Jamie gave her his hand to help her into the carriage.

Handkerchiefs flew, hands waved and voices called in love as the carriage started down the drive, Richard and Claire's following.

"So you're willing to give up dancing for me," Will teased, as if fearing she might succumb to a fit of the dismals despite their upcoming nuptials.

Samantha shook her head. "Oh no, my love. The way I see it, we have the rest of our lives to dance together. Today is only the beginning."

Will slid his good arm about her shoulder, and she snuggled against him. She had come to Dallsten Manor to say goodbye, and instead she'd come home at last.

* * * * *

Dear Reader,

Thank you for choosing *The Heiress's Homecoming*. I hope you enjoyed seeing the last Everard meet her match. I certainly can empathize with Samantha's bewilderment over her future. Making big changes in our lives is seldom easy. As I type this, my youngest son is about to head off to college and make me an empty nester, and my oldest son is about to make me a grandmother! I'm very thankful for them and for the opportunity to keep writing books I love.

If you'd like to learn more about upcoming books, be sure to stop by my website at www.reginascott.com or visit me on my blog at www.nineteenteen.blogspot.com. Blessings!

Regina Scott

QUESTIONS FOR DICUSSION

1. Samantha fears she has inherited more from her father and mother than the Everard legacy. What kinds of stories did you inherit from your family?

2. Samantha fights to keep her emotions from ruling her. When is it appropriate to lead with our feelings?

3. Will struggles to open his heart to love again after the tragic deaths in his family. How can we be open to love at any stage of our lives?

4. Will refuses to dwell on his past in the diplomatic corps. How can our past experiences enrich our lives rather than hold us back?

5. Prentice Haygood's ineffectual facade hides a cunning mind. How can we know a person's true character?

6. Jamie longs to be seen as an adult. How can we help the teens in our lives transition to responsibility?

7. The three male Everard cousins are very protective of their younger cousin Samantha. When does protection hinder our growth as individuals?

8. Samantha sees God's love in the rainbow. Where do you experience God's miracles?

9. Samantha feels as if she's carrying a heavy burden. What makes something a burden in our lives?

10. Samantha struggles with carrying her burden alone. How can we carry the burdens given to us without bowing under them?

11. Everyone in the Evendale valley looks forward to the Everard summer party. What traditions in your family or community do you look forward to?

12. Samantha fences—an unusual pastime for a lady in the early nineteenth century. What are your unusual pastimes? Why did you choose them? What do they say about you?

COMING NEXT MONTH
from Love Inspired® Historical
AVAILABLE APRIL 2, 2013

SECOND CHANCE PROPOSAL
Amish Brides of Celery Fields
Anna Schmidt

John Amman never forgot Lydia Goodloe when he left to make his fortune in the outside world. But when the prodigal son returns to his Amish community will his first love welcome him with open arms?

FAMILY LESSONS
Orphan Train
Allie Pleiter

Plain Jane school teacher Holly Sanders thinks no man will ever love her. But a catastrophe in her small Nebraska town leaves her wondering if she should take a risk with brooding sheriff Mason Wright.

HIS MOUNTAIN MISS
Smoky Mountain Matches
Karen Kirst

Lucian Beaumont is a jaded aristocrat, and Megan O'Malley is a simple farmer's daughter. The terms of his grandfather's will brought them together—and now she's challenging his plans and his heart.

THE BRIDE WORE SPURS
Janet Dean

Self-sufficient tomboy Hannah Parrish will do anything to save her ranch and give her dying father peace of mind, even if it means marrying a widowed rancher determined to protect his heart.

LIHCNM0313

REQUEST YOUR FREE BOOKS!

2 FREE INSPIRATIONAL NOVELS
PLUS 2
FREE
MYSTERY GIFTS

Love Inspired
HISTORICAL
INSPIRATIONAL HISTORICAL ROMANCE

YES! Please send me 2 FREE Love Inspired® Historical novels and my 2 FREE mystery gifts (gifts are worth about $10). After receiving them, if I don't wish to receive any more books, I can return the shipping statement marked "cancel." If I don't cancel, I will receive 4 brand-new novels every month and be billed just $4.49 per book in the U.S. or $4.99 per book in Canada. That's a saving of at least 22% off the cover price. It's quite a bargain! Shipping and handling is just 50¢ per book in the U.S. and 75¢ per book in Canada.* I understand that accepting the 2 free books and gifts places me under no obligation to buy anything. I can always return a shipment and cancel at any time. Even if I never buy another book, the two free books and gifts are mine to keep forever.

102/302 IDN FVXK

Name _____ (PLEASE PRINT) _____

Address _____ Apt. #

City _____ State/Prov. _____ Zip/Postal Code

Signature (if under 18, a parent or guardian must sign)

Mail to the Harlequin® Reader Service:
IN U.S.A.: P.O. Box 1867, Buffalo, NY 14240-1867
IN CANADA: P.O. Box 609, Fort Erie, Ontario L2A 5X3

Want to try two free books from another series?
Call 1-800-873-8635 or visit www.ReaderService.com.

* Terms and prices subject to change without notice. Prices do not include applicable taxes. Sales tax applicable in N.Y. Canadian residents will be charged applicable taxes. Offer not valid in Quebec. This offer is limited to one order per household. Not valid for current subscribers to Love Inspired Historical books. All orders subject to credit approval. Credit or debit balances in a customer's account(s) may be offset by any other outstanding balance owed by or to the customer. Please allow 4 to 6 weeks for delivery. Offer available while quantities last.

Your Privacy—The Harlequin® Reader Service is committed to protecting your privacy. Our Privacy Policy is available online at www.ReaderService.com or upon request from the Harlequin Reader Service.

We make a portion of our mailing list available to reputable third parties that offer products we believe may interest you. If you prefer that we not exchange your name with third parties, or if you wish to clarify or modify your communication preferences, please visit us at www.ReaderService.com/consumerschoice or write to us at Harlequin Reader Service Preference Service, P.O. Box 9062, Buffalo, NY 14269. Include your complete name and address.

LIH13

"You saved us," Holly said, as she moved toward Sheriff Wright.

He looked at her, his blue eyes brittle and hollow. She so rarely viewed those eyes—downcast as they often were or hidden in the shadow of his hat brim. "No."

"But it is true." Mason Wright was the kind of man who would take Arlington's loss as a personal failure, ignoring all the lives—including hers—he had just saved, and she hated that. Hated that she'd fail in this attempt just as she failed in *every* attempt to make him see his worth.

He held her gaze just then. "No," he repeated, but only a little softer. Then his attention spread out beyond her to take in the larger crisis at hand.

"Is she the other agent?" He nodded toward Rebecca Sterling and the upset children, now surrounded by the few other railcar passengers. "Liam mentioned a Miss…"

"Sterling, yes, that's her. Liam!" Holly suddenly remembered the brave orphan boy who'd run off to get help. "Is Liam all right?"

"Shaken, but fine. Clever boy."

"I was so worried, sending him off."

He looked at her again, this time with something she could almost fool herself into thinking was admiration. "It was quick and clever. If anyone saved the day here, it was you."

Holly blinked. From Mason Wright, that was akin to a complimentary gush. "It was the only thing I could think of to do."

A child's cry turned them both toward the bedlam surrounding Miss Sterling. The children were understandably out of control with fear and shock, and Miss Sterling didn't seem to be in any shape to take things in hand. Who would be in such a situation?

She would, that's who. Holly was an excellent teacher with a full bag of tricks at her disposal to wrangle unruly children. With one more deep breath, she strode off to save the day a second time.

Don't miss FAMILY LESSONS
by Allie Pleiter, available April 2013
from Love Inspired Historical.

Love Inspired HISTORICAL

In the fan-favorite miniseries
Amish Brides of Celery Fields

ANNA SCHMIDT

presents

Second Chance Proposal

*The sweetest homecoming.
He came home…for her.
A love rekindled.*

Lydia Goodloe hasn't forgotten a single thing about John Amman—including the way he broke her heart eight years ago. Since John left Celery Fields to make his fortune, Lydia has devoted herself to teaching. John risked becoming an outcast to give Lydia everything she deserved. He couldn't see that what she really wanted was a simple life—with him. Lydia is no longer the girl he knew. Now she's the woman who can help him reclaim their long-ago dream of home and family…if he can only win her trust once more.

Amish Brides

CELERY FIELDS

Love awaits these Amish women.

www.LoveInspiredBooks.com
LIH82959